# BITTER TRUTH
A Green Dory Inn Mystery: Book 3

### JANET SKETCHLEY
janetsketchley.ca

*Bitter Truth*, A Green Dory Inn Mystery, Book 3
© 2022 by Janet Sketchley

978-1-989581-07-0 (epub)
978-1-989581-08-7 (mobi)
978-1-989581-06-3 (print)

All rights reserved, in all media. No part of this publication may be reproduced or transmitted for commercial purposes, except for brief quotations in printed or electronic reviews, without written permission of the author.

Permissions requests may be directed to the author via her website: janetsketchley.ca/contact/ or via email at info@janetsketchley.ca.

The characters and situations in this book are works of fiction and are not intended to represent any individuals, living or dead. The Green Dory Inn is purely fictional and in no way intended to represent a real location. Where real locations are mentioned, they are used fictitiously for the purposes of the story.

Quotations and Scripture References:

Chapter 2: reaping what we sow: Galatians 6:7.

Chapter 8: not despising what God calls clean: Acts 10:15

Chapter 15: "The vilest offender who truly believes..." ("To God be the Glory," by Fanny Crosby, public domain).

Chapter 15: "Vengeance is Mine, says the Lord." Deuteronomy 32:35 NKJV, Romans 12:19 NKJV New King James Version (NKJV) Scripture taken from the New King James Version®. Copyright © 1982 by Thomas Nelson. Used by permission. All rights reserved.

Chapter 15: "Father, forgive them," Luke 23:34 NIV New International Version (NIV) Holy Bible, New International Version®, NIV® Copyright ©1973, 1978, 1984, 2011 by Biblica, Inc.® Used by permission. All rights reserved worldwide.

Chapter 17: "A cord of three strands is not easily broken." Ecclesiastes 4:12 CSB Christian Standard Bible (CSB) The Christian Standard Bible. Copyright © 2017 by Holman Bible Publishers. Used by permission. Christian Standard Bible®, and CSB® are federally registered trademarks of Holman Bible Publishers, all rights reserved.

Chapter 24: God speaking through a donkey: Numbers 22.

Edited by Brilliant Cut Editing.
Cover by E.A. Hendryx Creative.
Interior dory image: iStock.com/Gunay Aliyeva.
Author photo by Amanda Walker Photography.

Published in Canada by Janet Sketchley.

FICTION/CHRISTIAN/SUSPENSE

JANET SKETCHLEY
janetsketchley.ca

## BOOKS BY JANET SKETCHLEY

### The Redemption's Edge Series:

*Heaven's Prey*
*Secrets and Lies*
*Without Proof*

### The Green Dory Inn Mysteries:

*Unknown Enemy*
*Hidden Secrets*
*Bitter Truth*
*Book 4 (TBA)*

### Daily Devotions:

*A Year of Tenacity: 365 Daily Devotions*

*Tenacity at Christmas: 31 Daily Devotions for December*

### Readers Journals:

*Reads to Remember:*
*A book-lover's journal to track your next 100 reads*
(Available in two cover options, print only)

# Note to Readers

Lunenburg, Nova Scotia, is a real town—a UNESCO World Heritage site. The Green Dory Inn and most other places mentioned in this novel are products of my imagination and in no way intended to represent real locations. Thank you to the kind folks at The Ovens Park for permitting me to set some of the action there. This is a novel, and what happens at the park is pure fiction. The Ovens is a wonderful, safe family campground, and if you're ever in the area, do visit to walk the trails and see the sea caves. South Shore Regional Hospital and Fisherman's Memorial Hospital are also real places. If you've been inside South Shore Regional, you'll know that I've redecorated to suit myself.

I have also taken creative licence with the geography of the inn by elevating that part of the coastline to allow for the sea tunnel beneath it. One of the perks of writing fiction is being able to adjust the facts as needed, for the purposes of the story.

Also, for my non-Canadian readers, please note I'm using Canadian spellings in this book. You'll see words like colour, neighbour, licence, and travelling, and they're not typos. You'll also see some hyphenated words like mid-fifties and mid-size. That said, and despite the many eyes that have checked the manuscript, I can't guarantee perfection. But I've done my best!

## Dedication

This novel isn't about current events but it was birthed in a very difficult season. In view of that, I offer the following dedication:

To all those who lived through the years 2020 and 2021.

And in memory of those who didn't make it.

With gratitude to the God who carries us.

# Meet the Key Characters

**Anna Young:** owner of the Green Dory Inn

**Bobby Hawke:** Anna's neighbour

**Ciara Williams:** Landon's friend

**Dylan Tremblay:** local police constable

**Kenjiro (Ken) and Kimi Sanu:** Ciara's former boss and his wife

**Landon Smith:** Anna's friend

**Meaghan Lohnes:** Anna's part-time housekeeper

**Orran Ashwell:** Ciara's old friend and mentor

**Phil Kirkwood:** Ciara's stepfather

**Roy Hawke:** Bobby's grandfather, Anna's neighbour

**Shaun Riggs:** travelling motorcyclist

**Tait Hansen:** Orran's business partner

**Whitney Kirkwood:** Ciara's mother

**Zander Luca:** Landon's counsellor and mentor

# Chapter 1

*Thursday*

"WHAT IF I can't do this?" Landon Smith twisted her fingers together in her lap until they hurt.

"Don't let one toxic prof get inside your head." Bobby Hawke looped the Corvette around another curve in the narrow coastal road. "She's behind you now. Transferring to Halifax means a fresh start."

"I ran away."

"You made a strategic decision to regroup."

Landon snapped her stretchy bead bracelet against her wrist. How could she explain her mounting anxiety when she didn't understand it herself? She'd survived day one on her new campus. Next stop was a South Shore, Nova Scotia beach walk to unwind. Zero stress.

Except the drive from the city had given her time to think about the mountain of readings and the visible cliques among the other undergrads.

"Twenty-four isn't that much older, but I feel like..." The hypnotic unfolding of the faded pavement drew her gaze. The throaty power of the convertible's engine had them skimming the shore like a white seabird. "I feel like a trade-in car with dull paint and flat tires. What if I can't keep up?"

The rays sparkling off the Atlantic Ocean dazzled her vision and churned the nameless dread in her gut, compounding the slipstream effect from the open roof. She ground her molars against a rising tide of heat. Spewing in Bobby's Corvette was not an option.

Bobby slapped the vent control, and cool air blasted her cheeks. The car slowed. "Need me to pull over?"

Eyes closed, she inhaled deeply. The searing sensation ebbed, leaving a manageable queasiness. She gulped. "I'm good now."

He eased back up to the speed limit. "You were getting kind of green around the gills."

An oncoming police car chirped its siren once before whipping past.

Landon twisted to peer after it. "Was that Dylan?"

Bobby slowed again and jostled them onto the gravel shoulder, tires crunching to a stop. "Whoever it was just got a call. They're coming back."

Red and blue lights flashed, and the white cruiser paused alongside, its passenger window lowering. Constable Dylan Tremblay acknowledged them both with a nod. "There's a pull-off around the next bend. Follow me."

He cut the roof lights and drove on.

"Wonder what's up." Bobby signalled and eased the Corvette back onto the pavement.

Landon's heart flipped. "Something's happened at the inn."

With the trouble at the Green Dory Inn this summer, Dylan had been the responding officer so many times that he and Landon had become friends. When she decided to extend her stay in Lunenburg, he'd adopted a protective big-brother role. Not that he or Bobby had more than five years on her.

She focused on the cool air streaming from the dash vent, but her nerves coiled tighter and tighter until she could barely breathe. As soon as Bobby cut left onto a grassy area and stopped beside the police car, she ran after Dylan toward the lone picnic table.

"Dylan, what's wrong?"

He chose the bench with his back to the Atlantic. Behind him, the land fell away to where short, choppy waves sparkled like a net full of diamonds. The playful light contrasted with his unsmiling expression.

"Sorry about the theatrics. This needs more than a roadside chat. Anna thought I might catch you at the beach, and I was backtracking from there when we met."

Landon's breath caught again.

As if he'd sensed her fear, Dylan's lean features twisted into a wry smile. "She's fine, and she didn't want to call you."

Despite his reassurance, Landon's knees wobbled as she dropped onto the sun-warmed wooden bench opposite him. The way the sea air swirled, she had to tuck her skirt beneath her thighs to stop the loose fabric from billowing.

Bobby settled beside her, close enough to support, but not to crowd.

Dylan's dark eyes shifted between them, then focused on her. "Gord Lohnes was to be in Bridgewater today for a court hearing."

Not the inn after all. But Dylan's serious posture, his urgency to find them... Landon's skin pebbled despite the sun's heat. "Don't tell us he escaped."

"There's no easy way to say this." Brows crowding together, Dylan leaned on his forearms, fingers laced. "Gord was shot in the courthouse parking lot. He didn't make it."

"But—" Words flooded her mind, too many to channel into questions. She stared at the tabletop's wide grey planks until they slid out of focus. "It's finished, then. His case has been escalated to the Highest Court." No appeals, no mistrials. No dragging victims through their pain again in front of the judge.

Dylan cleared his throat. "The shooter deprived the living of the chance to see justice done."

"Dylan, the man tried to kill us. You want me to be sorry he's gone?" Remembered fear shook her breath.

Bobby shifted, the movement flexing the board beneath them. "You said 'the shooter'—the person got away? Or you're not revealing a name yet?"

"Gone. The investigators are working on it."

"Good luck." Bobby propped an elbow on the table. "I guess his old gang decided he was a liability."

"That's the most likely explanation. We'll be following up on local leads as well."

Gord—shot. So final. And while Landon might approve, Anna was probably crying.

In her mid-fifties, Anna Young had run the Green Dory Inn alone since her husband's death. He'd been the first casualty in Gord's plot to acquire the inn property. Anna had believed Gord was a caring friend until he tried to murder her six weeks ago.

Landon flattened her palms on the weather-beaten tabletop. "I have to get back to the inn."

Before she could rise, Dylan gave a quick headshake. "One more thing. As a formality, would you each make a list of who would have seen you in Halifax today from about ten on?"

"What?" From Anna's need to this abrupt request— Landon winced at the mental whiplash.

Bobby's frown matched the orange cartoon llama's on his faded tee shirt. "We do have motive."

She'd seen the protective fire in his eyes when Gord threatened to shoot her. But heroes didn't take revenge. Even geeky writers like Bobby who couldn't see that the word *hero* applied to them.

Dylan stood. "We have to cover all the angles. We'll need to verify your whereabouts and Anna's. Another officer will come by for that. But as a friend, I didn't want you to be blindsided about Gord."

As Landon and Bobby stepped away from the table, Dylan seemed to measure the distance between them.

"So are you two a couple now?"

Bobby's laugh sounded uncomfortable. "I just drive the getaway car."

A hint of pink flared under his beard stubble. With her resemblance to the poisonous girl in his past, he'd never want to date her even if he wasn't in a long-distance relationship with someone from home. "I keep telling you, you need to bring Jessie here for a visit so everyone will know you're taken."

His cheeks darkened. "Anna needs you. Let's go."

~~~

As the Corvette retraced the road's curves toward the inn, the wind in Landon's hair pulled and tugged, its turbulence matching her thoughts. She scooped blond tendrils from her cheeks and caught the tousled mass into a one-handed ponytail, twisting it into a rope.

How much more could Anna take? And she'd be so concerned for—

Landon slapped a hand to her mouth. "Meaghan." Anna's housekeeper, Meaghan, was Gord's daughter.

Bobby's fingers tapped the wheel. "Yeah, I was thinking about her. This'll be rough."

They crested a hill, and the Green Dory Inn's rope-edged sign marked the driveway on the left. At the top of a grassy slope, the grey two-storey inn stood well back from the road. Between the twin Cape Cod style dormer windows, an extended dormer jutted over the bright yellow door.

In the small lot, Bobby stopped beside the slate path to the rear entrance. "Anna would rather see you alone. I'll pass the news to Gramp."

"If he doesn't already know. He doesn't miss much." Landon clicked open her seat belt. "Thanks again for driving me. I owe you an ice cream."

A quick grin eased his serious expression. He gave a double thumbs-up. "I'll collect on it."

As she stood from the ground-hugging seat, the screen door banged, and rapid footsteps crossed the wooden deck behind the inn. Anna hurried along the path, plaid shirttail flapping, one arm outstretched as if to stop Bobby from leaving. "Did Dylan find you?"

"He did." Landon closed the distance between them.

Anna clung to her, then retreated, knuckling moisture from the corner of one eye. "Bobby, come and join us. I need to talk this through."

Slump-shouldered, she led them onto the deck and waved them into the padded wicker chairs at the table. "I'll be right back."

The past month's slower pace had given Anna time to recover from the mental trauma Gord had put her through. But perhaps the biggest difference came as her body rid itself of the low-level lead poisoning he'd added to her shampoo. Although she still wasn't wholly herself, the tiredness and the emotional fragility were mostly gone. Now the shock of his death could trigger a relapse.

The door opened, and Anna carried a tray of glasses and golden, sugar-topped cookies to the smoked-glass tabletop.

Bobby whistled. "Homemade gingersnaps. I'm glad I stayed."

Anna sank into her chair like a spent helium balloon. Her broad, generous features lost even the pretense of a smile. "We do need to talk about what happened but first, how did your classes go?"

The reminder stirred a fresh ripple of fear, but Anna didn't need anything else to brood over. "Both profs have high expectations, but they seem fair." As long as neither tried to use their power to squeeze the students into their own image. Landon's fingers closed around a cool water glass. "It helped to know Bobby was writing in the library in case I needed to bail."

He lifted his half-eaten cookie in salute. "You can thank me in your graduation speech."

Anna nudged the tray nearer to him. "Bobby, I haven't seen you or Roy since you came home. How was your road trip?"

"Gramp won't admit it, but the drive was tough on his leg. Good thing he flew out in the first place."

After Anna's neighbour Roy fell off a ladder in the spring, Bobby had come for an extended stay. With Roy mobile again, the two had set off for Ontario to visit his son and daughter-in-law, Bobby's parents.

Roy had been itching for a chance to drive Bobby's Corvette on the highway. Grinning, Landon pictured the mischievous old man behind the wheel. "So did he get a speeding ticket anywhere?"

"Nah, we took his truck. Even he can't make that thing fly. I had some things I wanted from my apartment."

Anna rested her arms on the table's wicker rim. "So you're staying longer? I thought with Roy mobile again we'd lose you."

"He said he'll put up with me for the winter. Provided I keep cooking."

From the few meals Landon and Anna had shared at Roy's place this summer, the joke held a kernel of truth.

Bobby stretched back in his chair, reaching overhead and dropping his clasped hands on top of his head, mashing his hair out like straw. "I like it here, and the writing flows well. Assuming you two don't find another mystery."

Anna palmed her chin-length bob away from her jawline. Released, it fell into the same lines, silver strands glinting among the brown. "We'll leave the mysteries to the police. But we do need to talk about poor Gord." She blinked back tears. "What did Dylan tell you?"

"That he'd been shot outside the courthouse." Bobby tilted his glass to catch the last of his water. "And that, although it's likely an outside job, they want an account of our whereabouts."

A wan smile tipped Anna's lips. "Motive-wise, we're all possible suspects: the three of us plus Hart, Meaghan, Elva, and Nigel."

Gord had coerced his daughter, Meaghan, and her boyfriend, Hart, into his plot. And he would have killed Anna's neighbour Elva if the ever-watchful Nigel Foley hadn't rescued her.

Landon gazed out over the short grassy lawn to the mixed forest behind the inn. Hart had skulked through the trees and fired paintballs at cars in the inn's parking lot, but that didn't mean he could hit a human target. Plus, he and Meaghan had avoided arrest by giving evidence against Gord. Shooting him now would lead to prison.

Watching the trees' gentle sway, she drew a deep breath of fresh country air. "I hope Nigel didn't do this."

Bobby laughed. "Now you're really reaching."

"You didn't see him the morning after the fire." The tang of smoke had clung to the man after he'd dragged Elva from the blaze meant to kill her. Nigel had sat at the inn's kitchen table, burned hands wrapped in bandages. Avenging fury in his face. Warning Dylan to find the culprit before he did. She shivered. "If he'd known Gord set it—if Elva had died—I think maybe Nigel could have killed him."

Behind the gunmetal-framed glasses, Bobby's blue-grey eyes widened. "Soft-spoken, metal-detector-toting Nigel, whose main goal is preventing the alien invasion?"

"Nigel, the protector of woodland creatures and wounded humans." She locked his gaze.

"I guess. But Elva lived and Gord was arrested. There's no need for vengeance."

Cold gelled in her chest. "Gord's death means she won't have to testify about their shared past."

"He couldn't!" Anna's vigorous head shake refused to allow the possibility.

"Somebody did, though." Landon placed a gentle hand on Anna's arm. "Gord is dead. Did Dylan give you any details?"

"He was being escorted from the transport van to the courthouse when glass shattered in the parking lot and car alarms started going off. Everyone turned to look. The deputy sheriffs kept hold of Gord so he couldn't run, but Dylan said all the shooter needed was a clear line of sight. Because they turned, the bullet impacted the back of his head."

Anna's clinical words came out heavy. She swiped at her eyes. "The court's in a quiet part of town, and the killer got away unseen. They found his sniper rifle, but Dylan didn't expect there'd be any prints."

It sounded like an execution. Who would have the precision—and the hate—to kill one man without harming his guards? In an area where there would be civilians too?

Bobby chose another cookie from the plate. "Remember he was trying to get himself reinstated in that gang. The gun supports the theory of it being an outsider. There are plenty of hunting rifles in Lunenburg County. Why spring for a high-end assassin's weapon?"

Half the tension drained from Anna's posture. "The court dockets are posted online for anyone to see. They'd have plenty of time to send a killer."

"Now you're thinking like a writer." But his expression stayed serious, and he made no attempt at his chin-stroking supervillain pose.

Landon waited. "What is it?"

"Remember in the barn? I told him he wouldn't see it coming." Bobby pushed his chair away from the table. "On that sunny note, I should go see if Gramp knows yet."

"He reaped what he sowed." As sad as this was for Gord's daughter and Anna, Landon couldn't regret his death. But Bridgewater, where he'd been gunned down, was less than half an hour from Lunenburg. If the gang considered Gord a risk, they might come after Meaghan and her boyfriend too.

# Chapter 2

*Friday*

"I FEEL LIKE we're intruding." Landon balanced the plate of tea biscuits in one hand and opened the apartment building's smudged glass entryway for Anna, who'd insisted on carrying the heavy stew pot.

"We won't stay if she doesn't want us. But she needs to know we care."

Anna was puffing by the time they reached the third floor.

Meaghan let them in, reaching for the pot. "Here, let me take that."

Landon followed her into the galley-style kitchen and set the biscuits on a scarred but spotless grey countertop before rejoining Anna at the door.

"Thank you. The stew smells good. Would you like to sit down?" A halo of frizzy red hair accented Meaghan's pale skin. Above the thin line of her mouth, her blue eyes revealed her need.

"If we're not in the way." Anna folded her into a hug. "I'm so sorry for your loss."

Meaghan rested her cheek on Anna's shoulder as if drawing strength to go on. Then she gestured toward the living room where a faded brown couch faced a wall-mounted big-screen television. A matching chair sat near the window.

Once Landon and Anna settled onto the couch, Meaghan angled the chair toward them and curled up in its depths. "I've spent all morning making arrangements for Dad. It's been a hard twenty-four hours."

Anna unfolded a piece of paper from her purse. "I brought a list of the steps I went through for Murdoch. The funeral director will have given you the basics, but there are a few other things I wish I'd known."

"Thank you. Especially—" Trembling lips pressing tight, Meaghan reached for the page.

Especially when her father killed Anna's husband and caused Anna to learn all this. The unspoken truth thickened the silence.

Anna flapped her hand side to side as if to clear the air. "This is a terrible situation, but even small things help."

The first sign of tears glimmered on Meaghan's lashes. "You're very kind. Both of you."

Landon flattened her palm against the couch's nubby weave. The last time she'd been in this room, she and Bobby had come to confront Meaghan about poisoning Anna. Gord had been controlling his daughter, and later Meaghan had done everything she could to help build the case against him.

Despite the awkwardness, Anna had convinced her to keep working at the inn. Now Meaghan's hours had reduced to accommodate a community college program. That should be a safe subject switch. "What do you think of your courses so far?"

"The first day and a half were great. Then Dad had to get himself killed." Meaghan pulled her denim-clad legs up to her chest, locking them with her arms. "He is not going to ruin this for me. He cost me the rest of this week, but I'll be in class on Monday and back at the inn tomorrow."

"See how you feel in the morning," Anna said. "We can cover for you if we need to, but I know sometimes it helps to be busy."

Did Meaghan even know she was grieving, or was she still too angry with the shock?

Between her crime-syndicate father and bad-attitude boyfriend, the girl needed a positive note in her life. No wonder she'd gone behind their backs to return to school. Gord couldn't stop her now, and for all his mouth, Hart wasn't the dominating type Gord had led them to believe. Hart might not be terribly supportive, though. "Is there anything we can do?"

"It's set. Cremation. No ceremony. He didn't have life insurance, and we're not going into debt for him. Besides, who'd come?"

"People who care for you, Meaghan." Anna slid forward, dipping the couch cushions. "To be what comfort we can."

"That's a small crowd these days. Most are talking about a 'gang-style slaying' and wondering if Hart and I are next."

Landon had been concerned about the same thing. "Did the police say you might be in danger?"

"We shouldn't be. He didn't drag us into anything until he moved back here when the syndicate kicked him out." Leaning an elbow on the armrest, Meaghan kept her feet on the seat and angled her knees to the side. "It might not have anything to do with his criminal ties. It could have been someone from around here."

"But—"

"He didn't say anything about the gang before." Ignoring Anna's protest, Meaghan drew her thick braid over her shoulder. "Why would they worry now? It's not like he could save enough jail time to make a difference. There's motive here in the community after what he did."

Motive aside, the method seemed more like organized crime. The police were taking the local angle seriously, though. They'd collected Landon's and Anna's statements this morning. Meaghan and Hart would have had to account for their whereabouts as well.

Anna stood, smoothing the button front of her pale mint blouse. "We have a check-in later this afternoon. Meaghan, the investigators will find this person, whoever it is, and the closure will help. For now, take things slowly and remember you do have friends. You'll get through this."

Meaghan fixed Landon with a steady blue gaze. "If it's someone local, will you find them?"

Already on her feet, Landon retreated half a step. "The police are on it."

"How hard are they going to work? The shooter saved the justice system a ton of money for court and prison."

Anna rested a palm on Meaghan's shoulder. "Our Lunenburg officers are thorough, and they care. They're already working with the Bridgewater detachment, and I'm sure they'll bring in any outside help they need."

"Please?" Meaghan kept her focus on Landon. "If you'd waited for them to clue in about Anna, you'd both be dead."

The words drilled cold into Landon's chest, the vibration raising memories of terror. Helping Anna almost cost her life. Even so, Anna nearly died. This September was about a restart. Safe. Predictable. School and friends. No mysteries. No more danger.

Landon raised shaky hands and retreated toward the door. "I can't."

~~~

"I hope I won't be too long." Landon ducked her head into Anna's sitting room at the rear of the inn.

Feet up in one of the teal recliners, mug of tea in easy reach on a side table, Anna looked up from her paperback. "Take as much time as Ciara needs. I'll be here in case the guests want anything when they return."

With a busy weekend ahead, a quiet evening would do them both good. Crossing homework off the list would help too. Instead, Landon followed the hardwood-floored hallway to the back door and let herself out onto the deck.

Timkin, Anna's black and white cat, rose yawning from a corner and bounded down the steps to the grass. There was no sign of the marmalade stray they called Mister.

Ciara drove a new-looking powder-blue VW Bug. A flurry of shrill barks burst through the open windows as Landon approached.

"Hey, Moxie." Her friend's amber and white Chihuahua always amused her. Ciara couldn't have chosen a more perfect canine match.

Ciara flashed a hot-pink smile. "Thanks for coming. It wasn't much notice, but it's not like there's a lot to do on a Friday night in the sticks." As soon as Landon's seat belt clicked, Ciara whipped the little car around and zipped down the driveway. "You'll like Orran."

More to the point, she'd be moral support as Ciara reconnected with this reclusive family friend. Not that Ciara would admit any such need. "Who is he, anyway?" The urgent texts before supper hadn't said.

"He was my tutor, maybe a mentor. Until he started travelling more."

"But you were always on the honour roll."

"Later I was." Ciara's pearly nails tapped the steering wheel. "Mom married Phil and moved us here when I was eleven. I had a hard time with all the changes."

"Good thing they recognized it and hired a tutor."

Ciara snorted, loud and harsh, earning a startled yip from Moxie in the back. "All they did was lecture." Colour tinged her cheeks. "I cheated on a test. Phil got all cold and disapproving, and I ran away. I fell down a bank in the woods. Orran found me."

A prickling started at Landon's hairline. The last young girl she'd heard of meeting a man in the woods... Was tonight a visit to reconnect—or to confront? "Did he hurt you?"

"Of course not!"

Landon breathed an inward sigh. How sheltered had Ciara's childhood been for stranger danger to be a shock?

"He took me to his place and cleaned me up and listened to me cry. Fed me peanut butter and jelly and convinced me I couldn't live in the woods with the spiders and bears. Then he said that first, faking wouldn't impress anyone so don't cheat, and second, I could learn math and he could help."

"So he's a teacher?"

"A security consultant. With a work ethic that wouldn't let me quit."

They'd skirted the main part of town, and now Ciara navigated through a cluster of well-kept bungalows on treed lots. "This is where we lived then, before Phil's firm made him a partner."

A series of turns brought them out of the subdivision and onto another two-lane rural road. Minutes later, the Volkswagen was jostling along a narrow dirt lane through the woods.

The plastic orange bobbly flower on the Bug's dash rocked like a sapling in a gale. Ciara slowed even further to splash through a puddle. "Orran needs to invest in some road repair."

She pointed to the cutaway bank an arm's length from her side of the car. "This is about where I fell. It's so deserted I stayed there in a lump, crying, until Orran found me on his way home from town." She sniffed. "He was so mad at first. Scared, I think, because he could have run me over. Then he saw the blood on my hands and knees and stopped yelling."

The way wound through more trees, mostly evergreens, then opened into a wide grassy clearing with a single dwelling in the middle. The lane continued as two dirt tracks leading to a detached garage.

"This whole road is his driveway?" Landon let out a low whistle. She'd go nuts this far from human contact.

"He has an ATV to get out in the winter. Snowmobile, if it's really bad."

A dark SUV occupied the space in front of the garage. Ciara parked beside it. She unclipped Moxie's harness from his doggy booster seat, cooing about what a good boy he was, and led Landon toward the house.

Wide chestnut-stained shingles on the front gave the impression of an ancient, rough-barked tree—as if the single-storey building had grown from the ground, part of the surrounding forest. A wooden railing ran the length of the front, marking the edge of a low deck. A solitary Adirondack chair in deep hunter green matched the front door. They stepped up onto the deck, and Ciara poked the doorbell. In her arms, Moxie darted his head this way and that, pink tongue lolling.

The man who answered the door couldn't be Orran. With short brown hair and a compact build that suited his form-hugging tee shirt, he wasn't much older than they were.

Instead of sliding into flirty mode, Ciara hiked Moxie higher in her arms. The tiny dog yipped. "Where's Orran?"

The guy matched her pose. "Ciara Williams, I presume? Nice to meet you. Tait Hansen, Orran's partner. Care to introduce your friend?" He tipped an eyebrow at Landon, dry amusement twitching at the edges of his mouth.

Landon kept a neutral expression. Baiting Ciara wasn't kind. Or wise. "I'm Landon Smith."

"Charmed."

Ciara huffed. "Partner?"

He let the pause linger, then shook his head like a kid who knew he'd pushed the teacher's patience far enough. "Business partner. What did you think? Dude's twice my age." His chin dipped as he gave Ciara a slow once-over. "Besides, I'm a ladies' man."

"Really." One thin eyebrow slid upward. "Then why—"

"Why am I here? Orr's having a rough day. We had projects to talk over, and it was easier for me to come to him.

Plus, I wanted to meet this chapter of his past." He stepped away from the door. "Please, come in."

Spine erect, Ciara marched past him, her heels clicking a sharp staccato against the ceramic tiles in the entrance.

Landon followed, uncomfortably aware of Tait behind her.

An arched opening to the right gave onto a spacious living room. Natural light spilled in through large windows on the front and far side wall, and two cream leather loveseats formed a conversation-friendly vee on a claret accent rug.

A grey-haired man with a pencil-thin moustache sat at one end of the farther loveseat. Clutching the armrest, he started to rise, then seemed to think better of it. "Forgive me for not getting up." He drew in a breathy rasp. "Welcome, both of you."

"Orran, this is my friend Landon. And Moxie." Ciara bounced the little dog in her arms.

As Landon settled beside Ciara on the opposite loveseat, Tait spoke from the doorway. "What can I get you? Coffee, tea? Wine?"

Once they made their choices, Ciara repositioned Moxie on her lap and crooked a finger under his sparkly collar. "Orran, are you sure you're up for a visit? We can catch up another day."

"I overexerted myself earlier and needed some oxygen, but I'll be fine." One hand swept the room. "What do you think?"

"I definitely don't miss that awful carpet. Or the heavy old furniture." She looked around. "It suits you. Understated and smooth. The landscape, is that your television too?"

Beyond admiring the blues and greens of the pond scene, Landon hadn't paid much attention to the large wall-mounted display screen.

Orran's fingertip traced one side of his narrow moustache. "You know me. I like my tech."

Clinking glassware announced Tait's return. He set a high-rimmed black lacquer tray on the coffee table, then took the seat beside Orran, stretching his legs to cross at the ankles. "Help yourselves."

Ciara lifted a wineglass, the ruby liquid catching light from the windows. "It feels weird to have an adult drink here. I haven't been in this room since I was fourteen. Before you took that long business trip."

Orran fingered one of the buttons on his camel-coloured cardigan. "And yet another father figure let you down."

Stretching an arm along the back of the loveseat, Tait flicked the back of Orran's head. "What did you do, you old scoundrel?"

"I went away. And didn't make contact when I returned." Orran studied her over tented fingertips. "I owe you an apology, Ciara, and an explanation if you want it."

The wine rippled in her glass as she set it on the tray. Both hands caressed her dog's short hair. "I was taking too much of your time."

"Not at all." A wheeze cut short his laugh. "Helping you allowed me to throw your stepfather's attitude back in his face. It also let this loner have a bit of parenting experience." He picked up the other wineglass but didn't drink. "You didn't need tutoring that last year or so. I was trying to give you a portion of the attention you weren't getting at home. But your parents thought a blossoming young woman shouldn't be hanging out with an older man. So I let the trip build distance."

Tait stirred. "That's when we met."

"You were much harder to teach." Orran switched focus to Ciara. "I knew you could make it on your own. I'd heard you moved away, but when I saw you in town this week, it felt like time to reconnect."

His index finger tapped his chest. "I could have decades left or days. It changes a person's perspective on what's important."

Ciara's fingertips fluttered on Moxie's back. "Don't say that. You're still young."

"Fifty-one isn't old. Despite what certain people say." He squinted at Tait. "But my lung condition changes the odds. Hence my bringing Tait into full partnership in the company."

Tait smirked. "Someone has to keep an eye on you."

"I've done fine on my own all these years."

Landon sipped her cooling coffee. For all her initial discomfort with Tait's attitude, he seemed fond of his partner. Ciara wasn't the only one to look to Orran as a mentor.

Beside her, Ciara sniffed. "You're a stereotypical bachelor. Remember when you were hurt and I tried to help? I practically had to ransack your kitchen to find anything."

"You were a good little nurse. I lived."

Tait hiked a brow. "I haven't heard that story. How'd you get hurt?"

"I'll tell you later. Spare the women the gory details." He set his glass on the tray. "So can I assume you being here on the East Coast means things are working out with your parents?"

Ciara's bitter laugh made Moxie yip. Eyes bulging, the Chihuahua planted his forelegs on her silky top, reaching to lick her face. She caressed his ears and eased him into a sitting position. "Sorry, little guy. No, I didn't even tell them we'd left Vancouver until Moxie and I had moved into our place here. It's temporary—just until I figure things out."

Orran huffed. "They have more space than they know what to do with. Most parents in that situation would give you the chance to save up for a fresh start."

"Phil keeps offering to rent me an apartment—in any major centre 'because that's where the better jobs are.' He'd pay for me to go back to school too. Anything to get me out of town and away from my mother."

The corners of Tait's hazel eyes pinched. "Nice family. So you drove all the way across the country in that little car? Or did you ship it?"

"We drove."

His lazy grin reappeared. "I'm impressed."

"You should be." Orran's cough shook his shoulders, and he whipped a white linen handkerchief from his pocket and pressed it to his mouth. "This girl can do anything she puts her mind to. Ciara, while you're here, don't be a stranger."

"I won't." Cuddling Moxie in her arms, she stood. "For now, I need to take this big boy home. You order Tait around until you feel better."

Tait surged to his feet and snapped a mock salute. "Yes, ma'am."

Outside, Ciara leashed the dog and walked him to the nearest tree before buckling him into his car seat. Tail wagging, he snuffled the sheepskin lining while Landon climbed into the front. One hand on the ignition, Ciara hesitated. She glanced back at the house before driving away. "He wasn't this bad on Tuesday. I can't find him just to lose him again."

Landon held on as they jostled along the wooded lane. "If he overdid it today, you may see an improvement next time."

"I hope. Hey, you had a busy week too, with classes starting. How'd that go?"

"A lot better than being in Toronto. But my first day was when Gord was shot—the man who tried to kill us in July."

"Now you don't have to worry about trials and stuff. I'll bet that's a relief."

"Anna's broken up about it. I don't know how I feel." Justice, yes, but murder... And Meaghan asking her to find the killer. The lane's sheltering trees turned to brooding sentinels, closing in.

Landon focused on the dirt track in front of the car. Each turn of the wheels brought them closer to open air. The same way each step, each breath, would carry her through this stress.

The police would investigate. Landon's job was to be Meaghan's friend. No way was she stepping back into danger.

# Chapter 3

*Saturday*

"**D**ID MEAGHAN TEXT yet?" Landon set her tray with the guests' dirty breakfast dishes beside the kitchen's double sink.

If Gord's killer had been sent by the crime syndicate, surely he wouldn't linger in the area. Each passing day made Meaghan and her boyfriend seem less like targets.

Anna flicked a soap bubble from the purple-potted aloe vera plant on the windowsill. "She'll be here in about an hour. She said she needs to be busy. I'm sure she could use the pay too."

If Gord's estate passed to Meaghan, life might get a bit easier. For now, his death was one more problem he added to his daughter's life.

As Anna rinsed, Landon stacked plates and glasses into the dishwasher. "You won't need me, then."

"Going to finish your homework before Zander arrives?"

"Maybe." She should hole up in her room and do just that.

Zander Luca was even more of a father figure to Landon than Orran had been to young Ciara. A former prison chaplain, he'd found a new calling in ministering to troubled youth in the Ontario justice system. Especially young offenders, runaways, and human trafficking survivors like

Landon. Zander's influence at the recovery centre, and Anna's long-distance care, had led sixteen-year-old Landon to risk trusting Jesus with the shattered pieces of her life.

*Risk.* From this side of the decision, she knew it was the safest choice she could have ever made. But the moment of commitment had felt like stepping off a cliff and hoping for an invisible safety net.

Years of prayer, therapy, and counselling had brought her now to a place she thought of as "I've been healed, I am being healed, and I will be healed." Here with Anna at the Green Dory Inn, she felt nurtured and could continue to grow. From his phone calls and texts, Zander wasn't convinced. A few weeks after she'd told him she was staying for the school year, he booked an impromptu weekend vacation at the inn. Meeting Anna, the other spiritual rock in her life, would reassure him. As would the inn's homey, restful atmosphere.

Even the kitchen, professional-grade in terms of food prep, invited friends to pull up a chair to the pine block farmhouse table. The vinyl flooring's rose and grey flagstone pattern softened the stainless steel appliances. This room, the inn's warm core, reflected Anna's heart. Zander would approve of Landon staying here because he would approve of Anna.

Anna hung her apron in the pantry cupboard and retrieved her sunflower mug from the table. "Time for another cup of tea before Meaghan gets here. Want a refill?"

"No thanks. I need to get back to my readings, but I keep thinking about Meaghan and Gord. It was a terrible way to die, and I know she's grieving. But I wish she hadn't tried to drag me into the mystery."

Anna left her mug on the counter and closed the distance between them. Giving Landon's shoulders a gentle squeeze, she held eye contact. "That was the grief talking. Our last mystery was one too many. She'll understand eventually."

"I know. I just... don't want to go there today." Landon rested a little longer in the warmth of Anna's gaze, then stepped back. "I owe Bobby an ice cream. Ready-made distraction if he's free."

Bobby responded to her text with a thumbs-up. That meant he wasn't writing—whether by choice or because he was stuck again.

Or she'd woken him up. It took half an hour before the white Corvette arrived from next door, and when she settled in the passenger seat, his hair was still damp. "Late night?"

"Huh? No, I've been up for hours. New video game."

"Well, at least I didn't interrupt anything important."

"I'll have you know gaming is serious business. It simply can't compete with ice cream." He dropped the car into gear and cruised down the long driveway.

The two-lane road snaked along the coastline, small whitecaps tossing in the bay on their left. Landon snuggled deeper into the leather seat, glad Bobby had warned her to wear a sweatshirt. Despite the strong September sun, the wind had teeth—especially with the car top down. She brushed hair from her face and tucked it behind her ear. A few blond strands fluttered forward to dance in her vision. "Can we walk too? Speed therapy isn't going to do it for me today."

"I don't know. Strolling the beach, ice cream in hand... Sounds like a recipe for happiness. Are you up for that?"

"You know you're an idiot."

"I do. Seriously, what's going on?"

Telling him about Meaghan's request brought the tension back, creeping along her muscles, tingling at the edge of her hairline. "I know she wasn't trying to upset me. But I don't even want to think about a mystery—about danger—ever again. I can't find out who killed Gord. It's unreasonable." Her neck started to cramp, and she rubbed the spot at the base of her skull. "I have to get this out of my head before Zander gets here, or he won't believe I'm safe to stay."

Bobby nosed the car into a parking spot at the edge of the beach lot away from the other vehicles. "You're an adult. He can't make you leave."

"No, but he went ballistic when he heard what Gord did to us in July." He'd urged her to return to Toronto at once, but she'd chosen to stay at the inn and help Anna back to health.

The long beach grass between the parking lot and the shore bent in the breeze, green turned silver in the sunlight. They followed a path through the grass and stepped into dry, light-brown sand that filled Landon's sandals. She slipped them off and hooked them with her index finger for the walk. After a few paces, Bobby was carrying his flip-flops too. Today, his shirt bore a black cartoon figure in a green skirt with a broom brush on its round helmet.

On a Saturday morning in September, Landon hadn't expected to wait in line for ice cream. She'd been a little afraid the stand would be closed. But the chattering swarm of preteen girls ahead of them chose quickly and clustered around a nearby picnic table.

When she saw the mound of triple chocolate in Bobby's cone, she was glad she'd ordered herself a small.

"Thanks for this. You've fuelled me for the day." His expression twisted into an exaggerated scowl at the cone in her hand. "How can you eat that stuff?"

Grinning, she slurped the side of the scoop. The sharp licorice and sweet orange melded perfectly. "When I was little, the brightest ice cream won. Tiger's the one I still like."

The tide was going out, and as they neared the water, they hit firmer sand, cool beneath their feet. Bobby angled into the shallows until they reached his ankles, but Landon kept to the shore near the surf's edge. Every so often, a rush of sea water would surge in and drench her toes.

The roar of incoming breakers made a soothing rhythm. Airborne gulls cried and wheeled. Small shorebirds scooted along the wet sand, chasing the receding ocean to turn and flee, stick-legged, from the next wave. Here in this expansive place, Landon's memory of Gord's crimes couldn't trap her. She spread her arms wide. No walls, only the horizon on one side and a line of beach grass on the other. Light, not darkness.

She inhaled a lung-straining breath of salt-tanged air. "Why do you suppose Meaghan would even ask me to help find Gord's killer?"

"See, now, you should have had the chocolate. It would have distracted you from all that."

She glanced sideways at his half-eaten cone. "What did you need distracting from?"

"No comment. But about Gord, I don't know. I mean, you figured out Meaghan was behind the poison."

"After you thought to check for poison in the first place. And it took both of us to escape from the tunnel."

"There went my chance to be a hero. Rescued by a girl." He sounded like a five-year-old boy complaining to his mother.

She refused to laugh. Instead, she jammed fists to her hips and planted her feet wide. "What's wrong with a female hero?" They'd talked enough for her to know he wasn't dismissing women. He was comparing himself with the larger-than-life character he wrote about.

Bobby left the shallows and plucked a pebble from the hard-packed sand. A quick swish to wet it, and he uncurled his fingers to reveal a tiny treasure that sparkled in the sun. "Sea glass."

"Quit dodging the issue. Besides, we rescued one another. Either one of us alone would have died." Even together, they'd only survived because Gord didn't stick around to finish the job.

"So we make a rocking team." Bobby dropped the bit of glass into the side pocket of his cargo shorts and picked up another sea treasure.

Landon scooped up a finger-length black stone, worn smooth by the tumbling surf. The thin oval fit into her palm, releasing the sun's warmth against her skin. "As kids, we never left the beach without a few shells or stones for our collection."

"Me too. To my mom's chagrin. She's a neat freak with a superpowered sense of smell."

"So you took home crab legs to be a brat?"

He splayed a hand against his heart and gave her a look of round-eyed innocence that dissolved into a smirk. "One or two."

"Did you come every year?"

"When we could. Mom couldn't take much time off. Sometimes it was Dad and me, and once I could fly unaccompanied, they'd send me for the summer." He stooped for another find, wet it, and lifted it to catch the light. "This one matches your eyes."

Landon peered at the pea-sized bit of sea glass. "I guess."

"Hey, I'm a writer. It's my job to notice things." He ground a heel into the sand, a dusky tide rising in his cheeks.

She stepped over a long strand of seaweed. "How's the new book coming?"

"I'm in edits for the one I wrote this summer and gearing up for the release of the one before it. Ideas are taking orbit for the next one."

"How long is the series?"

"I'll write Travers as long as people want to read him. It's not high-class literature, but it's good clean fun."

He'd hinted that something in their escape from Gord inspired part of this last book, but he wouldn't say what it was. She'd have to find out when it was published.

His steps slowed, and he stuffed his hands in his pockets. "So now that I'm here for the winter…"

Her phone chimed in the pause, and he shrugged. "Go ahead and check that."

"If you're sure." Shading the phone from the sun, she squinted at the text. "Zander says he'll be at the inn in about half an hour."

The hiss of Bobby's exhale echoed her frustration. Zander wasn't supposed to arrive until midafternoon. Plenty of time to get her head on straight and still make headway with her homework. "I'm sorry, Bobby. I need to go. Finish what you were saying on the way?"

"It'll keep. At least we got the ice cream."

The way to the parking lot stretched farther than she'd realized. As the tide receded, more people had arrived. Some sat in chairs or on blankets, but most strolled the shoreline or tossed balls or flying discs. Not surprisingly for September, the only ones in the water were a couple of energetic dogs.

If Zander reached the inn first, he'd ask Anna and Meaghan how Landon was doing. As part of her recovery team, that was expected. But if Meaghan expressed hope that Landon would find Gord's murderer, Zander would see a major red flag.

Bobby was right. Zander couldn't force her to move back to Toronto. His protective concern, however, could make for an uncomfortable weekend visit.

She had to keep him away from Meaghan.

~~~

A brown SUV with Ontario plates was parked beside Anna's sedan when they arrived. Zander. Meaghan's car wasn't there, but if Hart had dropped her off, that meant nothing.

"Thanks, Bobby. Say hi to Roy for me."

Landon hurried along the slate path and up the steps to the deck. When she opened the screen door, Anna's cat, Timkin, swished past her ankles in a black and white blur and strolled into Anna's sitting room. He must have followed her from the grass.

Anna poked her head out of the kitchen. "Did you have a good walk? I'm making Zander a coffee."

Coffee and tea fixings were available on the sideboard in the breakfast area, and guests weren't invited into the behind-the-scenes part of the inn. Anna must have decided Zander counted as a friend.

With his chair set diagonal to the square farmhouse table and one ankle crossed over the knee of his navy dress pants, he looked more like a visiting caseworker than a trusted friend and mentor. He'd folded his sleeves up to the elbows. Maybe that was his nod to vacation attire.

"Landon." As he rose to take her hands, he studied her the same way a doctor would check a thermometer or a pulse. With the same accuracy. Zander always knew when she wasn't okay.

A smile softened the angle of his jaw. "It appears you're thriving."

With Anna's cooking and the good sea air, not to mention eluding a toxic professor, how could she not thrive? "It's good to see you, Zander. I'm glad you can finally meet Anna."

Zander's presence always filled her with warm security. Behind his formal manners and his thin, earnest features lay a quiet and highly sensitive man who'd invested years of patience to support her well-being. He'd filled the role her father couldn't fill, much like Anna had stepped in for her mother.

Anna set a steaming mug of coffee on the table along with two wildflower porcelain mugs, then carried the teapot from the stove.

"No tea for me, thanks." Landon took a tall glass from the cupboard and filled it with cold water from the tap. The ice cream had left her thirsty. She settled in the chair between Zander and Anna. "How was your trip?"

"Very satisfying. I rearranged my schedule to leave a few days early, so I've been touring your scenic province."

Overhead, a floorboard creaked. Landon glanced at Anna. "How's Meaghan?"

"About what you'd expect." Anna's broad forehead creased. "Zander, you may have heard we had a shooting not far from here. The victim was my housekeeper's father."

His cheeks hollowed slightly, accenting the sharp cut of his chin, and he sat still as if sifting the information. "How tragic for her. Wasn't he the one who tried to kill you both this summer?"

"Yes. I hired Meaghan when I thought Gord was my friend." Anna's eyes welled. "Now he's dead. I should have visited. Talked to him about his soul."

"But something prevented you."

"I wasn't ready. I've forgiven him in my head, but it hasn't reached my heart. He'd have known I didn't fully mean it, and he'd have thought the gospel hope was false too." She palmed grey-streaked brown hair from her cheeks, accenting the sorrow lines around her mouth. "If God didn't have someone else to speak to him—" Her hands dropped to the table.

Gord's life choices led to murder. Wouldn't he have already rejected God too completely to come back? Landon covered Anna's nearer hand with her own. Focused on justice for Gord's crimes and the sniper's identity, Landon hadn't thought about judgment for his soul. No wonder Anna's pain ran so deep.

Zander watched Anna over the rim of his coffee mug. "God's ways are deeper than we see. And forgiveness takes time."

"Gord didn't have time." Anna's chin wobbled, then firmed. "But that's my problem, and I'm sorry to spoil the moment."

"I understand the struggle to forgive. I've experienced a significant loss of my own."

From the day Zander first spoke to her recovery group, his brooding expression and haunted eyes revealed a private sorrow. Despite his being male, Landon and the other girls knew he was no threat. He could empathize.

Footsteps in the hallway interrupted the conversation. Meaghan walked into the kitchen. "Anna, I'm—" She stopped short. "Sorry to interrupt. I'll just put this away." She opened the cleaning cupboard and stowed her blue plastic basket of supplies.

Anna swiped her eyes before turning. "Meaghan, let me introduce Landon's friend Zander."

Zander left his chair and rounded the table, extending his right hand. When Meaghan took it, he covered hers with his left. "My sympathy for your loss."

"Thank you."

As Zander moved out of her space, she flipped her thick red braid over her shoulder and lifted her chin. "He wasn't a good father, but he's all I had. I don't expect they'll look too hard to find his killer."

The accusation targeted Landon, but Zander wouldn't know that. He made a sympathetic sound. "I'm sure the authorities will do their best."

Her lips flattened. "For a murderer?"

"For any of us. Justice matters."

He stood in Landon's peripheral vision. "I have connections in law enforcement. They won't share details on an active investigation, but I can press for them to give this the attention it deserves. Things can fall through the cracks with so many needs vying for limited resources."

Meaghan stared. "You'd do that for me? After my father tried to kill your friend?"

"Absolutely. I respect your pain."

"Thank you." Meaghan's fingers bunched the hem of her baggy blue shirt. "If it was his old gang, we may never know. But if someone local killed him, they could come after me or my boyfriend. Dad made us help him. What if they don't believe that? Or don't care?"

Anna's forehead puckered. "You and Hart were only involved here at the inn. Anyone else's issue would be with Gord alone. But I can't believe anyone here would have done this."

Did the police? Investigating the locals in a case like this could be pure routine. On the other hand, how well did Landon and Anna know any of the others with motive?

Nigel had claimed innocence. With his strong, if complicated, sense of justice, he'd admit killing Gord and consider the jail time a small price. Elva? Hart? Landon had no idea what statements they'd made. Or if they'd told the truth. Hart had both attitude and motive. Did Meaghan fear her boyfriend had killed Gord? In revenge or in fear the man's coercion would somehow reach them from prison?

Landon squeezed her water glass, the smooth curve firm against her skin. She needed to be firm and cool too. Not reshaped into someone who'd jump into mysteries and take unnecessary risks. Dylan and the other officers here and in Bridgewater had the skills and training to find the shooter. She needed to stay out of the way.

She tuned in to what Anna was telling Meaghan. "Call me in the morning if you change your mind about coming in. Or if you'd like to try church with Landon, I'll stay home and cover breakfast cleanup. Grief is terrible, but walking through it with God helps."

"Thank you." Meaghan hoisted a roomy purse onto her shoulder and tucked a stray red curl behind one ear. "My ride's here. See you tomorrow."

After the back door shut, Anna sighed. "She's been through so much this year."

"As have the two of you." Zander carried his empty mug to the sink and rinsed it before returning to the table. "I trust this is the end of it."

Landon had held a similar hope when Gord was arrested. Now he'd gone from villain to victim. She swallowed the last of her water. Lunenburg County folk were friendly, hard-working, and fiercely loyal. Local trouble meant domestic disputes, petty theft or nuisance, or the occasional stash of illegal drugs. Not murder.

Now they'd had two within a year—Anna's husband and Gord. Plus Gord's four attempted murders.

She'd thought it was over. Gord's death had to be a contract hit. If not, there was a new killer in town.

# Chapter 4

*Sunday*

"THERE IS NO statute of limitations for evil." With the open barn doors at his back, the pastor roved his gaze across the knot of people in the inn parking lot as if wanting to make eye contact with each one. He sounded like a witness for the prosecution.

Landon's spirit hushed at the weight of his words. Around her, Anna's guests stood in solemn silence.

He raised a hand, index finger pointing upward. "There is no statute of limitations for evil. But thank God, there is also no expiry date for grace."

A ripple of soft exhales brushed Landon's ears like the faintest breeze. Her shoulder muscles loosened, and she relaxed into an easier stance. She'd almost died in that barn, but the small grey structure held no fear for her now. Not after so many trips in and out helping to empty its contents.

Anna wanted the building to have a prayer of cleansing and blessing, and she'd invited people from the community and her church to join in. Landon recognized a few neighbours, including Anna's friends, Tricia and Blaine—minus their grandson, Quinn, and his supersized attitude. Understandably absent was Elva, the other woman Gord almost killed this summer. Elva whose experience here as a teen left her unwilling to step onto the property even now.

At the opposite edge of the group, Dylan's uniform and on-duty stance set him apart. If Gord's assassin had come, the visible police presence was meant to spook them. The two plainclothes officers borrowed from the Bridgewater detachment were here to mingle and observe. So far, Landon hadn't been able to pick out either of them.

She focused on the barn. Gord's attempted murders here in July were nothing compared to the criminal legacy of the property's original owner. That man had died over forty years ago, but his legacy of abuse lived on.

Pastor Vern swept an arm toward the empty space behind him, lit by a string of weak bulbs. "Innocence was stolen. Contraband distributed. A life lost. This summer, more lives were nearly taken. Tonight, we cleanse the taint."

He plucked at the shoulders of his faded tee shirt. "I'm dressed this way because I expect to get dirty. We're going inside in a minute, and we're going to take back this building." His gaze cut to one end of the front row, to the white-haired woman in the sole chair. "Those of you with better fashion sense and anyone with dust allergies may wish to sit that part out."

He stooped, then lifted two tall galvanized metal pails. "We've claimed the cleansing blood of Jesus Christ over the evil perpetrated in this place. To symbolize that, on your way inside take a handful of rose petals to scatter over the floor. Red for the victory of the cross and white for purity."

Before following the others into the barn, Landon stopped to speak with the black-clad woman in the chair. Maria Hiltz was the end of the family line, daughter-in-law of the infamous Captain Hiram "Jack" Hiltz.

Cradling one of Maria's knobby arthritic hands, Landon studied her pain-lined features. "This is difficult for you, but I hope it's healing too. Would you like to spread a few petals in memory of David?"

They'd found the bones of Maria's long-lost son in a tunnel shaft beneath the barn. Gord claimed it had been an accidental death. They'd never know the truth.

Plastic blue glasses emphasized the paler blue of Maria's tear-bright eyes. "Will you show me the spot?"

The elderly woman leaned on Landon's arm as they approached the barn, their feet crunching on the gravel path. They reached the doorway as Pastor Vern swarmed up the ladder into the barn's half-loft. The pastor might have the shape of a couch potato, but he scaled the rungs like a pro. Like a warrior.

Maria chose the red petals. Landon scooped up some of each, their silky texture cool against her fingertips. She led David's mother through the shadowed space, its dusty air thick with the tastes of ancient hay and motor oil. Near the back, she stopped and toed the thin outline of a trapdoor in the wide floorboards. "Here's where he fell."

The weight on her arm increased as if Maria's grief would pull them both to their knees. Breath rasping, Maria stretched out her gnarled hand and let her petals rain like drops of blood.

Tears blurred Landon's sight as she stood in silent support. The lonely old woman had built her life around waiting for her son to come home. Since identifying his remains this summer, she seemed weaker each time Anna and Landon visited.

Maria straightened. "Thank you. I need to sit."

Most of the guests had already moved outside to where long folding tables held plates of finger food. "I can get you a plate in a minute, Maria, or help you over. I need to go back to the barn first."

"I'll be fine. Take me back to my chair."

After seating Maria, Landon chose the soft grass instead of crunchy gravel for a silent return to the now-empty building. She'd strewn her petals on the trapdoor as well, in praise to the God who didn't let her die down there. Now she poured the remaining red in with the white and stirred them with her fingertips, releasing a sweet fragrance.

Pail in the crook of one arm, she walked the interior edges of the barn, sprinkling the rose petals like holy water.

Somewhere in one of these corners, fifteen-year-old Elva had huddled, crumpled and used, violated by a man in his eighties. All these years later, Anna's neighbour had never recovered. With the past no longer hidden, Landon prayed the healing could begin.

When she'd circled the walls, she paced to the middle of the space and spun in a slow circle, eyes closed, tipping the pail to spill the last of its contents. "Amen."

"And amen." Bobby's soft echo came from behind her.

She hissed in a breath and whirled to face him.

He approached, holding out his hand, and she took it, somehow understanding his intent. They walked to the square of floor where Gord had forced them into the unlit tunnel. A memory of damp, mineral-heavy earth filled Landon's nose. She inhaled deeply, replacing the past with the bruised-rose-hay-oil present. As one, they stooped and gathered fallen petals, then let them flutter to the trapdoor.

Bobby released her hand. "I still have nightmares sometimes."

The dim light shadowed his features beneath his rumpled-haystack hair. He'd shaved for church this morning, and without the weekday layer of stubble, he looked younger and surprisingly vulnerable.

He'd been afraid of the gun. Her terror came in the tunnel. By God's grace, they'd rescued one another.

Nightmares. "Me too."

"What's Anna going to do with this place?"

"She's not sure."

When they stepped out onto the gravel path, they almost collided with Zander. Landon stopped. "Zander, I wanted to introduce you to Bobby. Bobby Hawke, Zander Luca."

Bobby stuck out his hand.

Zander shook it, his olive complexion darkening. "What were you thinking, letting her confront a killer?"

She tensed, but Bobby let out a soft breath. "I asked myself the same question in the tunnel. With all due respect, though, Landon's tough to stop when she puts her mind to something."

"I'm standing right here, and I hear you both." She pressed her palms into the soft cotton of her capri pants, refusing to make fists like an angry child. "Bobby didn't have to go anywhere near Gord. It wasn't his fight. It was mine. And if he hadn't, Anna and I would both be dead." Not waiting for an answer, she dodged around Zander and stalked toward the refreshments.

People stood chatting in twos and threes. A knot of damp-eyed older women huddled close as if sharing past pain. More than once Landon heard gentle scoffing about prayer and muttered epithets about Captain Hiltz. Nobody mentioned Gord, and no one looked guilty or satisfied to have killed him.

Nigel had been on the fringes earlier, perhaps to represent Elva. He'd likely spotted the two undercover officers. More importantly, had he observed any telltale clues?

Landon poured a red plastic cup of lemonade and strolled toward where Anna stood with Maria and Zander. Maria refused the drink, so Landon sipped it herself. From Maria's closed expression and her tight-folded arms, they'd been talking about Jack.

Anna continued, "He had a long, painful death. Plenty of opportunity for regrets and repentance."

"He deserved no such chance. Where's the justice for his victims?" Maria pushed herself up from her chair and hobbled toward the tables.

Anna started after her, then turned back, shoulders sagging. "I didn't mean to upset her."

Behind Anna, Bobby's grandfather detached himself from a cluster of people and intercepted Maria. His white head dipped toward hers. Then he offered her his arm and escorted her up the stairs to the deck.

Landon touched Anna's wrist and nodded toward the inn. "Roy's got her."

Roy's gruff compassion had warmed Landon to him when they first met. He'd lived next door for years, even when the inn was still Maria's private home. Long enough to remember Jack as an old man.

Landon rested her fingertips on the back of the empty chair. Anna's tender heart wanted everyone to be saved, but no wonder Maria took offence. "Hurt finds a level of comfort in justice, but what it wants is punishment."

"Even revenge." Zander glanced at the barn. "Anna, this was a moving ceremony. I know you didn't plan it to coincide with my visit, but I'm glad I could participate."

"I hope you're more secure now about Landon being among friends here."

"Indeed." He rubbed his knuckles against a smudge on his sleeve. "In hindsight, your pastor had the right dress code for the evening."

Landon hadn't seen Pastor Vern come down from the loft, but when Bobby had ventured up there in June, he'd shot out of the barn slapping cobwebs from his hair. Bobby had been so supportive all along, to her and to Anna. And to Roy, moving in to help while his leg was in the cast. He didn't deserve Zander's blame.

He stood balancing a plate of food, in conversation with Meaghan. Observing her drooping posture, Landon stepped closer to Zander. "Gord caused a lot of harm in his life, but killing him adds to Meaghan's and Anna's pain. It's not right."

"These things are difficult." Zander rocked back on his heels, hands clasped behind him. "We can't condone the means of delivery, but justice is served. The hurting are free to heal."

Lips compressed, Anna peered out across the bay.

How could Anna heal when she feared for Gord's soul—and blamed herself for not doing more to reach him? The fact that the responsibility lay with Gord's own choices wouldn't comfort her. Landon looped an arm around her shoulders and squeezed.

"Thank God for you being here." Anna drew a tissue from the pocket of her denim skirt and wiped her eyes. "I hope the investigators find the shooter soon. Meaghan needs closure."

Despite Meaghan's fears, there'd been no sign of danger for her or her boyfriend. If Gord's former syndicate had ordered a single hit, the shooter should be long gone and might never be found.

What stirred Landon's dread was the chance the person was local after all. And had been here today.

# Chapter 5

*Monday*

"Ciara, look, a deer." Landon pointed to a doe standing at the edge of the broad dirt road.

Ciara screamed and stomped the brake. The little Volkswagen skidded on the unpaved surface, raising a cloud of dust as another deer leaped across their lane to join the one Landon had seen.

An engine roared behind them, and a motorcycle slewed past their bumper. The black-helmeted driver stabilized his ride and slowed to flash a rude gesture before accelerating away. Gravel sprayed from his tires.

Ciara sat chalk-faced, clutching the steering wheel. "I—" Her head swivelled from side to side. Looking for other drivers or other deer? She guided the car to the side of the road. After a couple of ragged breaths, she twisted to focus on the whining Chihuahua in the rear. "Are you okay, buddy?"

He gave a subdued yip.

She turned to Landon, her brown eyes brimming. "I barely saw that second deer. Did not see the bike at all." Another shuddery breath lifted her chest. "We could have been killed. Are you hurt?"

Shaking her head, Landon eased the seat belt strap away from where the jolt had dug it into her shoulder and slid her fingers down to loosen it across her hips. She'd have bruises tomorrow. Her heart still thudded. "How about you?"

"Just scared."

A van approached, heading for the main road. Once it passed, Ciara drove toward the park. "I need to make sure Moxie didn't wet the pad in his booster seat. Poor little guy."

Landon found herself scanning both sides of the wooded road for deer. Her adrenaline-taut muscles wouldn't relax until she could stand on her own two feet, sunshine on her skin and fresh air in her nostrils.

Her limited class schedule, all on Tuesdays and Thursdays, gave plenty of buffer against overload. She'd powered through the last of her reading assignments this morning once Zander started for Ontario, and Ciara's invitation for a day out made the perfect reward.

A blond wooden sign welcomed them to The Ovens Park. Ciara slowed still further and approached the admission gate. Ahead, three motorcycles stood parked among the cars.

"That has to belong to Mr. Road Rage there, the green one with the California plate. I'm glad he didn't wait around to bawl me out."

"You didn't see him. It's not your fault."

She chose a spot facing the water, well away from the bikes. "Did he look like he'd agree with you?"

"He was probably scared too." Landon stepped out of the car, pebbles crunching under her feet.

Crooning to the dog, Ciara unclipped his harness from the car seat and fastened it to his leash. She wrinkled her nose and passed the sparkly teal leash to Landon. "He had a little accident. It happens when he's scared. This'll only take a minute."

The Chihuahua snuffled around Landon's canvas sneakers as Ciara replaced the cream fleece pad in the pet seat and bundled the soiled one into a plastic bag.

Bag sealed and stuffed in the trunk, Ciara rooted in the glove compartment and produced a scrap of paper and a pen. Using the car roof as a table, she scribbled a note, bracketing the word *sorry* with sad faces. "I'll leave this on his bike."

With the paper wedged in place on the dusty motorcycle, they descended wooden stairs to a rocky beach. A woman in a wide-brimmed canvas hat sat on a low folding camp chair, peering into a tambourine-shaped gold-panning sieve. She paused at their approach. "Beautiful day."

Ciara kept Moxie away from the woman's buckets. "Is there still gold around?"

The woman rubbed her forehead with the back of her hand. "Not enough to get rich on. There's a flake here and there, but most of us regulars come because we like the sunshine and the sea air." She laughed. "Besides, if I'm out here, I'm not home doing housework."

Jagged tree-lined cliffs walled the left side of the crescent-shaped inlet, but straight ahead, the ocean stretched deep blue. This bit of shore felt like a pocket of peace.

The woman added another handful of small rocks and a splash of water, then swished the panning tray side to side in a slow rhythm. "It's a good pastime."

They left her to it and let the dog roam the water's edge, his tiny feet weaving around the larger rocks and broad strands of rusty seaweed. Ciara picked up a stone and tossed it into the shallows. "I know this was mining territory, not smuggling, but gold reminds me of that guy, Gord. Any news yet about who killed him?"

"I haven't heard. For Meaghan's sake, I hope they find the shooter soon. She acts like it doesn't matter, but it has to hurt."

"Families can be complicated. Hey, you could try to solve the case."

Jaw clenched, Landon turned toward the horizon so Ciara wouldn't see her eyes flare. Meaghan's request had at least been legitimate. She knew Landon and Bobby had discovered her part in Gord's plot. Ciara's carefree suggestion said it was all a game to her, like a movie she'd watch and forget. No emotional investment, no danger, maybe a laugh or two along the way. Four people had nearly died. Anna's husband Murdoch *had* died, almost a year ago now.

"No more mysteries for me." Landon tried to keep it light. Today was supposed to be about recreation, not argument.

Ciara shrugged. "I suppose the police have all the ballistics experts and techs like you see on TV."

With the murder weapon left at the scene, ballistics might not come into play except to confirm it wasn't a decoy. Landon gave her head a shake. No more mysteries meant not thinking about the details.

The sharp-edged rocks underfoot became bigger as they reached the base of the cliff. Close up, white quartz, likely the source of the gold, veined the rough-cut grey face. Slabs of flat rocks lay at their base. Moxie darted around, poking his nose between the larger rocks, tail waving in a blur.

Landon stood looking up at the clifftop. A thin strip of brown was all the soil available, yet hardy evergreens thrived right up to the edge. In places, they hid the rail fence that marked the hiking trail.

She and Ciara retraced their steps and climbed back to the parking lot. Skirting the cars, they found the start of the trail. Wide enough for two, the dirt path angled upward into the trees, with the ocean on their right. Moxie scampered around Ciara's feet, trying to investigate everything at once.

Soon they came to an opening in the trees overlooking the strip of beach where they'd walked. Landon stopped and leaned her forearms on the top fence rail, its sturdy wood aged to a smooth grey. The incline hadn't felt steep, but the gold panner seemed child-sized from here.

Ciara joined her, gazing over the water.

Bright blue in the depths, at the base of the cliffs it was almost tropical green and so shallow they could see the bottom. Puffy white clouds made a perfect scene.

Landon touched her empty pocket. "I left my phone in the car, and I want to take a picture. Could I have the keys?"

"Sure. We might even see another deer." Ciara unzipped her leather backpack. The metal ring held as many ornaments as keys—a silver ball that jingled when it moved, a spiked rubbery one that might light up, and a broad pink leather strip with her name stamped into it.

Keys in hand, Landon jogged the distance to the Volkswagen and grabbed her phone from the cup holder. She'd just locked the car when a scream split the peace and lifted the hairs on the back of her neck.

Her head whipped around. The high-pitched cry had come from the trail area. Where she'd left Ciara. Shrill, frenzied barks—Moxie.

Landon took off running.

It couldn't be a coyote or a bear. Not with so many people around. Maybe the little dog slipped over the edge.

She dodged a tree root in the trail. Ciara was enough of a drama queen she could have screamed at an insect sting and scared her dog.

Skidding around the last turn, Landon flung out her arms for balance. Ciara was gone. Moxie stood beneath the fence rail, his tiny body shaking with each bark.

"Ciara?" Landon caught the trailing leash and peered over the cliff.

Her friend lay on her back on a narrow ledge halfway down the steep incline, her knees supported by a scrawny tree that bent out from a crack in the rock. One foot dangled in thin air.

A black-clad man clung to the jagged cliff at her shoulders, swearing, one hand to her throat.

"Hey!" Landon activated the video on her phone. "Get away from her—now."

He scowled upward, a shake of his head flipping black hair from his eyes. "Call 9-1-1. She's unconscious, but I found a pulse. Lousy cell service dropped my call."

"So move away from her and call again." She kept recording. Ciara wouldn't have jumped, and no way could she fall over this waist-high fence.

He glared at her, lips tight. "If I move and she twitches, she'll be in the water. You think I'm perched here like a crazy pigeon for kicks?"

Steadying himself against the craggy rock face, he thumbed his phone screen. "No service. What kind of pathetic—"

As he shoved the phone into the back pocket of his jeans, Landon cut the video and keyed in the emergency call. She drilled the guy with a stare. "How do I know you didn't push her? She sure didn't fall on her own."

"Brilliant deduction, Lady Detective. Someone did push her—but if it was me, don't you think I'd have shoved her the rest of the way? Dude ran off along the path."

"Hey!" A shout came from below. The gold panner stood waving an arm above her head. "Is she okay? The 9-1-1 operator wants to know her status."

Before Landon could cancel her own call, it went through. She muted the line and yelled down to the woman on the beach. "I'll update them. Go tell the office."

The man on the cliff maintained his position in front of Ciara's prone form, answering the questions Landon relayed from the phone. Both of his hands now pressed against the rock, fingers wide. Maintaining that squat must be killing his legs.

Phone wedged between her ear and shoulder, Landon knelt, gathering Moxie's leash until she could reach the frantic dog. "Shh... She'll be okay." *Please, God.* She stroked from the top of his head along the length of his spine, firm and steady, repeating until the rhythm calmed him. He stood panting, focused on the edge of the cliff.

In another minute, he allowed her to scoop him in her arms and stand. His heartbeat tapped through his ribs, and sweat matted his short fur. He twisted to look down at Ciara.

Landon secured him with one arm and transferred the phone to her other hand. The operator had instructed her to stay on the line, so she thumbed the speaker icon and rested her arms against the railing.

The man below might be thirty, dark-eyed with vaguely exotic features. A black leather bracelet circled his left wrist, and the tip of a tattoo showed under the sleeve of that arm's tee shirt.

He was right—Ciara could tumble further without a guard. Thank God he'd seen her fall and acted so fast. But even at this distance, his aggressive vibe had Landon's fight-or-flight instincts quivering with the need to run.

Still... She swallowed some of her apprehension. "I'm sorry I overreacted when I saw you. Thanks for helping her. Her name is Ciara."

His expression didn't change, but he dipped his head. "I get it. I'm Shaun."

"Landon. This is Moxie." She repositioned the Chihuahua so the fence rail took more of his weight. Nobody would call him heavy, but her arm muscles needed a break.

"Good thing he was scared to come down here. Sounded like he wanted to take a bite of me." The first hint of a smile touched his mouth.

"Did you see who pushed her?"

"Just his back. When she screamed, I ran over, but he didn't stick around."

Feet pounded on the path. A middle-aged park employee appeared, breathing hard, the gold panner a few steps behind. The park employee rushed to the fence and peered down. She unfolded a grey blanket and dangled it over the side. "Can you reach this? We need to keep her warm until the ambulance arrives."

"How long?" An angry bite clipped Shaun's question. Or maybe that was muscle strain.

The worker's thin shoulders shifted. "They're on the way, but we're isolated. Could be twenty minutes or so. Can I get you anything? Water?"

"I'm good. Just hope she stays unconscious. If she starts to flail, we could both go down."

Landon made eye contact with the gold panner. "Did you see what happened?"

"I looked up when she screamed—in time to see her land." She took off her hat and started fanning herself with it. "It was terrible. I thought she'd keep going right to the bottom. Then I saw him climb down, and I hoped he'd know not to move her."

The park employee stepped away from the edge. An embroidered badge on her uniform shirt identified her as Judy. "Nothing like this has ever happened here. We're a safe family campground. Did you see anything, miss?"

"No, I'd gone back to the car for a minute."

Moxie squirmed in Landon's arms. Remembering the soggy pad in his car seat, she set him down but kept a firm hold on the leash. He scooted to the side of the path and wet a tree, then raced back to look down at Ciara, whimpering.

Good thing Ciara dropped the leash when she fell. Fell— the attacker must have picked her up and heaved her over the side.

Landon shook her head. "This can't be random. I'm sure your other guests are safe. But she's never mentioned any enemies, and I don't know how anyone would have followed us here."

Judy caught her lower lip in her teeth. "I need to let my boss know. I'll send up water bottles for you and another blanket. Maybe the young man can put it under his knees or something to be a little more comfortable. I hope that ambulance gets here soon."

Before the emergency crew arrived, Judy had supplied a metal dish of water for Moxie, who lapped half of it up without stopping. Landon and the gold panner, who'd introduced herself as Emmalee, stayed at the fence so Shaun would know he wasn't alone.

They heard the sirens a full five minutes before the sound cut off. A long red fire truck stopped at the stairs to the beach, and figures lugged equipment down to the base of the cliff. The ambulance would have parked at the trailhead, out of sight from here.

The firefighters positioned a soft mat to catch a falling body while two white-shirted emergency medical techs wrestled a wheeled gurney along the path. A couple more firefighters followed.

Landon scooped up the Chihuahua and moved aside with Emmalee to give them access.

Despite the danger and urgency, the first responders' calm talk and movements drained the fear from the atmosphere. After the high alert of Ciara's fall and the drawn-out tension waiting for help to arrive, the rescue felt anticlimactic. A lanky EMT cross-checked the details while firefighters attached ropes to sturdy trees. A second EMT stepped into a safety harness and climbed over the fence, grey ponytail swinging. Swift, careful motions took him out of sight as he spoke with Shaun.

Minutes later, Shaun's dishevelled hair appeared above the cliff edge, and he clambered up and over the fence. He slapped dirt from his skinny black jeans and the front of his shirt and then stood flexing his hands. Gripping the rough rock for so long must have hurt.

Landon hurried over to him. "Ciara will want to thank you. Could you give me some contact information?"

He waved her away, the braided leather bracelet bouncing on his wrist. "No need. Anybody would have done the same. Anyone but the creep who dumped her over in the first place."

He half-turned to the trees as if to take the quickest route out of there, then glanced toward the fence. His feet followed his gaze, and he stood, elbows on the wooden rails, looking down at the rescue workers.

Voices drifted up from the rock, and Shaun retreated to the trees, keeping his distance from Landon and Emmalee. A series of choreographed actions brought Ciara up the cliffside and over the fence to safety.

Ciara's dark hair and lipstick emphasized her pallor. Straps secured her blanketed body in place, but she lay still as death. The ponytailed EMT knelt to reassess her while the other disengaged his safety harness and helped coil the ropes.

Shaun was sidling past the EMT at the stretcher, toward the farther reach of the trail, when a new voice called out.

"Please, nobody leave until we can take a statement from each of you."

He stopped, but with that schooled-patient expression, he'd considered running.

Constable Zerkowsky joined the group, offering Landon a flat-lipped smile. She nodded, relieved to see him but wishing for the extra comfort Dylan brought. Still, Zerkowsky was capable and thorough.

As he organized the witnesses and began taking information, Landon knelt at the stretcher's free side. "Moxie's okay, Ciara. I've got him."

Ciara's lashes didn't even flicker.

The little dog fought to break free of Landon's arms. "Could he lick her cheek if I held him?"

The EMT's eyes softened. "Be quick. She's ready for transport. We need to get on the road."

Moxie strained forward, whining as she lowered his nose to Ciara's face. When she eased him away and stood back to give the EMTs room, he whimpered like a child.

Once the EMTs elevated the stretcher and guided it toward the parking lot, she raised the dog to eye level. "What are we going to do with you while Ciara's in the hospital? The inn cats would eat you alive."

## Chapter 6

A POST-ADRENALINE headache brewed, but Landon was too edgy to rest. Cradling Ciara's little dog, she paced at the rear of the park's small café while Constable Zerkowsky conducted interviews. She pinched off another bite of ham sandwich and fed it to Moxie.

Ciara would be horrified.

Seeing her draped across the rocks, so vulnerable and still... The hollow sensation lingered in Landon's stomach. Maybe Shaun felt the same way. While she'd chosen to wait, he'd demanded to go first and get it over with. Without trying to eavesdrop, she'd learned his name on paper was Edgar John Riggs, with Shaun being an unusual derivative of John.

Now, after Emmalee the gold panner, Judy the park employee, and a few campers who'd wandered onto the scene and either heard the scream or seen someone running, Zerkowsky beckoned Landon to the corner table he'd claimed as a desk. Broad-framed and on the short end of the police height spectrum, he always projected calm and order. "You okay? You look like you've got something on your mind."

Landon perched across from him and braced Moxie on her lap. "They've been so kind to let me bring him in here."

"They're good people." He took a sip of water. "How's Anna?"

"Much better, thanks. She's almost her old self again. Hearing about Gord set her back, but she'll be all right."

"And you?"

"I thought this was a safe place. Not the park but the whole region. Rural, edge of nowhere. Safe. But I've been nearly drowned, held at gunpoint, trapped to die in the dark. I almost lost Anna—then Gord was killed. Now Ciara's been attacked. All this in less than four months!"

Heat flooded Landon's chest. Blinking, she snapped her mouth shut. Where had all that come from, and how could she have spewed it at him?

He held eye contact, his features impassive. His head dipped in a small nod.

The nod did it. Calm touched her spirit like a cool, gentle breeze across fevered skin. She was seen. Heard. And it was okay. Her ribs unlocked, and she could breathe again. Somehow she felt that to apologize would be to negate the gift. "Thank you."

"Any time. So what can you tell me?"

Fingertips smoothing the dog's short hair, she gave him every detail she could, which wasn't much. She'd seen no one in the area prior to the attack.

Zerkowsky's heavy brows drew together. "Nobody passed the two of you on the trail? You didn't meet anyone on your way to the car?"

"I heard people off toward the campsites, but otherwise no. And the trees aren't thick. I'd have seen anyone lurking near the path."

"He could have ducked down the steps to the first cave or deeper into the woods, and you wouldn't have seen him. We'll canvass all the campers and scout possible hiding places, but his footprints will look like anyone else's."

"So you'll be a while yet." She'd hoped he could drive her home. Anna couldn't come until today's guests arrived, but

Bobby or Roy would pick her up. Not that a four-legged passenger would be welcome in the convertible.

"Dylan said to tell you he'll take you back to the inn. He's out looking around now. I'll finish up when we're done here."

"Thanks. I should learn to drive. It didn't matter in Toronto." She fished Ciara's keys from her pocket and plunked them on the paper placemat. "What do we do about her car?"

"Leave it here for now, and someone can pick it up later. I'll clear it with the park people."

"Then I'll keep the keys. I need to get Moxie's booster seat anyway."

"Booster seat, huh? My dog's a shepherd. All she needs is a harness clip so she doesn't go flying if I stop short." Zerkowsky extended his index finger for the small dog to sniff. Moxie stood tall, tail wagging as if he'd made a new best friend. "Dogs like me. It comes in handy once in a while."

"You couldn't take him while Ciara's in the hospital, could you?"

"Man, I wish I could. But my wife and I both work, and our dog's not mature enough to be left alone with him. I can recommend a kennel if you need it."

Ciara treated her pet like royalty. Sending him to a kennel, however nice, might feel like another assault. Could she even afford it on her gift-shop wages?

Zerkowsky gathered his notebook and pushed back his chair. "I'll go find Dylan. Take it easy on yourself the next little while, okay? Your system's had a shock. And give my best to Anna."

Landon collected the rest of Moxie's sandwich from the other table and led him toward the door.

Judy waited at the entrance, balancing an empty brown tray. She stepped aside to let Landon pass. "He says I can clear up now and reopen. Suppertime crowd is small this time of year but they'll be in tonight and looking to trade stories."

"Thank you for everything. You've been so kind."

Judy scowled. "This person harmed an innocent woman on our property. He's scared off a few campers and we've had to bring in security to patrol the trails. We want him caught almost as much as you do."

People didn't toss random strangers off cliffs. This had to be personal even if they didn't see the connection. Yet how could they be sure? The park staff had every reason to be concerned.

Out in the fresh air, Landon scooped up the dog and carried him to the far end of the parking lot. With her back toward the cliff, looking out over green grass and sparkling blue ocean, she extended his leash so he could roam and sniff. She was staring seaward, praying for Ciara, when Dylan called her name.

Moxie spun, yipping furiously.

Dylan gave his head a slow shake. "The things I do in the line of duty. Let's go."

"Not a dog person, huh?"

"Dogs are fine. That's a lap ornament." He stopped Landon with a touch to her shoulder. "Bridgewater hospital reports she's awake but in a lot of pain. How are you?"

"You know I wasn't with her, right?"

"Zerkowsky briefed me."

Had he mentioned her mini-meltdown? "Right now, I'm concerned about Ciara and about what to do with this pup I've inherited. Unless you want him."

He snorted. "The line of duty only extends so far. If Anna can't keep him, find a kennel."

"Dylan, some creep just threw Ciara down the side of a mountain. If everyone rejects her pet, she'll feel like we're throwing him away too." She shut her eyes, forcibly unclenching her jaw. "I'm not asking you to take him. I just—

any attack is a form of violation. We can't do anything that makes it worse."

Cupping her elbow, Dylan started them moving toward the patrol cars parked at the trailhead. "I understand. Between you and Anna, you'll find him a place."

"Let me get his stuff from her car."

"He rides in the back. You can sit in front."

In the time it took to figure out how to detach the booster seat and secure it in the rear of Dylan's cruiser, Moxie sprayed the nearest tire.

Dylan snickered. "One less thing to worry about on the road."

Once Landon clipped the dog into his seat, he snuffled the fluffy lining and curled up. "Poor little guy, he must be exhausted. That fleece probably feels like a security blanket."

"Yeah, he's smart enough to know she's hurt. Too bad he can't talk. We'd have a good witness."

"Shaun saw the attacker from behind. Did you find anyone who saw more?"

"Not so far."

Dylan opened the front passenger door for Landon and swept papers off the seat. He tucked them into his pocket and tossed a brown paper takeout bag into the rear. "Welcome to my mobile office."

"You'll be checking on Ciara tonight, right?"

"After I drop you off."

She held out Ciara's key ring. The silver ball bauble jingled as she passed it over. "Take her these?"

Rolling his eyes, he scooped it from her palm. "Will do."

He slid behind the wheel. As they passed through the gate, he said, "Why don't you lean your head back and rest? You must be tired too."

Landon watched the passing trees instead. Anything to keep from imagining Ciara and the crime scene.

She hadn't told Dylan the full truth. Sure, she was troubled by the attack. But she was also angry. More angry than made sense. Something about seeing Ciara's sparkle crushed had lit a protective fire.

Not that Landon could do anything. Even in a fair fight, the weak always lost to the strong. And this sneak assailant didn't fight fair.

She couldn't make it right. But she couldn't let it go.

~~~

Landon barely glanced at the bright orange marigolds and yellow pansies in the inn's signature green fishing dory as Dylan passed it on the way up the driveway. Any other day, the vibrant colours were like an energy drink for her spirit.

Dylan pointed to the dirt-crusted car parked beside Anna's silver sedan. "Somebody's been cruising the back roads." He stopped in front of the barn. "I'll help you unload the dog seat. Hope the official vehicle doesn't scare these guests."

In June, he'd been here to follow up on Anna's prowler trouble when a couple arrived to check in. One sight of the police car had the wife acting like they'd be murdered in their beds, and Anna had to find them another spot in town.

With Dylan carrying the bulk of Moxie's travelling gear and Landon holding the squirming animal, they followed the slate path behind the inn. Dylan set his load in a corner of the deck. "I have to get going, but I'll check in later."

"Thank you. For all you've done."

As he drove away, she tied Moxie's leash to a deck rail. "I'll bring you a drink in a minute."

The little dog busied himself sniffing everything in reach.

She was filling a plastic bowl at the kitchen sink when Anna came in. "I thought I heard Dylan. Did he go too? How was the park?"

If Anna had seen the vehicle he was driving, she'd have known he was on duty. Landon shut off the faucet and turned, careful not to spill the water. "Ciara's hurt, so Dylan brought me home. I have to find a place for Moxie."

A sharp bark drifted through the open kitchen window in response to his name.

Anna's expression clouded. "Timkin won't tolerate him here. But what happened to Ciara?"

"Let's go outside."

Moxie stood stiff-legged as close to the door as he could get, white tail waving.

Landon set the bowl at his feet. Then, instead of joining Anna at the glass-topped wicker table, she prowled the wooden deck, her steps short and choppy. Retelling the story drove the anger deeper. When she finished, she leaned against the railing, back to the forest, facing the inn.

Anna's broad forehead furrowed. "The poor girl. Which hospital did they take her to?"

"Bridgewater. The EMTs said she might need a CT scan."

"I imagine they'll keep her at least overnight. We need to find a spot for her dog. Preferably before Timkin decides to show up."

"I wondered about Quinn. He has a soft spot for strays." It could well be the sullen teen's one positive feature.

"No, Tricia has too much on her plate right now, and she's not as well as she could be."

Quinn lived with his grandparents a few houses away. His attitude appeared to be softening since the prowler incident, but Tricia and Blaine still seemed worn down and anxious.

Landon withdrew her phone from her pocket. "I'll text Bobby and see if he and Roy can help. If not, we'll track down Nigel."

"I hate to interrupt his writing."

Bobby always said he wouldn't stop for a text alert if he was working, but she rarely waited long for a reply. Today, she had time to walk an antsy Moxie to the tree line, keeping a lookout for the inn cats, before he called. Five minutes later, as she unwound the dog's leash from the base of a sturdy pine, Bobby emerged from the path connecting the two houses through the woods.

"You told me about Ciara, but not about yourself. Are you okay?" Here under the trees, his blue-grey eyes were dark and searching.

If he detected her troubled emotions, he'd understand. But she didn't need to make it obvious. "It's a lot to process. I'll feel better when we know how badly she's hurt."

"I can drive you in to see her if Anna's tied up here."

"For now, it's huge that you'll take Moxie."

"Yeah. About that." He snapped a dry twig from one of the trunks and twirled it between his fingers. "He'll be confined to my room except for potty breaks. I forgot Gramp's allergic."

The amber and white Chihuahua nosed the leaves of a poplar sapling barely taller than his head.

"Poor little guy. I'll try to find him another spot." She pictured Ciara unconscious on the stretcher. This was the one thing she could do.

"Is it just him, or does he come with food and stuff?"

"I guess for tonight look online for what human food he can eat and don't tell Ciara? She's pretty particular about him."

"I hope His Royal Highness can handle wearing the same jewelled collar two days in a row. Her last job must have paid well."

"Leave his car seat here so it doesn't affect Roy. If Nigel will take him, Anna'll need to deliver him anyway."

Bobby held out his hand. "I'll take escort duty from here."

She passed the leash over with exaggerated dignity. "The little prince is officially in your care."

"As you wish." His lips quirked into an odd grin. "Keep me posted. Come on, little dude."

Moxie stood still, oversized eyes fixed on Landon. She knelt and rubbed his ears. "It's okay, buddy. She'll be here for you soon."

He swiped at her wrist with his tiny pink tongue, then gave in to the taut leash and trotted away beside Bobby.

Landon collected the pet paraphernalia and headed inside. Step one—wash the wet seat pad. Step two—contact Nigel, who refused to use a phone. But as she closed the basement door on the sound of water pouring into the washing machine, the inn's landline rang.

Anna's "Good afternoon, Green Dory Inn" filtered from the private sitting room. Getting Nigel's mother's number to leave a message would have to wait. Landon walked along the hallway toward the front of the building, sneakers squeaking on the aged-honey hardwood, and jogged up the stairs.

A door latch clicked as she reached the second floor. A man and woman stood outside the Schooner Room. Landon stepped toward them. "Welcome. I'm Landon, Anna's helper. I'm in the Butterfly Room, across from you." She pointed to the rear of the inn.

The petite black-haired woman extended a hand, a silver bracelet accenting her delicate wrist. "Kimi and Ken Sanu. Pleased to meet you."

Their handshakes both carried the restrained confidence of long-term business success. No need to impress or one-up, just a security and a sense of purpose. In his mid-to-late sixties, Ken kept himself clean-shaven with short grey hair. Crinkles at the edges of Kimi's eyes suggested a similar age, but her glossy pixie cut was a perfect midnight black.

A slight paunch padding Ken's golf shirt added to the impression of a comfortable life. He nodded as if in recognition. "Anna mentioned you're a friend of Ciara Williams. We knew Ciara in Vancouver, and we hope to reconnect while we're here."

What if Ciara didn't recover? She'd been so pale. Could a person die of internal bleeding? Bracing her core, Landon shunted the fears away. Dylan had promised to let her know as soon as the doctors let them take a statement. Calling before then would be useless.

Ken's eyes had narrowed, his brows drawing together. "Is there a problem?"

"Ciara's in the hospital in Bridgewater. Someone pushed her off a cliff today."

While Kimi gasped, Ken's posture took on a stillness as if he were listening. Or waiting. Then he strode toward the conversation nook. "We need to hear the full story."

Kimi reached out as if to stop him. "Our dinner reservations."

"Will wait." He claimed one of the three blue fabric club chairs facing the dormer windows above the front door.

After placing her designer handbag on the wooden coffee table, Kimi sat beside him.

Landon perched on the edge of the third seat, hands on her knees. "I'm sorry to give you bad news." Out on the bay, stiff little waves marched in formation. Impersonal. Life kept moving while the weak got tossed aside.

For once, the sight of nature repelled instead of comforted. She concentrated on the Japanese couple, straightened her spine, and forced her anger deeper. This was about Ciara. Landon's emotions had to stay out of it.

The basics didn't take long to tell. "My friend on the police force will let me know when it's okay to call."

Ken leaned back in his chair, elbows on the armrests, fingers spread and steepled. "So it's not known if she saw her attacker."

"The police may know by now." Unless her injuries required emergency surgery. Landon ground her teeth. "She didn't deserve this."

"Nobody does." Kimi rose and circled the coffee table to kneel beside Landon. She held Landon's hand in a soft grip, a faint citrus fragrance sharpening the air. "Your friend is hurt, and it hurts you too."

The gentle affirmation almost undid Landon. Eyelids squeezed tight, she tensed her whole body. Letting the tears out meant another win for the attacker. He wouldn't know or care, but this was the one fight she had left. One tiny act of resistance. She strained for one deep, silent breath after another, blessing these compassionate strangers who waited with her in the battle instead of fussing or trying to fix everything. Kimi kept a light pressure on her hand.

At last, Landon met the woman's warm gaze. "Thank you." She glanced over at Ken, still seated as if he had no plans to move. "But I know your reservation's waiting. This evening I should be able to tell you more."

"I hope so." Kimi squeezed her hand before releasing it. She rose to her feet with a dancer's grace. "It sounds like a frightening experience."

Ken stood and passed his wife her purse. "We can stop by the hospital after we eat. I want to see for myself how she's doing."

"We'd better not. The surprise could distress her."

"Did she know when you were coming?" Ciara hadn't mentioned anything to Landon.

Ken shook his head. "We haven't spoken since she left. She recommended the inn to a mutual acquaintance."

For all Ciara's confident persona, some kind of trouble lurked in her past. She'd told Landon her reasons for returning home were complicated, and the other night visiting Orran, she'd spoken of coming back to figure things out. Things here or things from her time on the West Coast?

Landon studied Kimi and Ken. "How did you know Ciara?"

One corner of Ken's mouth pulled down. "I was her boss. Kimi's right. A surprise visit wouldn't be appropriate. We're here until Friday. Plenty of time to reconnect before we leave, and I trust it won't have to be in a hospital setting."

They said goodbye, and Ken ushered Kimi to the stairs, fingertips at the small of her back.

Landon pulled the pewter butterfly key fob from her pocket and unlocked her bedroom door. The warm peach walls welcomed her, lit by sunlight from the window at the base of the sloped ceiling. Through the glass, trees in the mixed forest stood strong and patient—waiting with her in this pause.

She kicked off her canvas sneakers and flopped backward onto the four-poster bed. One hand dragged the butterfly-shaped accent pillow to support her head. If Dylan didn't call soon, she'd try the hospital anyway.

Her phone's vibration woke her with a jolt. Dylan? Ciara? Sitting bolt upright, she peered at the display.

Zander. Stifling her impatience, she accepted the call. "Hi, Zander. Are you home yet?"

It was a two-day drive. Two long days. But before he left this morning, he'd been bragging about the distance he could cover, and the joke might divert him. He did not need to know anything else dangerous had happened in her vicinity.

"I'm in Quebec. I stopped for gas and checked the news feeds—I see a woman was hurt at The Ovens today. Wasn't that where you were going?"

Landon dropped her forehead into her palm and closed her eyes. Ciara's name would be made public soon, and Zander would recognize it. "Someone attacked my friend when I left her alone."

"Hold on." A muted clicking sounded on the line. Zander's turn indicator. "The news report said she fell. What happened? Is she all right?"

Telling her trauma story in therapy had been part of releasing the past and leaving it behind. Telling Ciara's, over and over again while it was so fresh, pumped lava through her veins. By the time she finished answering Zander's questions, heat radiated from her skin. Ciara's attacker was strong, but her anger felt stronger.

"I'm going to find him." She snapped her mouth shut so fast her teeth clicked. Opened it again to take the words back.

The burn in her heart wouldn't let her. She focused on the canvas prints on her wall. A monarch butterfly and a Canadian tiger swallowtail. The monarch's vivid orange and black pulsed in her vision like a rising, avenging fury. She blinked it into stillness and flattened a hand to her thudding heart. She was going to do this. No matter what she'd told Meaghan about being done with mysteries, she would fight. Because Ciara couldn't.

The phone still rested against her ear. Silence. Had the call dropped?

Then Zander cleared his throat. "I know you want to help your friend, but you need to trust the authorities to do their job. Promise me you'll stay out of their way."

Her gaze lingered on the vibrant butterfly prints. Earthbound creatures transformed to take flight. She hadn't come out soaring from her experience, but maybe she'd emerged stronger. It was time to find out.

"I won't interfere. But Ciara must know something that'll help us identify him. She'll open up more to me than to a stranger." Even to Dylan, despite her flirty ways.

"Landon, please..."

"I saw her on the stretcher." A shudder rocked her. "Limp and pale and helpless. Broken."

When they first met, Zander said Landon reminded him of his dead daughter. In those days, she'd thought helping her was a form of tribute to the love he'd lost.

This drive to defend Ciara, to bring justice—maybe this was why Zander did what he did. Not out of compassion for the present victim, although he had that. Because the link to his pain made it personal.

Because it was a way to fight back.

Landon surged to her feet. "I will protect and support my friend. You, of all people, should understand."

"I do understand. But remember what happened this summer. Don't risk your life—or your ongoing recovery."

"I'll only be asking questions. Anything I learn will go right to the police. Don't worry. I may want to pound this guy into meatloaf, but I wouldn't seriously risk confronting him." Been there, done that. Learned the hard way.

"Fine." Clipped. Decisive. Harsh in her ear. "I have a few fires waiting on my desk. I'll get home, put them out, and be with you Friday. Thursday, if I can. Don't do anything rash."

Her stomach clenched. "You don't have to—"

"Landon, you do what you have to do. But allow me to do the same. I can't lose you too. See if Anna has a room for me." He cut the connection.

With a slow whistle, she dropped the phone on the bed. She'd defied Zander. One of the people she most respected.

But she needed to do this for Ciara.

## Chapter 7

*Tuesday*

IN THE SOUTH Shore Regional Hospital lobby, Landon scanned the signs until she found one pointing to the elevators. She'd spoken with a very drowsy Ciara last night and texted with her today between classes. Once the doctors agreed to keep her another night, the frantic volume of texts had settled down.

Ciara's stepfather had hired a guard in case the attacker tried again. The uniformed woman checked Landon's name against her list before allowing her to pass. Landon rapped her knuckles on the wooden door. "Ciara? It's me."

"Come in."

The injured girl lay propped up against pillows, her short brown hair flattened against her skull. As pale as the linens, her skin took a sickly hue from the faded seafoam hospital gown. Her left hand lay on the blanket, pinkie finger in a silver splint.

She set her phone on the side table and mustered a pitiful smile. "Thanks for coming. They stuck me in here all alone where they can ignore me, but it's better than kicking me out in this much pain."

Landon scooted a chair nearer and settled into the moulded plastic seat. "Last night you said your stepfather paid for a private room for better security."

"Okay, he did. But they're still avoiding me. And before you think he did me any favours, having a family member languishing in a crowded ward wouldn't reflect well on his successful lawyer persona." She yawned. "Plus, the sooner I recover the sooner he can push me out of town."

A few gentle breaths kept Landon from rolling her eyes. Whatever painkillers Ciara was on weren't helping her filters. "Does it still hurt a lot?"

"My ribs are the worst. Or the headache. The shoulder not so much now." Her lipstick-free mouth quivered. "What hurts most is knowing someone attacked me."

Landon hadn't asked about clues on the phone, and she hadn't planned to now. Today was about comforting her friend. The investigation could start tomorrow. But since Ciara brought it up… "Dylan said you didn't see your attacker. Do you have any idea who'd want to hurt you?"

"None." A tear tracked down her cheek. "I was leaning on the fence rail watching the gulls fly. He picked me up and just—threw me."

"I heard you scream from the car. Did Dylan tell you about the guy who helped you?"

"Yeah, some people still help strangers. Who knew?"

"When I found him crouched beside you, I yelled at him— I thought he'd attacked you. But he kept you from falling further."

"I woke up in the ambulance. It was terrifying!"

"The EMTs were great. The fire department showed up too."

"I missed hot firefighters? Now I'm really sad."

Landon laughed. At least Ciara was trying to rebound. "Recover fast and go down to the station to thank them. Take food."

"Great idea." But she lay against the pillow, her breath shallow, her hands limp on the blanket.

Pink roses on the windowsill spread a sweet fragrance. "Gorgeous flowers. Who brought them?"

"Mom sent them this morning. She even talked to me for a few minutes when I phoned. But she's not coming in."

"Sometimes we need our moms." Or dads. Landon's parents weren't there for her either. "But hey, guess who I met today? Ken and Kimi Sanu are staying at the inn. You recommended it to someone they know. They didn't think they should come to the hospital, but they asked me to pass on their care."

Colour seeped into Ciara's cheeks. Her eyes sparked a faint fire. "So you know about his company."

"He said you worked for him in BC, but they both seem more interested in enjoying their vacation than talking about work."

Ciara flattened her palms into the sides of the bed and pushed herself higher on the pillows. A wince hitched her breath. "Last time I saw Ken, I was in a designer sweater and killer heels. I can't face him in a hospital gown on pain meds."

A knock edged the door open enough for the security guard's head to appear. "Orran Ashwell and Tait Hansen?"

"Aww..." Emotion choked Ciara's voice. "Yes, please."

The woman retreated, and Orran stepped inside, carrying a tall vase of peach and yellow glads. "Some people will do anything to make the news."

Tait followed.

Orran set the flowers on the sill where they towered above the roses. "Good to see security at the door. The news coverage didn't say much. What happened?"

As she stared at the flowers, Ciara's expression lost its guarded look. Then she hiked her chin. "I didn't fall, and I wasn't doing anything stupid. Someone attacked me." Her defiance turned plaintive as the story poured out. When she finished, the rigid cast of her jaw revealed how hard she fought the tears.

Frowning, Orran approached the foot of the bed. "What does the doctor say?"

"I'll live. It'll just hurt for a while. Three cracked ribs and a punctured lung, various scrapes, and a monster headache from a concussion." She wiggled the splint on her baby finger. "They think I broke this and dislocated my shoulder trying to grab the fence and let go of Moxie's leash at the same time. I'm glad that bully didn't throw him too."

As Ciara's cheeks crumpled and the tears came, Landon grabbed the tissue box from the side table and set it in Ciara's lap. "Do you want us to go?"

"I don't want to be alone." The words came through a double-fisted wad of tissues.

Orran's breath rasped in the silence. "Can we do anything?"

"Take care of Moxie." She blinked tear-heavy lashes. "He has a spot, but it's not ideal."

"I suppose your parents won't take him."

"Phil said to kennel him. After all the poor boy's been through."

With a low growl, Orran took the second visitor's chair. "I'll keep him for you."

"I beg to differ." Leaning against the hospital-beige wall, Tait scowled at his partner. "Pet dander and your lungs are not a good match." He shot Ciara a saucy grin. "Good thing one side of the partnership is healthy. Your pup can stay with me till you're better."

Ciara's eyes had rounded. "Oh, Orran, I didn't think—why didn't you tell me when we were at your place? He could have waited outside."

"Don't worry about it. I have puffers for short-term. More than a few hours would be a problem though."

Her lips trembled, then firmed. "In the future, he'll stay home. And, Tait, thank you. So much."

"Someone has to protect Orran from himself." Tait bobbed his head lightly against the wall as if he'd been still too long. "What I want to know is why someone would try to kill you."

Her fingertips covered her mouth, but a thin whimper escaped.

Tait scrubbed his hands down the sides of his jaw and bunched them into his pockets. "I shouldn't have been so blunt. But it seems obvious that a person who'd do this wasn't simply trying to scare you. I've been to The Ovens. That's a mighty drop from the cliff trail."

"The police asked me about enemies, but couldn't it be a random mugger?"

"Did he steal anything?"

"My bracelet's gone." She slid the hospital ID band up her arm to reveal a red line on her wrist. "But he didn't touch my backpack."

Orran gave his head a slow shake. "Ciara, I've been in the security business a long while. I don't believe in random. Think about who might have a grudge, real or imagined."

Fingers worrying her ID band, she pouted. "I don't know."

"Was your bracelet valuable?" Landon hadn't noticed it. Leave it to Ciara to wear expensive jewellery on a hike.

The name Ciara mentioned meant nothing to Landon, but Tait and Orran inhaled simultaneously. Tait spoke first. "There's your motive."

"But who'd know I had it on? It's not something to flaunt."

Wasn't it? Ciara had always been about having—being—the best. Designer clothes and accessories had been her tools of the trade in school.

"What about a professional jewel thief?" Landon watched Tait as she spoke, building from the motive he'd identified. "Someone stole a fancy brooch the other day in Liverpool. If he's scouting around, he could have noticed Ciara's bracelet at the store or anywhere he happened to see her with it. Maybe he followed her."

Tait had stiffened at first as if to nod agreement, but he relaxed against the wall again. "Good idea, except that other theft was an antique taken from a collector. Plus, a professional would have lifted the bracelet from Ciara's jewel box, not torn it off her wrist. There goes his resale value."

These two were security experts. They could be a great resource in finding Ciara's attacker. Tait's questions showed he was already thinking about it.

He folded his arms. "Some street thieves take jewellery, and they'd have an eye for what to grab. Maybe he left your backpack because he couldn't separate it from you in a hurry. Not like a shoulder bag."

"Maybe." Ciara sniffed. "Was the Liverpool brooch one of your clients?"

Orran let out a harsh laugh. "Not on your life. I don't work with fools of that magnitude."

Interest sparked in her eyes. "There's a story there."

His lip curled as if he tasted something foul. "When someone posts an image of a valuable item online with the hashtags eighteenth century, cameo, and private collection, what do you think will happen?"

"You follow him online?"

"I monitor certain keywords as a way to identify potential clients. Thieves can do the same to find targets."

"Did you contact him about installing a security system? He might have appreciated your advice."

With a lazy lift to the corner of his mouth, Orran glanced at Tait. "There are times you have to let nature take its course."

Ciara's brow puckered. "Did he have any security at all?"

"He seemed to think so. We do manage a few private East Coast homes, but our fees are higher than the mid-level collectors can stomach."

Tait snorted. "And worth half that again. Private sector owners require a lot of hand holding."

He might be thinking of specific clients, but his dismissive attitude seemingly put Ciara's emotional reaction in the same throwaway box. Landon dug her fingernails into her palms to keep from retaliating. Tait wasn't the enemy here. "Maybe they take their treasures more personally. A loss may hit their hearts even more than it damages their net worth."

"Exactly!" Ciara's cry brought more colour to her cheeks. "Museums and corporations are all about the ledger and prestige."

"Public or private, for the true collector, it's always about the heart." Orran spread his palms. "Although the heart holds pride and jealousy as well as affection."

Grimacing, Ciara wriggled herself higher on her pillows. "Says the man who insists everything be strictly functional. If your television didn't double as a big digital frame, there'd be nothing. No art, no trinkets of any kind. Even the ruby goblet I was so excited about as a kid was a simple prop for your girlfriend's theatre group."

Orran's eyebrows rose. "Fancy you remembering that. But you always did have a taste for pretty things. I have a picture somewhere from the play. The fake jewels caught the stage lights like liquid fire."

Ciara traced the scratch on her wrist. "I do like pretty things, but I also appreciate them as investments. I guess I shouldn't try to have the best of both worlds. Wearing a few months' rent on a hike didn't end well."

A few months' rent? Landon choked. "Tait, you said breaking the bracelet ruined its resale value. So should the police be checking the pawnshops? Ciara, did you give them a description?"

"No." Her fingers clasped her wrist as if she could will the bracelet back into place. "I wasn't thinking about a thief. I thought I'd lost it in the fall."

Voices sounded in the hallway. A food services worker in pastel blue scrubs opened Ciara's door. "Hello, folks. It's mealtime."

Landon jumped up and rolled the mobile bed table into position for her friend.

"Thank you." The man deposited a plastic-filmed meal tray on the tan laminate surface and offered Ciara a warm smile. "It tastes better than it looks. Enjoy."

His rubber-soled shoes squeaked on the polished tiles as he left.

Orran eased to his feet. He seemed to catch his breath before speaking. "We should leave you in peace. I didn't mean to stay so long. Listen, kid, have you been into Halifax for that new gallery opening?"

"I meant to."

"They have a Burmese ruby pendant on loan that'll take your breath away. The exhibit closes this weekend. You obey the nurses and get yourself discharged, and we'll go. Maybe Friday."

"I'd love that."

Tait threw a vague salute toward the bed. "While you recuperate, I'll tend to your dog. Is there anything I should pick up at your place? Where do I find him?"

"Landon, pass me my backpack?"

Ciara fished the jingly key ring from the outer pocket of the supple leather bag. She held out the keys to Tait. "The square one with the dot opens the apartment building and the plain square one is for my unit."

She recited the address and directions and rattled off so many care instructions for Moxie that Tait's lips took on a pinched look. "The poor little boy needs someone to comfort him. I'm sure Bobby's doing his best, but he doesn't have the vet-prescribed food or the doggy bed or anything. Plus, his grandfather's allergies aren't very hospitable."

Tait swallowed visibly. Regretting his offer? Nonetheless, he keyed Ciara's and Bobby's addresses into his phone.

Landon said, "Stop at the inn beside Bobby's place first. I kept Moxie's car seat. If I'm not home yet, Anna will get everything for you. I'll text her now."

As his eyes widened at the word *everything*, she grinned. "Moxie may be small, but he comes with a lot of worldly goods."

"And a huge heart." Ciara produced the brightest smile Landon had seen today.

After the men left, Landon checked the time on her phone. Dylan wouldn't be here for another half hour. Today was his day off, and he was still spending it driving around and stopping at the hospital. At least Anna had brought her over after the commuter van delivered her home from the city.

Still standing, she texted Anna about Moxie's things and returned her phone to her pocket. "Want me to let you eat in peace?"

"Can't you stay a little longer? It's so lonely here."

"Okay, but don't let your meal get cold. Is hospital food as bad as they say?"

"As bland, anyway." Ciara lifted the cover from the plate, releasing a savoury aroma.

Landon settled into a chair. "Bobby said you put it on social media about yesterday. Were the police okay with that??"

"I didn't say anything about the investigation—if they can find anything to investigate. Just that I'm hurt and in the hospital." Ciara poked her fork into her mashed potato and swirled it around. "Virtual sympathy is better than nothing." She pointed her utensil at Landon. "But then you came and so did Orran and Tait. Thank you."

"I was feeling bad for you here alone and in so much pain. You'll do better when you can be home with your furry friend."

Ciara replaced the fork and plucked a brownie from its small white dish. "Days like this call for eating dessert first."

"Amen, sister."

It was almost time to go when the guard knocked again. "Shaun Riggs?"

"I don't—"

Landon interrupted, sitting forward to grasp Ciara's hand. "He's the guy who saved you."

"Oh." Ciara drew the bed sheet up to cover her thin hospital gown. "I—yes."

Shaun hesitated in the opening, one hand in the pocket of his leather jacket, dark bangs hanging low on his forehead. When he saw Landon, he seemed to lose a bit of tension.

"Okay if I come in?"

Ciara opened her mouth, but the tears came first. She pressed the paper napkin from her meal tray to her eyes, shoulders shaking.

Beckoning to Shaun, Landon reached to comfort her friend. "Try to breathe slower. Be careful of your ribs."

"And lung." The words came out watery.

Shaun edged toward the hall. "I can come back."

He'd driven all this way from the campground. "Maybe give us five minutes? I know she wants to meet you."

"Yup." Then he was gone.

Stroking the sobbing girl's hair with a gentle rhythm, Landon whispered, "You're safe now. Shaun will understand this isn't about him. And it isn't who you really are. It's the hurt and the fear." She hauled a fistful of tissues from the box, jostling it onto the floor. "Here."

Gradually Ciara's breathing levelled, and her little squeaking hiccups ceased. She mopped her cheeks, sniffled, and mopped again before raising a glass of water to her lips. Some sloshed onto her gown, darkening the pale green.

Tears clung to her lashes, and a dusky shade tinted her rounded cheeks. "Great first impression."

Landon squeezed her hand. "This was a second impression. The first is what he'll remember—you needing protection." She offered the wastebasket, and Ciara tossed the wadded tissues. The box had landed right side up, so she set it in Ciara's lap.

Her friend plucked another two and dabbed her eyes. "I'll bet I look horrible."

"Like someone who belongs in a hospital. But alive. Would you rather meet him later, once you're discharged and dressed in your own clothes?" Maybe she shouldn't have been so quick to invite him in.

Ciara drew another slow breath, deep enough to make her wince. "After this performance, I'd never have the nerve to go find him." She leaned forward. "Help me with these pillows so I can sit straighter?"

"Do you have a brush or makeup in your bag?"

A watery giggle burst free. "Rule number one—don't make it look like you're trying too hard."

Pillows adjusted and bed table positioned like a shield—food tray and all—Ciara nodded. "It's showtime."

Landon poked her head into the hallway and spotted Shaun loitering in front of a bulletin board. "Psst."

He shuffled toward her. "I'm not sure this is such a good idea."

"She's embarrassed, but she wants to thank you. She's in a lot of pain and isn't at her best right now."

He curved an eyebrow. "You don't say." One corner of his mouth twisted to match the brow. "I'm not at my best either. Here goes nothing."

Thumbs hooked into the front pockets of his skinny black jeans, he sidled past her and approached the foot of Ciara's bed. "So I'm Shaun, and I saw you fall."

Landon leaned against the wall where she'd have a clear view of Ciara's reaction. If this wasn't a good idea, the mysterious rescuer would be out the door, gratitude or no gratitude.

Ciara gave him a fast once-over and half-raised her hand to flutter her fingers in a timid sort of wave. "Thank you for saving me. I'm sorry for my meltdown."

"What meltdown? I just got here."

Her fingernails, marred from the rocks, tapped the bed table. "They said you couldn't identify the guy."

"I saw him from behind. Don't you know who it was?"

"I don't have a clue. One of my friends thought it could have been a robbery." She held up her banded wrist. "My bracelet's gone. The chain left a mark when it broke."

"Fancy move, seizing it off a falling victim. Why not knock you down and unfasten the thing?" He glanced at Landon, then Ciara. "I'm from the States, but our laws can't be that different. Wouldn't murder or attempted murder pull a heftier jail term than theft? If he's caught?"

"Then someone was after *me*. That's worse." Ciara's fists clenched. Her face scrunched into a fierce scowl as if to defy a second outburst in front of Shaun.

The effect would have been comical if it wasn't so tragic. Landon breathed a quiet growl. Whoever had broken this perky spirit had a lot to answer for.

Shaun hiked a shoulder. "It feels like you should know if anyone hated you this much. Maybe it was random after all. Some dude having a breakdown. Or who mistook you for someone else. You don't have any enemies? No evil ex?"

Ciara's chin came up. "He has better things to do. But if we were both at the edge of a cliff, I wouldn't be the one going over."

An approving nod moved his whole body. "You hold onto that fighting spirit, and you'll be fine. I'll get out of your space now that I know you're okay."

He started for the door, then pivoted. "If you need anything, I'm camping at The Ovens. You can get a message to me through the office."

As soon as his shadow cleared the doorway, Ciara sniffled. "I'm scared."

Landon tried to infuse comforting warmth into one last meaningful look as she scooped up her purse. "My ride's been waiting. I didn't want to leave you alone with him, but I have to go. Text me later tonight?"

A couple of tears escaped. "Thanks for being here."

The elevator took forever. Once it reached the ground floor, Landon quick-marched to the exit.

The fluffy clouds from the afternoon had darkened, shedding a dismal drizzle. As she stepped outside, a green motorcycle emerged from the parking lot. The black-helmeted driver cleared the crosswalk and swerved out toward the road, revving the engine.

The biker who dodged Ciara's car on the way to The Ovens rode with the same swagger. Same colour machine and helmet, with California plates. Not many people would drive so far on a motorcycle. Shaun's clothes matched too. And he'd said he was from the US.

By the time she found Dylan's Jeep in the parking lot, the bike was long gone. The road incident was a flimsy motive for murder, but if Dylan wanted to check it out, they knew where to locate Shaun.

## Chapter 8

*Wednesday*

DRIVING TO THE Ovens the next morning gave Landon an uneasy stomach. Even without deer on the road or an aggressive biker, an eerie sense of déjà vu had her on edge.

Bobby kept his speed low, the occasional bit of gravel kicking up at the Corvette's undercarriage. Heavy rain in the night had left the road damp and puddled.

A larger rock thumped underneath, and she cringed. "I should have warned you about the road."

"I forgot it wasn't paved, but we're fine." He patted the top of the steering wheel. "One luxurious wash and wax coming up this afternoon."

He navigated through the admission gate and parked at the edge of the lot. Walking toward the trailhead, they passed the stairs to the beach. Landon glanced down. No sign of Emmalee or anyone else panning for gold.

This felt like an exercise in futility. The investigating team had already scoured the path and surrounding woods for signs of the attacker. Still, they could have missed something. Or he could have returned the next day to erase any evidence and dropped a clue then.

On Monday, a few people had gathered before the EMTs rescued Ciara from the ledge. Had he doubled back to watch with them? Landon rubbed a sudden chill from her arms. Constable Zerkowsky had brought the onlookers into the restaurant for statements. It'd take a bold—or foolhardy—person to associate himself with the scene and risk being interviewed.

Forbidding in the morning light, the cliff loomed over the water. Or perhaps the attack tainted Landon's view. She glimpsed movement on the rock face. "Look! That's where Ciara fell. Someone's there."

"Don't run until we reach the trail. If it's her attacker, we don't want to spook him."

"Where's security when you need them?" But they'd be patrolling, not hanging out here in the parking lot.

Approaching the final bend in the path, Landon put on a burst of speed. The site was etched in her memory from Monday's vigil. She planted her feet and peered over the rail. Below, a dark-haired figure in black clothing crept across the rock.

Beside her, Bobby had his phone trained downward, elbows steadied on the wooden railing.

The man worked his way over the surface, then stilled. One arm stretched, plucked at a rocky outcropping, then eased back. With a soft grunt, he tucked a flash of gold into his pocket.

He started for the top.

Landon touched Bobby's arm. As one, they eased away, splitting up to cover both directions on the trail.

Shaun's head crested the edge. His gaze hit Landon, whipped toward Bobby, then locked on Landon. He climbed onto the gravel path and stood braced against the weather-bleached railing. "We meet again."

"What were you doing?"

His chin jutted. "What are you, some kind of amateur sleuth?"

Landon's arms snapped into a tight fold across her ribs, and her posture stretched taller. Stiffened. She focused a glare to burn. "What I am is finding answers. Someone tried to kill my friend. Convince me it wasn't you."

At the edge of her vision, Bobby flashed a thumbs-up.

Shaun swore. "What is your problem? We covered this when she fell. Why would I hold her steady if I'd pushed her?"

"Maybe to rob her. Or maybe you went down to finish the job, but I got here too fast."

"Oh, for—" Narrowing his almond-shaped eyes to mere slits, he shook his fists. If he were a cartoon, steam would be pouring from his ears.

"We did cover this before. I believed you. Until I saw your bike yesterday." Landon jabbed a forefinger at him. "Monday, on the way here, Ciara stopped to avoid a deer. This maniac biker swerved around her, spitting gravel and rude gestures. How angry were you, Shaun? Angry enough to kill her?"

"So... what? I beat it to my campsite and lurked near the trail for a chance at revenge? That's serious road rage." Head shaking, he rocked onto his heels. "She's a bad driver, but not the worst I saw—not even that day. People have no respect for bikes."

"The deer jumped out in front of her. What was she supposed to do?"

"Pay more attention and anticipate a second deer. But, yeah, it was too big to hit. And maybe I was too close." He shrugged, his scowl fading. "She left an apology on my bike. I had no idea she was the same girl as on the cliff."

"I reported your bike."

"They know where to find me."

Dylan might not even follow up on it. He'd thought it was a thin suspicion. "If you're so innocent, why were you down there again?"

"As it happens, I was doing another good deed." A toss of his head shook the hair from his eyes. "My friends would never believe it. No surprise you don't either."

"What did you find? We saw you put it in your pocket."

One hand eased toward his jacket. "Don't freak out and think I'm going for a gun."

On the other side of him, Bobby was still recording.

Shaun's fingers emerged from his pocket, dangling a thin chain, the gold glinting in the sun. He extended it toward her. "Ciara's bracelet, I assume? No wonder she was so unstrung about losing it."

Landon stepped closer and pinched the delicate strand, struggling to decipher the letters stamped on the flat metal tag. The same European-sounding name Ciara mentioned yesterday. "Should that mean something to me?"

His lip curled. "Should mean a couple grand. Minimum."

For this simple gold chain? "How do you know?"

"High-priced exes." He reached for it. "I'll get it cleaned up and see if it can be fixed."

"So you can sell it?"

"So I can give it back. Your friend is in the hospital after being attacked. Don't you think she could use a nice surprise?"

Landon couldn't read those exotic brown eyes.

Inhaling a deep, salt-heavy breath, she relaxed her stance. Shaun wouldn't have thrown Ciara over the cliff and then gone after her, even if he wanted her ridiculously expensive bracelet. And even if he'd been furious with her driving.

But hearing about the bracelet yesterday could have sent him here for his own benefit now that the rain had stopped. Nothing about his hard-edged behaviour encouraged her to trust him. Nothing except his resignation when he acknowledged her distrust. As if somehow being trusted mattered, at least here and now.

How often had she longed for the benefit of the doubt from people who misread her past and used it to judge her present?

"Bobby?"

"He makes a good point."

Shaun huffed. Stood waiting, hand out.

Landon let the thin gold strand puddle into his palm. "I want to nail the creep who did this."

His fingers closed around the chain. "Me too. When I climbed down there... she was so limp. Helpless as a kitten."

Bobby had joined them, no longer recording. "Don't let her hear you say that when she's better. Thanks for saving her. And for understanding today."

"Yeah. It's good she has friends who'll fight for her." He tucked the bracelet into his leather flight jacket. "Give me a few days to find a good jeweller. In the meantime, don't tell her."

He crossed the path and strode among the trees toward the campsites.

"That went well." Landon crossed her arms, watching him out of sight. "He's the sort of guy who could mess with my head. Trigger-wise, I mean. But I'm so angry about Ciara—I guess that kicked in first. Instead of going submissive, I went..."

Bobby smirked. "Warrior angel is what came to my mind. Remind me never to cross you." He pointed along the trail toward the sea caves. "I haven't been out here for a while. Want to walk?"

"Second time here in a week? It'd be nice to be able to enjoy it."

Side by side, they strolled along the pebbled path as the morning sun caught sparkles from raindrops still clinging to twigs and leaves. Landon trailed her fingertips over the supple needles of a young evergreen, and droplets shivered to the ground. Steps slowing, she inhaled the sharp clean scent of the foliage and underbrush.

She tried to roll the tension from her shoulders. "I wonder what the Good Samaritan would have said if the next person on the road accused him of the assault. I did it to Shaun twice."

"I had the same doubts about the guy."

"You stopped to think before blasting him."

"So you fired at the wrong target. He wasn't happy, but I'll bet he understands." Bobby picked up a fallen branch and tossed it into the undergrowth. "Too bad Ciara didn't see you take him on. She'd love to know she has a friend fierce enough to stare down her enemies. Travers would be proud."

Travers. The hero in the sci-fi novels Bobby wrote. She needed to read one so she could talk intelligently with her clever neighbour. And maybe so she could convince him he wasn't second best to his imaginary friend. "What would Travers have done about the bracelet?"

"Kept it and had it fixed himself. He has more cash than we do. In case Shaun decided not to return it."

"He'll have to now. You have video evidence."

"One would hope."

On the fence rails ahead, yellow letters on a green sign read, "Tucker's Tunnel, enter if you dare." A narrow track angled downward.

Landon didn't do small spaces. Especially in the dark. She and Bobby had almost died in a dank, pitch-black tunnel beneath the inn. Funny how surviving that and then choosing to walk in later to defy the fear gave her a reckless sense of power over this challenge today.

Bobby had praised her for being fierce. She'd need to be that and more to find whoever attacked Ciara. She pointed to the sign. "Let's do this. We've seen worse."

"You've got to be kidding. You're not kidding." Shaking his head, he gestured toward the way down. "After you."

At the end of the narrow path, a short set of concrete steps descended into a rock passage. Ducking instinctively, Landon kept a hand on the metal railing. At the base, a wooden barricade rimmed a flat ledge in the cave-like opening. Black water sloshed beneath their feet. Filtered daylight from the sea entrance created a gloomy half-dusk.

Beyond the barricade, a narrow chasm cut to the left, deeper into the cliff. Bobby knocked his knuckles on the wood. "Saved by the fence."

The heavy, damp air washed goose bumps across her bare arms. She rubbed them away, feet planted, exploring with her eyes. Overhead, green and rusty stains patched the mottled grey rock. In places on the walls, the layers of slate ran nearly vertical, bands of brown and grey. Stark and jagged.

Bobby toed a pebble toward the barricade. It skidded underneath and plopped into the water. "I can't help thinking of Gord. Ciara's attack kind of pushed his death aside."

"For us. I wonder how Meaghan's doing. She said she'd be in class again this week."

"I know they weren't close, but he was still her father. It has to be tough not knowing if they'll catch the shooter."

"Dylan said they found discarded clothing that may have been part of the killer's disguise. They're not releasing that information yet."

Bobby traced a pale diagonal seam in the rock wall. "Seen enough? It's cold down here."

Climbing back to the main trail, they passed a clump of tiny purple asters growing in a pocket of the rock. The sun felt good after the shadows.

As they walked, a sound like thunder echoed from the further sea caves. Landon took in the blue expanse of ocean and distant land to her right, green scrub forest to her left.

"Talk about picture-perfect." On Monday, she'd wanted a camera. Today, she'd rather saturate her senses in the here and now than store up a copy for later.

Bobby tapped the outline of his phone in his pocket. "Next cave. I'll send Dad a photo. Show him what he's missing in the high-rise jungle."

"He grew up here, right?"

"Left and never looked back."

That would have been Landon if Anna hadn't needed her. Filling her nostrils with a slow, tangy breath, she trailed her fingers along the weathered fence rail. "I missed the ocean."

"Me too. And the slower pace." He scooped up a brown stone and passed it from hand to hand. A few steps later, he chucked it into the trees. "So... Dylan... just friends, or has he asked you out?"

She cut him a glance. "Friends! Where did you get that idea?"

"Sounded like you had inside information there, about the investigation. And he kept a close eye on you when he broke the news about Gord."

"Because he sees the girl who survived being human trafficked. He thinks I'm even more fragile than I am."

"That's not usually what that look means."

She caught him at the end of an eye roll. "Don't be ridiculous. He knows what happened to me. No decent guy's going to want me now."

They'd reached a descent to another cave, the source of the hollow booms. Below, a viewing platform jutted into the sea. Bobby started down, pulling out his phone. "Here's a good spot."

Landon followed him to the waist-high metal railing. Chin up, she faced into the wind. "I'm single, and I'm okay with that."

He lifted the phone, aimed, and clicked. "Single by choice is fine. But—" Angling toward her, he leaned a hand on the rail. "Don't despise what the Lord has called clean."

"I have a pretty healthy self-image, thanks."

"Not if you're writing yourself off like that." His stubble-framed lips curved downward. "What they did to you was awful. But the past doesn't have to define you for life. Remember the tunnel at the inn. We crawled out filthy. Rank. It took a long while to soak the dirt off. I don't know about you, but I carried the tang in my nostrils for days. Maybe that was my imagination."

Arms folded, she butted a hip against the concrete wall that held the railing. "I smelled it too."

"Well, restoration's like that, right? The hurt can linger in our hearts once the healing has come. God has you, Landon. Cupped in the palm of His hand. And He's making something beautiful."

"I'm not saying He's not holding me. That's the whole reason I'm able to stand here having this insane conversation instead of throwing myself over the side like happened to Ciara."

Misery swam in his eyes. "Jesus calls you clean. If He says it, then why wouldn't the people who care about you be able to see it too?"

"My friends do. But come on. Not for a romantic relationship."

Frowning now, he matched her folded-arm posture. "Someone who looks at you through your abuse doesn't deserve you."

As his mouth opened for more, she jerked her palm up like a wall, stiff-armed. Her vision narrowed. "When they took my innocence, they poisoned my future. There's no Prince Charming for me."

She spun toward the water so he wouldn't see her tears. Her childhood longing for a fairy-tale romance had shattered into dust too small to see—but still sharp enough to cut deep. An impossible dream, now a wraith, hopeless but refusing to fully disappear.

"It's been nine years. You wouldn't believe how long it took with therapy, counselling, and prayer to start unlocking my emotions. To learn how to cry again." And then to stop crying.

"So if someone was interested, you'd shut it down and walk away? Not even give the guy a chance?"

She focused on the light glinting on the choppy waves. Standing shoulder to shoulder with Bobby, it'd be easy to lean in. Share his strength. Friends did that. But in this, she stood alone.

"Sorry for the info dump." It wasn't the first time he'd been exposed to the mess she tried to save for the professionals. "You're a good friend, Bobby Hawke. Most of my friends in Toronto are women. It's good to have met a couple of safe guys here."

After a minute, he coughed. "Define *safe*."

"Dylan's a police officer protecting someone vulnerable. You're in a relationship, which means you're not available. Safe." Swivelling on her toes on the concrete platform, she punched his arm. "I always wanted a brother. Now I have two. Sort of."

The expression in his eyes was unreadable before he turned back to the sea. His shoulders hunched. "I'm not. In a relationship."

"Oh."

His white-knuckle hold tightened on the curved iron rail. Brilliant response. *Oh.* "When?"

So much better. She glared at the blue ripples below them. He needed support, and she'd been loading her problems on him. Again.

"Labour Day weekend. When Gramp and I went home."

"I'm sorry." Two words this time, but at least intelligent.

"Thanks."

"You okay?"

"It's best for both of us."

Of course he'd be brave about it. "Do you want to check out this cave, or should we walk?"

"Let's walk."

They climbed to the main trail and turned right. Away from the parking lot, along an empty path with lots of space to spread out. The track led past more caves before curving away from the water. Light gravel crunched underfoot as they strode in among the trees, arms swinging, pace brisk. As if to leave the awkwardness behind.

Landon finally found some words. "I never met Jessie, and I'm sure she has lots of good qualities. But she didn't sound like she ever understood you. One of these days, the right girl will come along who'll value you for who you are and not want to change you."

She picked up her pace. How insensitive could she be, to spew a sob story of broken dreams to a guy who'd just been dumped? He hadn't said anything, but the signs had been there since he returned from Ontario. He'd been on edge, and she'd never asked why. What kind of a friend did that?

Almost running, she hurtled into a clearing. An empty campsite carpeted with short grass and ringed with trees. Beside a wooden picnic table stood a doe, liquid brown eyes staring. Ears perked but tail down.

Landon stopped and stuck out her arm to warn Bobby. They stood still, watching the deer watching them. After a long moment, the doe lowered her head to munch on something in the grass.

"Apples," whispered Bobby. "See, they're all over the ground."

Small and green, they'd be a feast for woodland creatures.

He gestured to the side, toward the trees. "Let's cut through there and leave her in peace."

The low undergrowth cushioned their steps as they threaded between slender grey trunks, aiming for another open area ahead. Instead of rejoining the path, they found a clearing with rough-hewn benches and a podium at one end.

A forest chapel, furnished in grey, weathered wood. A half-dozen benches lined the space before a simple pulpit. Landon walked to the front and stopped. Arms outstretched in worship, inhaling the evergreen incense, she lifted her face to the sun.

When she turned, Bobby had dropped to the rearmost bench, elbows on thighs, head in hands.

She strolled the perimeter, picking up the occasional early fallen leaf and rolling the stem in her fingertips before freeing it to fall again. Here in this timeless place, heaven felt near. When her steps led around to Bobby's bench, he lay on his back, knees bent, facing the sky.

He scrambled upright. Lines still etched his features, but the pinch had left his mouth. "Sorry if I kept you waiting. God and I needed a little chat. This seemed like the perfect place."

"I could stay here all day. Except I told Anna I'd cook tonight. And I have homework. And I need to check in with Ciara." She gazed around the chapel, trying to absorb its stillness. "This place is a gift. I want to come here again."

A tiny smile flickered. "Me too."

The smile spread into a full-on grin, and Bobby was back. Complete with what Landon thought of as his supervillain chin stroke. "Meanwhile, we have a mystery to solve. Justice for Ciara."

## Chapter 9

CIARA'S APARTMENT BUILDING was a tidy blue four-storey near the town limits. Outside the main door, Landon hefted a cardboard box of food from the rear of Anna's sedan. "If she still can't think of any suspects, I don't know what to do."

"I wish you'd leave it for the police." In the driver's seat, Anna twisted to make eye contact. "Text me when you're ready to go. I might stop in to see Maria instead of going home."

Once a groggy-sounding Ciara buzzed her in, Landon found the elevator. She and Ciara had spent time together the past month or so, but always out somewhere or at the inn.

A fist-sized polyresin hedgehog with a pink bow rested on a shelf outside the apartment door. Only Ciara... Landon knocked, and the door swung open. A weak hello floated toward her.

Elbowing the door wider, she edged inside, then closed it with her foot. Beyond the galley kitchen, Ciara lay curled on a pale grey loveseat, a tangerine throw covering her. She flopped a hand toward Landon's left.

"Just put the food in the fridge. I can't eat anything right now."

"Does it hurt a lot?"

"You have no idea."

With the soup and other perishables refrigerated, Landon unscrewed the lid of a Mason jar smoothie and popped in a green silicone straw. She set it on the floor beside Ciara. "You need nutrients."

Ciara's effort to sit drew a sharp gasp. "Tonight'll be brutal."

Landon scooted the armchair nearer and took a seat. "I have classes in the morning, but I could stay until then."

"No, I need to be able to do this myself."

"Keep your phone close. If you need help, the superintendent could let 9-1-1 in."

"Hello, hot firefighters. I've got your number." Ciara's giggle trailed off.

So pale... Landon leaned closer. "Why did they let you go?"

"If my stepfather hadn't insisted, they'd have kicked me out yesterday. My injuries aren't 'significant enough to merit long-term admission.' Yes, that's a direct quote." Her voice shot high, tinged with hysteria.

Landon frowned. "Ciara, you're not mixing alcohol with your pain meds, are you?"

"Of course not! Someone tried to kill me. I am not going to help him."

"Good. Another way not to help him would be to keep your door locked."

"I opened it when you texted you were on the way." Her lower lip poked out. "So I have Phil to thank for the extra night's hospital bed, but he and Mom want me to clear out my things from the house. Tomorrow."

"Why so soon? They know you're not recovered yet."

Faint pink lit her cheeks. "I may have set the deadline myself to undercut his power play. Bobby and Tait are coming after work."

"I can help after school. If Roy's not coming, Bobby will have space. I assume you want Roy's truck."

"And Tait's bringing Orran's van."

Landon spread her fingers on the chair's broad charcoal armrest. "Did you ship all this from BC or buy new?"

"It followed me across country. My place in Vancouver was bigger, so I sold some things to downsize. I was lucky to get this spot." Gingerly, Ciara reached for the jar Landon had moved to the coffee table. "Mmm. Tasty."

"I made smoothies for Anna when she came home from the hospital. She didn't have much energy for meals at first."

"She's okay now, right?" Ciara took another sip.

"About ninety-eight percent. You'll be up to a hundred soon. And we'll find the man who did this." Saying it stoked the fire in her heart.

"How? I have no idea who could hate me so much."

"Are you sure your ex-boyfriend couldn't be behind it?"

Ciara tossed her head, then clapped a palm to her forehead. "Concussion headache. The ribs make me forget." She dropped her hand and blinked pain-dulled eyes. "No, he got what he was after. He's still on the West Coast, enjoying his revenge."

Landon bit back her questions. "Do you need me to go? Sleep might be the best thing for you. We shouldn't be talking about this tonight."

"Well, I'm thinking about it now. Anyway, Tait's bringing Moxie for a little while. I can't keep the little guy yet, but I miss him so much."

"I'm sure he misses you too. He was really upset at the park."

Ciara took a slow sip from the creamy pink drink. "Moxie is the best thing that happened to me out west. Ken was a great boss—he and Kimi sent those orchids over there."

She waved toward the table. Orran's glads and the arrangement from Ciara's parents were there too, with a bright cluster of Gerbera daisies.

"They're beautiful." Especially the daisies' orange and red palette.

"People have been so kind."

Ciara's phone chimed. She answered, brightening as she listened. "Come on up." She dropped the phone beside her on the loveseat. "They're here."

Landon stood. "I should go so we don't overstimulate you."

"I barely know Tait. I'd be a lot more comfortable if you stayed."

At a light rap on the door, Landon hurried to open up. Tait stood bouncing the little amber and white Chihuahua in his arms. "Visiting hours." Moxie's open mouth looked like a happy homecoming grin.

She squeezed against the wall to let them pass, the spicy scent of Tait's cologne teasing her nostrils.

Ciara's joy-filled squeal pulled a matching bark from the dog.

Landon caught one of the high bar stool chairs from the charcoal-washed dining table and pushed it into the conversation circle. Tait had already claimed the lounge chair. Moxie danced a tight loop from Ciara's lap to the cushion beside her.

Contentment glowed on Ciara's face as her fingers tried to keep up with the dog's wiggling back. "Tait, this is so good of you to look after him and to bring him to see me."

He leaned into the chair, khaki-clad legs stuck straight out to cross at the ankles. The toe of his top loafer wagged side to side. "Couldn't let Orran take him. And the Boss here is a nice little fella."

Moxie planted his forefeet on Ciara's chest and lunged to lick her. Laughing, she squeezed him into a hug. "I love you too, little boy."

At the Chihuahua's wriggling bliss, Landon smiled. The feral marmalade cat at the inn preferred to keep his distance.

Anna's cat, Timkin, was far more approachable, but if he was ever pleased to see her, he hid it well.

"Oh, yeah." Tait rooted in his jacket pocket and drew out Ciara's keys. "Don't want to forget and take these home. Your car's outside in your parking space. We dropped it off this afternoon."

The key ring jingled as he set it in an intricately carved green dish on the coffee table. "Is that jade?"

"Yup. Moxie's too little to reach it, and I don't have kids—so I can leave my treasures out on display."

The corners of his eyes crinkled. "Like wearing high-end bracelets on a hike."

"Like that. Yes." Ciara shook her right wrist, jingling thin silver bangles. "What's the point of having something if you can't enjoy it?"

"A little prudence goes a long way, but I take your point." He roamed across the open space to a curio cabinet tucked in the corner where the kitchen wall met the dining nook. "I saw these when I picked up Moxie's things. Beautiful stuff. Looks like you've been collecting for a while."

"Since Mom married Phil." She sniffed. "My middle name is Jade. It amuses him to buy me a piece each birthday and Christmas."

Landon hadn't paid attention to the cabinet earlier. Now she went to stand by Tait. The simple case probably came from a big-box store. But the glass shelves showcased carved jade figurines from tiny turtles to a mountainscape the size of a coffee mug. Scattered among the standard green were other greens, glossy whites, and even a few stripes of violet and orange. "They're lovely, Ciara."

"Thanks."

Tait kept the conversation flowing with anecdotes about the unusual security challenges he and Orran had tackled—and some of the neurotic clients. As they chatted, Ciara slouched lower on the loveseat, one hand resting on the dog in her lap.

After about fifteen minutes, Tait stood. "Time for me to get out of your hair. I'll bring him tomorrow night before going to your parents' place to load up. They'll know what you want brought?"

"Yes. I'll have to figure out what to do with it once I'm better. I can't think about it right now."

He reached for the little dog, who whined as he was lifted from Ciara's hold. "Concentrate on healing first."

"For sure. While I'm off work, I hope I can reconnect more with Orran."

Tait settled Moxie in the crook of his arm. "Orran's situation isn't as straightforward as he portrays. Be careful not to bring up anything that would worry him or cause him stress."

Ciara squinted as if trying to read the reasons behind the warning. "Okay."

"Good. We owe him too much."

Palms on the upholstery, she levered herself upright against the back of the loveseat, breath hissing through her teeth. "You heard part of my story the other night. I'd like to hear yours."

He clasped one of the Chihuahua's front paws and waggled it like a human wave. "That's a tale for another day. Sleep well."

After Tait and Moxie had gone, Landon rinsed the empty smoothie jar in the tiny kitchen. "I should go too. I'll text Anna."

Grimacing, Ciara braced hands on knees and stood in slow motion. "Let me get ready for bed before you leave. Then, once I set the deadbolt, I can crash."

A few gasps penetrated the bedroom door before she reappeared in burgundy pyjama bottoms and a loose tee shirt. "I've never hurt this much in my whole life." The movement had drained what little colour she'd had, and she swayed on her feet.

"Are you sure you'll be okay alone?"

"I'll be fine once I get down. One of the nurses showed me how to roll to get out of bed." She sighed. "I wish I could have kept my little buddy."

"You'll have him home soon. He seems to like Tait." Landon grinned. "Tait seems to like you too. Cologne, and he was wearing his ladies' man smile."

Instead of Ciara's standard flirtatious comment, she bristled. "The smooth ones are the ones you can't trust. Especially when they make the first move."

"Your ex?"

Her countenance softened, not in warmth, but in wide-eyed, wounded hurt. Betrayal. "I trusted like a fool. A blind one. He was so attentive. Considerate and caring. Right up until his true motives were revealed."

A buzz on Landon's phone said Anna had arrived. She collected her purse. "I'm sorry that happened, Ciara. And I pray that, as your body mends, your heart will too."

Ciara would never expose such loneliness. Or vulnerability. This attack had split her broken heart wide open. Her pain followed Landon to the car.

Finding the attacker wouldn't undo the damage. But it could be an important step toward healing.

~~~

With Ciara's former boss staying at the inn, Landon might find out about the ex-boyfriend. The guests were still out when she and Anna arrived home, so Landon brewed herself a cup of jasmine tea and took it upstairs to finish the last of her reading for tomorrow. She settled in one of the club chairs in the conversation nook where she had a view of the driveway.

She'd slogged through the rest of her chapter when the guests' mid-size sedan returned. Either they'd taken it through a car wash or last night's rain had been even heavier than she'd thought.

The entrance chime sounded. Landon drained the cold dregs from her mug and closed the digital textbook as Kimi Sanu ascended the stairs. The petite woman started for the Schooner Room before catching sight of Landon. She angled toward the cluster of chairs.

Ken followed. "How is Ciara today?"

They made no move to sit, so Landon stood and filled them in. "Once she can have her dog home, she'll be okay."

"Little Moxie. She kept a photo of him on her desk. I'll text her in the morning. We'd like to see her before we leave."

"I think she'd appreciate that. The flowers you sent were beautiful."

"Kimi's choice." He tucked his arm around his wife's waist. "I defer to her expertise."

"Did Ciara have a photo of her boyfriend at work too?"

His expression blanked. "No."

Short. Clipped. Discussion closed.

Time to reopen it. Landon anchored her weight in her heels. "She said he betrayed her, but she won't say more. Do you know anything about him? Was he abusive, or do you think he might have followed her here? Attacked her?"

Glancing between them, Kimi stepped to the side.

"He orchestrated a hostile takeover of my former company. He hurt us both." Ken passed a hand in front of his eyes as if to wipe away the warrior she'd seen there. His posture softened. "Spencer Costain is a lot of things, but I can't see him attempting murder."

"Kenjiro—"

"What's done is done. This kind young woman is trying to help her friend. If reading about my shame helps her rule out a suspect, the price is not too high."

"All I need is a name and description. The police will do the research, and whatever happened, they've seen worse." Landon caught her breath. Heat swept her from head to toe. "I'm sorry—I didn't want to minimize your situation. I meant, don't worry about what they'll think."

Although Kimi still radiated tension, Ken's genial expression was back in place. "Understood." He drew his wallet from his light jacket's breast pocket and extracted an ivory business card. "If you have a pen, I'll give you what they need."

Landon had been taking notes on the laptop. She'd stepped toward her room to find a pen when Kimi supplied one.

Ken wrote, then passed the card over. *Spencer Costain.* With a website and a social media link. "My contact information is on the other side, should they need to reach me. But physical assault isn't his style."

Kimi's lips thinned. "He wouldn't get his hands dirty. But would he hire it out?"

He returned the slim gold pen. "My love, he takes far more satisfaction in leaving us alive. Good night, Landon."

Once the Schooner Room's door clicked shut, Landon texted Dylan the information. Despite what Ciara and Ken said, a partner or ex-partner were often prime suspects for a reason. She keyed Spencer's social media link into her browser. If he showed up, she wanted to recognize him.

## Chapter 10

*Thursday*

"That must be Tait now." Landon clicked open her seat belt. Moving Ciara's belongings offered the perfect chance to question her parents about possible clues to the attack. And to see if they were as antagonistic as Ciara claimed.

Bobby had parked Roy's pickup facing outward, truck bed aligned with the broad cobblestone walkway. The silver van reversing in from the street stopped beside them in the double driveway. Tait stepped out.

When she and Bobby joined him, Landon asked, "How's Orran?"

Tait grimaced. "Doing better than Ciara. She was in a lot of pain when I dropped off the dog."

"Maybe I should have gone to stay with her instead of coming to help load." Except she'd wanted to investigate.

She followed Tait along the walk toward the house, her steps slower so she could take it in. Enclosed by a white wraparound veranda, the fairy-tale Victorian was half windows, half creamy yellow wooden shingles. Pristine white trim framed each glass rectangle, and a pale grey roof over the veranda drew the eye to the upper floors and their matching roof.

Fit for a princess. Landon could see Ciara living here.

In response to the doorbell's faint Westminster chimes, the ornately carved wooden screen door opened. Landon and Bobby hurried onto the veranda as a blond man emerged.

Tait handled the introductions. Dressed for labour in a snug, soft-looking grey tee shirt and dark blue jeans, he matched the confident bearing that clung to Phil Kirkwood with his open-throated button-down dress shirt and casually held black coffee mug.

Landon tried to palm the creases from her cotton pants. A glimpse of her sneakers' stained toes made her feel like she belonged at the servants' entrance. With Bobby, whose shirt of the day was a moose in a biplane.

She followed the others into an immaculate hardwood-floored foyer. Their footsteps echoed on the stairs as Phil led them to an upper-floor corner room. Evening light filtered through the sheer curtains on both exterior walls, softening the impersonal effect of stacked two-foot-square boxes and a bare mattress in a four-poster bed.

Ciara could live in this house and avoid her parents for days. Why were they so bent on removing the last traces of her presence?

Phil stood with his back to a window, feet apart. "Whitney helped me with the boxes, but we left the bed for you men to disassemble."

Tait heaved the mattress and box spring off onto their sides against the wall and bent to assess the wooden frame. "We'll need tools."

"There's some in the truck." Bobby ducked toward the stairs.

Landon approached the boxes. "Tait, is the van unlocked? I can start loading these."

After she buckled a stack of boxes into his passenger seat, she started lining more against one side of the cargo area. On her next trip inside, Bobby and Tait were jockeying a solid oak bookcase on the stairs.

Listening to them grunt and gasp, she wandered the foyer, resting her spirit with the soft landscapes on the walls. Beyond a white-framed doorway, glossy dark wood shelving displayed crystal or blown glass sculptures. She drifted in for a closer look.

"Hello." The soft word came from an adjoining room. A petite woman uncurled from the corner of a divan. She crossed the Persian carpet, one white hand outstretched. "You must be Ciara's friend Landon. I'm her mother, Whitney. Thank you for helping her."

Whitney's chestnut hair hung in loose curls halfway to her waist. Her careful makeup couldn't disguise an underlying pallor. With her lacy pink blouse over navy pants, she resembled a collector doll.

Landon clasped her hand lightly, introducing herself. "The heavy lifting you hear from the stairs is Bobby and Tait."

"It's so good of you to do this for her. We suggested she wait until she's recovered from that dreadful fall, but you know Ciara. She can be stubborn."

"She needs to be right now."

It sounded like the bookcase had reached the main level. Time to fetch another box. But this was her opportunity.

"Mrs. Kirkwood—"

"Whitney." Pink-glossed nails flashed in a dismissive gesture.

"Whitney, do you know anyone who'd want to harm Ciara? Someone did this, and she needs justice."

The woman's full lips trembled. "My daughter is strong. An achiever. She's positive—not the sort to backstab or make enemies. I don't know how anyone could try to hurt her."

"There you are, darling. Has the commotion disturbed you?" Phil strolled in from the foyer.

She beamed at him. "It's fine, dear. It'll be good for Ciara to have her things again and fully leave the nest."

Finding her attacker would be good for her too. Landon focused on Phil. "We were talking about the lack of suspects in Ciara's fall."

His nostrils pinched. "Ciara lives her own life. We weren't informed she'd left her job to return to Lunenburg until it was a fait accompli."

Landon's breathing quickened. She forced her lungs to draw deep, to hold and exhale in a steady flow. His harsh response was not aimed at her. She'd heard frustration. Anger. Not control. Not abuse. Concentrating on each breath, she moved her gaze around the room. Anchoring to the reality of the setting.

Safe. She was safe. Feet planted on a glossy parquet floor. Surrounded by works of art and elegant furniture.

With Bobby and Tait for backup.

The sight of them in the doorway unfroze her spine.

She looked straight into Phil's glare. "I understand you wouldn't have information about Ciara's current contacts, but what about her past? Do either of you remember any specific trouble from her childhood? She wasn't always kind at school."

His chin lifted until he was sighting along his nose. "Do you seriously suggest a long-ago grade school resentment could lead to attempted murder in the present?"

Whitney squealed and clapped long fingers to her mouth. Phil rushed to hold her. He stood, head bent, murmuring in her ear.

Without glancing toward Bobby and Tait, Landon drew on their support. "We can't rule anything out, and family may be Ciara's best hope of figuring out who this is. What if he tries again?"

Arm locked in place around his wife's waist, Phil pointed toward the stairs. "This discussion is over. Finish the job and leave us in peace."

Tears glistened in Whitney's eyes. "Phil, I wish you'd hire an investigator."

"The police are fully competent." He tipped his face toward hers with a tender smile.

"Yes, dear, but they're spread so thin. Especially with that shooting in Bridgewater. A girl who lived isn't going to get much attention."

"The investigators assure me they have a full complement of staff to handle these and the other cases. We need to trust them to do their jobs and not allow the events to distress us." He stroked Whitney's hair as if to smooth the furrows from her forehead. With an "Excuse us" to Landon, he shepherded his wife farther into the house.

Ciara hadn't mentioned her mother's fragility. Did she know?

Landon spun and hurried for the foyer. Whatever unintended harm she'd done, the best thing now was to finish loading and remove themselves from the scene.

Bobby and Tait lingered at the door. Tait cocked his head. "Wonder what that was about."

"All I did was ask if they had any ideas about Ciara's attacker. Somehow we have to find who's behind this." She jogged up the stairs.

A cluster of boxes remained in the bedroom. Tait scooped two into a stack against his chest and headed out.

Bobby's touch stopped Landon as she reached for another. "Don't worry about Ciara's mom. It's the attack that hurt her, not you."

"Thank you." She picked up the box.

He cut his gaze toward the stairs. "Tait. Is he a person of interest to Ciara?"

"For the crime?" What had Bobby seen that she hadn't?

"Bad choice of words. Just…" He hefted a couple of boxes. "Cologne and fairly dressy casual clothes for a dirty job. Like he's trying to make a good impression on her. Or her folks."

"Or he likes to look good. But maybe. She's skittish, though."

Bobby snorted. "Huh. Never was with me."

True. No matter how often they'd mentioned his girlfriend. "Was she serious, or just trying to make you uncomfortable?"

"Dunno. You didn't tell her I'm single?"

"If she didn't care before, she won't now. How are you doing with it all?"

He peered at her around the edge of his boxes, beard stubble rasping against the cardboard. "Sounds like you assume I got dumped. Thanks for that."

Tait burst through the doorway. "Let's move. Ciara's waiting."

Bobby's steady gaze fixed on Landon. Unreadable.

With a grunt, Tait gathered more boxes and left.

As he clomped down the stairs, Landon shifted the load in her arms. "From what you've said, I never thought Jessie appreciated you."

Bobby took a step toward the door. "She's not that bad. But ending it was my choice."

"How'd she take it?"

"Not well."

"Heartbreaker."

He glanced back from the hallway. "Hearts weren't involved on either side. We'll both miss the convenience, that's all."

Landon followed him onto the stairs. "Is that why you decided to stay longer with Roy?"

"I couldn't go back to the same town, the same church. With the same friends. It wouldn't be right."

Tait zipped inside as they reached the main floor. "Still one left? I'll get it."

Fifteen minutes later, they lumbered in a slow convoy through quiet streets toward the inn. Anna had offered to store everything in the barn until Ciara could decide what to keep and what to sell.

As they left town, Bobby cleared his throat. "Mad at me?"

"For what?"

"Breaking up with Jessie. Did I let her down or something?"

The truck jounced into a pothole. Bobby yelped and did a quick shoulder-check through the rear window. "Didn't launch anything."

They'd tied it all down, but he'd seemed nervous about the straps. He blew out a noisy breath. "In the tunnel, waiting to die, I thought about Gramp. My parents. Travers and his crew. Never once about Jessie. That told me I had to let go and give her a chance to find someone who'd really love her."

Lacing her fingers in her lap, Landon traced a thumb along her opposite palm. "So that's why you wouldn't call about what happened. You had to see her in person."

"Exactly. And the longer I waited, the more certain I was. Here is where I want to be."

"I'm sure your parents were glad for the chance to see you and Roy."

His fingers lifted on the steering wheel, curled, lifted again. "They were less than thrilled about me moving here. Short-term help for Gramp made their lives easier. But staying when he doesn't need me…"

"What?"

"It may have been suggested I'll lose myself in the backwater of a have-not province. Not the kind of success they've hoped I'd pursue."

"But your writing—"

"Isn't a real career, apparently. Not that working an IT help line was much better, but at least it came with a regular salary." Turn indicator ticking, he slowed for the inn's long driveway.

With both vehicles parked tail-in to the wide barn door, offloading was easy. When they finished, Landon surveyed the neat stacks along one wall. "We just emptied this. But it saves Ciara storage fees."

Tait glanced around the interior. "So there's a floor hatch for the old smuggler's tunnel."

While Bobby pointed out the concealed trapdoor, Landon retreated to the exit. "We could have used your advice in June when we were looking for lights and cameras."

After they followed her onto the crushed gravel path, she clicked the padlock into place. "I know you and Orran deal with higher-end security, but could you give Ciara any shopping tips? Or don't you think she needs anything in her apartment?"

Tait squinted toward the trees. "You think her attacker will be back?"

"Unless it was a random weirdo, won't he try to finish what he started? She has a deadbolt, and it's a secure-access building. But she's there all alone."

"I'll talk to her. If she wants an off-the-shelf kit, I can set it up for her." He strolled toward the van. "For now, I'll collect the Little Terror and head home. She wasn't in any shape to keep him long."

Hand on the door latch, he stopped. "Come with me and see what I mean? I think she's worse."

"Let me tell Anna first."

Landon tossed the basics into a canvas tote bag in case Ciara needed someone overnight, accepted a foil package of Anna's lasagna to deliver, and headed out.

Bobby and Tait stood talking in the dusk. Bobby met her eyes. "I could come too. Then Tait doesn't have to divert all the way out here to bring you home."

Tait shrugged. "I don't mind. No sense in us all going."

Something in the angle of Bobby's jaw said he wasn't happy. Concerned, maybe. That she'd be uncomfortable alone with a virtual stranger? More likely concerned for Ciara's health.

Landon smiled her reassurance. "I'll text you once I see her."

Truth told, she wasn't all that comfortable with Tait. But he kept the conversation focused on Ciara as he drove. Landon couldn't tell him much from past or present that might offer a lead to the attacker, but at least he took an interest in talking it through. The more people who cared, the better.

When they stepped into Ciara's apartment, a single lamp lit the interior. Ciara sat on the couch with Moxie curled between her feet on the floor. She fluttered a weak wave. "Landon! I'm so glad you came. I can't stay alone tonight."

Landon passed Anna's care package to Tait and hurried to the injured girl's side.

Fiery red splotched Ciara's cheeks, and her eyes shimmered. "It hurts so much."

Moxie yipped as Landon sank onto the couch. She took Ciara's hand, hot against her own, and glanced up at Tait.

Brows low, he shook his head.

Landon tucked the blanket around Ciara's shoulders. "You have a fever, and the pain shouldn't be this bad."

"They should never have sent me home." Tears streamed down her cheeks.

"I can drive you to the hospital, or we can wait for an ambulance." Tait was already fastening Moxie's leash to the little dog's sparkly collar. "The Boy was coming home with me tonight anyway. Want to ride with him in the van?"

With a watery sniffle, Ciara pushed away the blanket and plucked at her happy-face pyjama pants. "I can't go like this."

"Hospitals could use a bit of cheer." Tait's expression didn't soften. "Let's go."

## Chapter 11

*Friday*

Yawning widely enough to make her eyes water, Landon leaned her elbows on the deck rail and cradled her second cup of coffee. The morning sun washed the tree trunks behind the inn with golden light while here in the building's shadow condensation skimmed every surface.

She'd taken Anna's advice to sleep instead of helping with the guests' breakfast, but Ciara's text woke her anyway.

After waiting in the local emergency room last night for triage, a protesting Ciara had been transferred by ambulance back to the larger regional hospital in Bridgewater. She'd been admitted with pneumonia, put on oxygen and antibiotics. This morning, she alternated between self-pity and concern for her dog.

Landon had promised to go when she could. For now, watching the trees sway and listening to the birds and squirrels felt good. The September air carried a cleansing crispness.

A muted cry stilled her thoughts. Soft yet sharp, like an animal in pain.

It came again. From behind the barn, where they fed the marmalade stray. She left her mug on the railing and slipped down the stairs and onto the grass.

When he strolled into her life earlier this summer, battle-scarred and aloof, she'd named him Captain Jack. Until they discovered the truth about the real Captain Jack, builder of the inn. Now they called him Mister.

Landon had built a fragile trust with the animal, but he wouldn't let her care for an injury. She eased around the corner of the barn. His stainless steel food dish lay arm's length from where it belonged.

In a dark blur, an arm snaked out from the shadowy wall. A gloved hand clamped her open mouth before she'd even drawn breath to scream. Her assailant's other hand dug strong fingers into her upper arm. He spun her face-in to the wall.

"Don't struggle, and you won't get hurt." His whisper hissed against her cheek.

Cold sweat slicked her body. The trafficker had employed that menacing tone whenever he was about to mete out punishment to any of the girls.

"Good." The word carried satisfaction.

Her thoughts ricocheted in crazy flight. Fear. Cage. Pain.

Her trafficker—dead. Zander gripping her hands as he gave her the news.

The memory jolted her from the cycle. She was free. Safe.

But the scent of leather clogging her nostrils and the grip on her mouth and arm said no. Not safe.

If one of her trafficker's friends had found her—

Landon's legs buckled.

The man held her upright, mashed against the grey barn wall. "I have a message for your friend."

Friend?

"Pushing her was a mistake. Let it go and she'll be safe."

The words buzzed in her brain. Little balls of light. They meant something. One truth burned clear. This was no trafficker. That light sliced her terror. Brought strength to her legs to stand.

"Mmm?" She squeaked the sound.

"Your friend." He shook her. "Back off and so will I."

"Hey!" The shout came from behind and to the left.

The man spun Landon and shoved her toward the sound. Footfalls thudded away behind her.

Her palms broke her fall. She pushed off the soft grass to her knees, twisting to catch sight of him. A dark figure fled into the woods behind Roy's place.

"Are you hurt?" Nigel. Quiet. Nearby.

Straightening, she looked around. He stood just out of reach. She hadn't heard his approach even though his chest heaved from his sprint. His sharp eyes, hooded under bristly salt-and-pepper brows, watched her like he would a wounded forest creature. Waiting for her response.

"I—" Ciara. This was about Ciara. Now that the mind-numbing terror of a sex trafficker's revenge had dissipated, she could understand his words. Their meaning.

"I'll be okay. Did you see him?"

Nigel blinked twice. "Come to the inn. To Anna. He was masked."

She placed her hand in his large rough one and let him lead her to safety. Her knees wobbled on the stairs, and she made for the nearest chair at the patio table. But Nigel steered her to the door and into the kitchen.

With the gentleness of a host, he settled her in one of the white hoop back chairs and squeezed her shoulder. "Wait for Anna. And tea." He hurried from the room.

A minute later, Anna burst through the doorway with Nigel a silent shadow.

The air fled Landon's lungs, and she lunged to her feet—and into Anna's embrace. Warm arms held her tight until her tremors stopped. Finally she gathered herself. "I'm okay."

"You will be." Tight-lipped, Anna led her back to her seat. "And there will be a camera behind that barn. This will not happen again." She rubbed her hands along Landon's forearms as if to warm her. "Thank God Nigel came by. Anything could have happened."

Eyes closed, Landon massaged her temples. "He said it was a message. That Ciara's attack was a mistake. That if we drop it he'll stop."

Anna dropped into a chair beside her. "Why would he come to you?"

Nigel chuckled. "Our Landon is persistent. He may have more to fear from her than from the police."

Anna placed a warm hand between her shoulders, fingers shifting side to side. "You know you can trust Dylan and the others to do their job."

"Of course. But civilians share information among ourselves that an officer would never hear." Landon inhaled through her nose, visually tracing the grey strands in Anna's brown bob. Strands that had multiplied over this ten-month ordeal. Continuing to ask questions would worry Anna—and jeopardize Ciara.

But the defiant burn in her mind pushed for answers. "I can't let it go—because it can't be 'let go' from Ciara's emotions. Dropping it would be saying it didn't matter." She flattened her palms on the glossy pine tabletop, fingers stretched wide. "Besides, the minute he touched me, he made it personal."

"I have to call this in." Anna plucked the landline handset from the counter. "Zander arrives today. What's he going to think about you being involved? And this man terrorizing you right here at the inn?"

Zander's quiet pain when he'd said he couldn't lose her... A weight lodged in Landon's stomach. "I hope he'll help me."

~~~

Landon set her phone on the kitchen table. "Bobby was going to take me to the hospital this morning. I told him it'll be a while yet."

Nigel studied her over the rim of his special tea blend. "There's another one who won't be happy about this."

Anna ushered Constable Zerkowsky in from the hallway. He settled his husky frame on the chair opposite Landon. Radiating stillness and solid strength, he leaned in like a friend inviting a confidence. "You know the drill."

Her throat tightened. It wasn't what had happened—it was what her triggered mind had thought was happening. The soul-blanking horror of the past reborn.

She concentrated on the feel of the contoured wooden seat beneath her. The smooth pine tabletop. The pale pink wall. The faces. Zerkowsky's, broad and patient. Anna's, drawn but determined. Nigel's, alert and questioning.

Nigel's scarred hands. Burned to save a life.

These people were on her side. She couldn't ask for better.

Her words came unstuck.

Once Zerkowsky absorbed her story and Nigel's, Landon tried to think of everyone she'd asked about Ciara's fall. Family, friends, none of whom seemed to have a motive. "That's all, I think."

He listed each name in his notebook. "Plus anyone they may have mentioned it to. The ripple effect can spread a long way." The tip of his pen dotted the margin. "Who was the guy I saw walking up the drive when I came? Dark pants, dark sweater tied around his waist... A brazen move if he's your attacker, but stranger things have happened."

"Oh." Anna's expression cleared. "That must have been Ken, one of our guests from BC. He walks every morning. I heard the front door chime before I let you in the back."

"So he'd have no connection with Ciara."

Landon grimaced. "He's her former boss."

Zerkowsky positioned his pen beneath the entries on his list. "Tell me his full name."

After he and Nigel left, Anna went online to order another security camera to add to the ones already in place. "In the interim, we'll feed your stray together."

It wasn't a suggestion. Landon wandered into the common room and slouched into the leather club chair by the bookcase to watch for Bobby. When the Corvette eased up the drive, her thoughts and emotions were still swirling. She called goodbye to Anna and hurried out the rear door.

Nigel was right. Bobby wouldn't take this well.

He greeted her from the driver's seat. "Anna draft you for cleaning duty?"

Instead of buckling in, she twisted toward him. "We had an incident. *I* had an incident. The police were here."

A too-casual breath lifted the skateboarding snowman on his shirt—a snowman, in September—and he cut the engine. "Are you all right?"

"I'm fine. But I'm not." The story tumbled out in fragmented sentences, jumbled words. Why was telling Bobby harder? That same blue-grey gaze had held hers in the barn when Gord intended to kill them both.

Bobby's stubbled jaw clenched so tight it pulled his lips into a line. "Objectively, an anonymous quasi-apology and message that Ciara was safe could have seemed harmless to him."

"Except he grabbed a trauma survivor." And stirred flames she thought she'd quenched. Landon's fingers quested the spot where her neck met her hairline. Where the trafficker's brand marked her as property—until she'd had the tattoo covered with another.

"Today—he threw me right back into that pit. I am so angry." The breath hissed between her lips like venting steam. The man had no idea what he'd unleashed. She swiped her hair away from her face. *She* had no idea what he'd unleashed. "He made this personal, and I will bring him down."

His eyebrows eased upward. "I hope you didn't express that to Anna. Or Dylan."

"Zerkowsky. But no." She rubbed her neck again. "What am I saying? The strongest person wins, and that's never me."

Bobby restarted the engine. "There's no point asking you to sit this out? To get your revenge in court?"

"I can't."

He guided the car down the driveway. "Then don't sell yourself short. You defeated Gord this summer."

"*We* did, together, but not head-on. If he'd stayed, we'd have lost." Her fingers twisted together in her lap. "Seeing Ciara so helpless... I thought I was sticking up for her. But this is still about me. About wanting to lash out at the men who hurt me."

"Hey." His knuckles tapped her arm. "You told me in July we were heroes. A hero may have reversals, but she does not quit."

"What does that even mean?"

"You are stronger than you know, my friend. And you have someone even stronger in your corner."

He couldn't be talking about himself, not when he kept comparing himself to the character in his novels. She cut him a weak grin. "You do realize Travers isn't real."

"Jesus is. Guaranteed stronger than this troublemaker. And stronger than any hate you still need to let go."

"For now, I need Him to find this guy. And keep us safe."

## Chapter 12

CIARA LOOKED WORSE than she had after the attack. Eyes shut, she lay against the pillows in a hospital bed with the head elevated. A bag of clear liquid suspended from a silver pole fed into the crook of her arm. Another tube underlined her nose.

Landon tiptoed nearer and settled in the solitary grey vinyl chair near the window.

Ciara's lashes fluttered. "Thanks for coming. I'm sure you have homework and stuff."

"How do you feel?"

"Breathing is like a knife slicing my lung open, and my head's still pounding with the concussion. Which means I can't look at my phone much and I have to lie here like a blob." She touched the line feeding oxygen into her nostrils. "At least I've graduated from the mask."

"Anna and Bobby send their best. We thought too many people today wasn't a good idea."

Landon was about to bring up this morning's brush with Ciara's attacker when a nurse breezed in to change the IV bag. His cheery chatter seemed to help Ciara respond in kind, but she blew out a slow sigh as soon as he disappeared through the door. "They're so kind to me, but I feel awful."

"There you are." Shaun stood in the doorway. "Hey, what happened? That cannula is new."

Staring at Ciara, he must have caught Landon's puzzled expression. "The oxygen tube. It's called a cannula."

The shoulders of his black leather jacket lifted in a shrug. "Spend too much time around hospitals, you pick up the jargon. But you..." He cocked a finger toward the bed. "First, I walk in on a stranger in your old room, and then I find you here all tangled up in tubes. What'd you do, pick a fight with the night nurse?"

Her pale lips twitched. "Please, laughing hurts. Ribs and pneumonia. I was sent home and had to come back."

"That stinks." He strolled closer, one hand in his jacket pocket. At the foot of her bed, he produced a treat-sized cloth lilac bag and flipped it onto her lap. "This might cheer you up."

"Ooh, what is it?" Reaching for it brought a swift gasp. Ciara eased onto the pillows and held it to eye level, loosening the drawstring and dipping her fingers inside. She pulled out a thin gold chain, rotating it to peer at the diamond-shaped tag.

"My bracelet!" Rounding it into a circle, she stared through it at Shaun. "Where was it?"

"Halfway down the side of the cliff where you fell." With a barbed look for Landon, he said, "Jeweller in Halifax did a rush repair job, and here it is."

"This is—I don't know what to say. Thank you so much." Ciara traced her fingers around the length. "Did they say what a repair will do to resale value?"

His cocky grin slipped. "I figured it was sentimental. Didn't ask. But, hey, if you'd rather have the insurance money, I can lose it again."

"No!" She fussed with the clasp. Once the gold strand wrapped her wrist, she looked up. "It has sentimental value now."

"Well, you're welcome. Maybe I'll see you around." With a half wave, he strode into the hallway.

He'd done what he said—had it cleaned and repaired, which couldn't have been cheap. Whoever this guy was, he couldn't be the attacker. Unless fixing the bracelet was another part of fixing his mistake.

Landon shook her head at her own paranoia. "We saw him at the park, Bobby and I, when we went to look for clues. He said he wanted to surprise you."

Ciara was still sliding her index finger around the fine gold links. "I'm nothing to him. Why would he rescue a stranger and then put the time and money into finding and restoring a bracelet he could have pawned?"

"To help you feel better?" They could try to figure Shaun out later. For now, Ciara needed to know about the attacker's apology-slash-warning. If she wanted to let it drop, Landon would find another way to identify him. For her own sake. She leaned forward in her chair, elbows digging into the thinly padded armrests, and tried to keep her emotions out of the story.

Ciara listened in wide-eyed silence, her fingertips frozen on the bracelet. "It was a mistake? Like he meant to kill someone else?"

"I don't know. I was too scared to think straight. But telling me to stop means he knows I've been asking questions. And everyone I approached is connected with you."

"So it's me." The faint lift in Ciara's cheeks had vanished. Pearl-white teeth worried her lower lip. "I feel terrible that you were accosted like that. For helping me."

Landon spread her fingers on her jeans, pressing into the soft denim. "Now I want to find him for both our sakes. You haven't thought of any possible local enemies, past or present? And you're sure your ex is still in BC?"

"I looked online, and he's in a bunch of high-profile meetings this week."

"Could he have hired someone to kill you?"

Ciara's lips twitched. "Honey, he surrounds himself with the best. If he outsourced, I'd be dead. There'd be no mistake."

"I don't know what to do with the idea of the attack being a mistake. Like he misunderstood instructions to scare you or to attack someone else? Or he thought you'd done something you hadn't..."

Palms to temples, Ciara squeezed her eyes shut.

Landon was about to go find a nurse when Tait arrived. He closed the door behind him. "How's the patient?"

Ciara's eyelids sprang open. "Thanks for driving me last night."

"Glad to help." He mimed a casual salute and stepped nearer to the bed. He put a finger to his lips, then lowered the zipper on his brown cloth jacket. Moxie's head popped into the opening. Tait's fingers clamped his muzzle in time to stifle a yip.

Ciara stared, tears running down her cheeks, as the little dog vibrated with eagerness.

Tait nestled Moxie into Ciara's non-IV arm, and the Chihuahua climbed to lick her chin. Once Tait repositioned him, he stayed in the crook of her arm, tongue lolling, tail a blur.

She accepted a bunch of tissues from Landon and dried her face. Sniffling, she beamed at Tait, sunshine after the rain. "Thank you so much. I feel so terrible, but these gifts have made this the best day."

"Seeing double? There's only one of him."

That brought a watery giggle and a painful gasp. She raised her wrist, dangling the bracelet. "Shaun was here—the guy who rescued me. Look what he found and fixed for me."

"That was decent." Tait stuffed his hands into his jacket pockets, elbows out. His brows drew together. "Listen, he could be a fine person, but..."

"But what?"

He shifted his weight from foot to foot. "It's just you don't know him or anyone who can be a character reference for him. Like I said, probably an upstanding man. But he could be using all this to get close to you."

"Why? I'm nothing." Colour seeped into Ciara's cheeks, and her breaths picked up a sharp wheeze.

"Access to your wealthy parents? Or to influence your stepfather's extended family?" He shrugged. "Security is my business. Most of the time the potential trouble I see doesn't happen, but I'd be remiss if I didn't bring it up."

Ciara ruffled Moxie's fur, her fingertips gliding over the soft amber and white hair. "Believe me, I've seen ingratiating behaviour. Shaun's not it."

"Good."

"Thanks for caring, though. And for bringing my little buddy. I don't dare keep him long."

"Could get awkward."

Ciara's free hand drew the oxygen feed farther away from the dog. "Tait, I wanted to ask you—is Orran still together with his girlfriend?"

"What girlfriend?"

"I guess that's a no. Seeing him living alone now that he's ill... I was thinking of the one he used to see when he travelled and hoping they still had a long-distance thing going. The one he picked up that fancy goblet for, for her theatre group."

Tait hiked a shoulder. "He was single when I met him."

Landon's phone buzzed a text. She peeked while Ciara and Tait chatted. Instead of Anna or Bobby, it was Zander. He'd already stopped at the inn and was now waiting in the hospital parking lot "because I need to know you're okay. But take your time. I have calls to make."

Some of her tension drained away. Zander was her Orran. He'd help find Ciara's attacker, especially now that the man had made it personal. A shiver slid down her arms. His reaction to this morning's encounter wouldn't be fun. She tapped a reply to his text, then slid the phone into her pocket.

Hallway noise penetrated the room. The door swung open.

Moxie chose that moment to bark.

As Tait was reaching for the dog, a nurse strode to Ciara's bedside. "What do we have here?"

Tait's movement continued without a hitch. "Therapy animal. See how much better she's doing?"

The nurse's scrubs stretched across her slim shoulders as she adjusted Ciara's position in the bed. She checked the monitors. "Remove it now, and I'll forget to report this."

He scooped the dog into his jacket and closed the zipper. "Gotta go. Ciara, I'll give Orran your love."

The nurse turned to Landon. "It's time for her breathing therapy. I need to ask you to leave too."

Landon stood. "Thanks for taking care of her. See you tomorrow, Ciara." She hurried into the hallway. "Tait, wait up."

They ducked into a free elevator. "That meant so much, bringing Moxie today." She grinned at him. "Smooth extrication under fire."

"Not my first escape routine."

"Do you have a minute outside? I want you to meet a friend who's going to help find Ciara's attacker."

"For that, I'll make time."

A sturdy maple shaded Zander's brown SUV. As Landon and Tait approached, the driver's window slid down.

"Zander, this is Tait, one of Ciara's friends. He's in security systems. Tait, Zander has contacts in corrections."

Tait stuck out a hand, the other one keeping gentle pressure on his jacket.

"What do you have there?" Typical Zander, observant and direct.

Unzipping, Tait gave Moxie space to breathe. "Unauthorized visitor for the patient."

Zander rested a pale blue sleeve on the window rim. Cuff buttoned today, not even a pretense at being on vacation. "I've been to see the investigators. They have nothing yet."

Tait unrolled a sparkly leash from his pocket and clipped it to Moxie's collar before setting the dog down. "Manly task, minding this brute."

With Moxie sniffing the pavement around his feet, Tait flapped the slack leash against his pant leg. "You two have clearly put thought into this. Any suspects?"

The possibilities were so far-fetched, naming them felt like slander. "Her former boss and his wife have been staying at the inn. Instead of leaving today, they moved to a housekeeping unit in Bridgewater. And what did you think about her parents last night? Do they want her out of town as badly as she thinks?"

"Her stepfather's on edge, but I think it's concern for his wife. Not sure what the issue is there. I'd add that Shaun guy too. Rescuing someone in the heat of the moment is one thing, but going back to find a piece of jewellery and then paying for repairs... all for a stranger? My gut says he wants something."

Zander's lips pinched. "Ideas?"

"Influence with her family? I don't know, abduction for ransom?" Tait spread his palms. "You can tell I'm reaching. He could be a private investigator for all I know."

Landon scuffed her canvas sneaker against the pavement. "That's the problem. Nobody seems to have a motive. Do either of you have the connections to check into these people?"

The two men eyed one another. Zander said, "They're on my list."

"I can run standard internet checks, but I do security systems, not investigations."

Tait's words opened a new angle. "If you looked at video footage at The Ovens, might you see a clue the police missed?"

"Maybe. If they even have cameras there. There wouldn't be any on the trails."

"It's worth a try." Landon caught her hair in a one-handed ponytail. "Tait, you don't know this, but Anna will have told Zander. Ciara's attacker grabbed me this morning and claimed the fall was a mistake. He said if I'd stop asking questions she'd be fine."

The familiar burn flared. Her arms clamped across her ribs. "That's much less severe than what he did on Monday, but it's still an assault. He has to be found. And stopped."

Tait mirrored her stance, bouncing slightly on his heels as if absorbing her tension. "You okay?"

"I'm a trauma survivor. He triggered the memory so badly, I could barely process what he said." Focusing on the broad maple leaves overhanging Zander's SUV, she steadied her breathing. "I still wonder if it's someone from Ciara's past before she went away to university. Orran hasn't mentioned anyone?"

Tait shook his head.

"Could you ask him?"

"Will do. If she chattered as much then, he'll have heard all kinds of youthful drama." He bent to collect the dog. "I'll let you know what he says. Text me your number?"

Once she unlocked her phone, he recited the digits. Then, with a nod to Zander, he walked off across the lot.

Landon rounded the front of the vehicle and climbed into the passenger seat, bracing for Zander's reaction. She couldn't blame him for thinking she'd be safer in Toronto with her trusted support network, but she'd made her choice. No matter what he said, she was staying here. And helping to put this attacker away.

He gave her a long look. "How are you really?"

Breathing deep against her nerves, she held eye contact. "Angry. Zander, I was so scared he was a trafficker—come to take me back." Speaking it aloud set her heart hammering.

He nodded, narrow jaw tensing. "I'll stay as long as you need me. Your questions rattled him, or he wouldn't have approached you."

When she opened her mouth to say she wouldn't quit, his raised index finger stopped her. "Let me do the asking. I'll work with the police."

"I can't sit this out." Not now.

"I understand. All I'm asking is that you work behind the scenes."

~~~

Landon cut a piece of roast beef and swirled it in the mushroom sauce before popping it into her mouth. Enjoying a meal with friends while Ciara ate something bland and uninspiring alone in the hospital felt wrong.

Glass bowls of peas, carrots, and mashed potatoes surrounded the oval platter of sliced beef on Roy's dark oak table. His chair anchored one end, with Landon and Anna on one side and Zander and Bobby on the other. Bobby's skateboarding snowman shirt and Zander's button-down made an unusual pair.

As Roy's outlandish anecdotes flowed, Zander's naturally stern expression relaxed to allow a small smile. He forked another slice of beef onto his plate. "This is delicious."

"Come back in November. Maybe we'll have venison."

"You hunt?"

"I clear some of the neighbours' driveways when it snows—you've noticed they're not short city things—and somehow food mysteriously shows up at my door." Roy waved in the inn's direction. "Elva lives down past Anna. Crack shot. Always provides me with a roast or two."

A chill spread from Landon's spine across her shoulders. "Elva?"

"That woman always gets her deer. Often the first day of the season."

Landon set her fork on the edge of the stoneware plate, stomach queasy. Elva had more motive than most to want Gord dead. He'd tried to murder her, and he knew things from her past she didn't want shared.

"Do the police know? How well she can shoot?"

Roy's sea-blue eyes sharpened. "I wonder."

"She wouldn't!" But Anna's knife clattered against her plate.

Landon sipped her water, her gaze finding Zander's over the rim. "Zander, the shooting before you first arrived. Gord, who tried to kill Anna, Bobby, and me? He also tried to kill Elva."

"Ah." He patted his lips with a plaid paper napkin.

"Dylan hunts. He may already know." Landon felt her hips settle heavier onto the wooden seat. "I'll text him later."

Anna shook her head. "Didn't you say his vacation started today? We can phone the detachment in the morning."

Frowning at the remaining peas on her plate, Landon said, "He cancelled his leave when Zerkowsky told him what happened at the inn this morning. He said they needed a full staff rotation with Gord's killer and Ciara's attacker."

"Proper thing." Roy's water glass rapped against the table. "And I feel better knowing Zander will be next door to keep watch on our Landon."

Landon kept focused on her plate. Her friends loved her. They cared. But if they didn't stop jostling to protect her, she was going to explode. Even Bobby was bristly tonight. Did they think they could out-testosterone this attacker?

Zander cleared his throat. "Thank you, Roy. I'll do my best. Landon and I did a bit of brainstorming today with another of Ciara's friends."

"Tait. Hansen, I think," Landon supplied.

Anna sniffed. "For Landon's safety, she needs to stay out of this. Zander, I can't believe you're encouraging her."

"It's not my first choice." He offered a rueful smile. "I'll make myself the visible target asking questions. If I become a threat, the attacker should refocus his attention."

"All I did was introduce Zander to Tait, and the conversation went from there. We came out of the hospital together." Landon grinned. "He smuggled Moxie in to see Ciara."

Mischief sparked in Roy's sea-blue eyes. "Wish I'd seen that."

Later, as they lingered over coffee, tea, and an apple-caramel bread pudding, Zander told how he'd first met Landon and how they'd bonded over the years. His cheeks hollowed. "My daughter died in tragic circumstances. Seeing Landon find wholeness, new life, has helped me as much as I hope I've helped her. You'll understand why I'm committed to keeping her safe."

He glanced around the table. "I believe you feel the same. God has given her good friends here."

Roy rapped his spoon against the rim of his dessert dish. "Robert, why don't you and Landon clear up and let your elders relax? A meal like this doesn't happen without a body slaving in the kitchen all afternoon." When Landon glanced at the elderly man, he winked.

With the others in the living room and Bobby running water into the sink, she butted a hip against the counter. "You cooked, didn't you?"

"Yup."

"Then what's up, *Robert*? Are you in trouble?"

"Not that I know of." He rinsed a few more plates from the stack and loaded them into the dishwasher. "Gramp wants to get a better feel for Zander. It's hard to know how to take him."

She tucked a length of blond hair behind her ear. "He's very protective. That's why he came to visit when I decided to stay—to be sure I was okay and in a safe place."

"Hey, I'm not questioning his integrity or motives. He's just so intense."

"What would Travers think about Zander?"

"I wish I knew. It feels like there's a darkness there, but what he said about his daughter would cause that." When they finished loading the dishwasher, Bobby started scrubbing pots. "Zander wanted to check things out here. Since he's involved in this mystery, your local friends have the same questions about him."

He shot her a stern look, then grinned. "What? You didn't think we staged this meal because we were worried about you after this morning?"

Landon grabbed a tea towel and flipped it at him.

He sidestepped. "Seriously, you're okay?"

"Yes, and more determined than ever."

A slow exhale. "I figured you would be. Let me help."

# Chapter 13

*Saturday*

"Meaghan says there's still no lead on Gord's killer." Landon clasped her thin cardigan against a sharp breeze as she and Bobby hurried up the concrete steps toward South Shore Regional Hospital.

"How's she holding up?"

"Strong but sad, you know? Like she's acknowledged it hurts even though their relationship wasn't good. I think she's still mad that I'm not helping investigate, but what could I do?"

Bobby held open one of the glass entry doors for her. "Does she know you're asking around for Ciara? That'd burn."

"She didn't say. But I did tell Dylan Elva can shoot."

His light touch on her arm stopped her in the hospital foyer. "You're not going to approach Elva about this, are you?"

"No way. But I hope she didn't do it."

In the elevator, Bobby dangled a mid-sized pink gift bag against the side of his jeans. "Thanks for not making me visit alone. As flirty as Ciara gets, I wouldn't want to give her the wrong idea."

"Aw, but you're so cute when you're uncomfortable." Landon snickered. "Maybe that's why she does it. That and habit."

His face pulled into an exaggerated grimace. "Thanks for the ego boost."

The elevator shuddered to a stop, and Landon stepped out. She smirked at him over her shoulder. "Hey, friends are for keeping you grounded."

Today's private guard recognized Landon. Once Ciara okayed Bobby, they entered the room.

Ciara's features lit when she saw them. A faint rose entered her cheeks, although it didn't reach the grey hollows around her eyes. "Thank you so much for coming."

Wincing, she hitched herself taller against the elevated pillows and rearranged the length of clear tubing leading to her nose. A green bangle on her right wrist stood out against her pale skin and the pastel hospital gown. "They say my oxygen count is getting better, but I could be days in here."

Bobby strolled to the bed and offered the gift bag. "Maybe this'll make you smile."

"For me?" Eager fingers scooped out the tissue paper and lifted an eight-by-ten picture frame. "Oh, Bobby, thank you. I miss him so much!"

She reversed the frame for Landon to see Moxie sitting tall and proud, a circle of cloth like a tiny nest beneath him on the tile floor. His wide-open mouth and lolling tongue mimed laughter.

Bobby laughed. "That's Gramp's favourite hat. Old guy wasn't too impressed."

"He didn't... leave anything, did he?"

"Just allergens. It's all good."

"Did Landon tell you Tait smuggled him in here yesterday? You should have seen the nurse. But it was worth it."

It *had* been worth it. Landon smiled. "I think he likes you. Tait, I mean."

Ciara shrugged. "He's kind, but it's more for Orran than for me. But speaking of Orran—" She lifted her wrist with the bright bangle. "See what he brought me last night."

"Yeah, I saw your post online this morning." Bobby leaned a shoulder against the wall. "Very nice."

Before long, Bobby excused himself. "I'll give you two space for a little girl talk."

Once he left, Landon scooted her chair nearer to the bed. "So what's wrong? Other than being tossed off a cliff and getting pneumonia on top of your injuries?"

Ciara's shuddery, drama-queen-worthy sigh ended with a sniffle. "Bobby noticed too, didn't he? That's why he cleared out."

"He's going to work on his book in the cafeteria while he waits for me."

"Don't writers need quiet?"

"His idea, not mine. But it might be easier to talk about what's troubling you while we're alone."

"Orran said my bracelet was an early inheritance—while he's alive to see me enjoy it." Ciara caressed it with her fingertips. "It's beautiful and I love it. But now I'm even more worried about his health. What kind of life expectancy does he have if he's talking like that?"

"And the two of you have just reconnected."

"He's been more like a father to me than my real one—or Phil. He helped me believe in myself." Ciara's mouth trembled.

"A good mentor is a treasure." Landon thanked God every day for Anna and Zander. "Even with his lung problems, though, Orran seems do be doing okay. Tait doesn't act worried."

"Protective, but yeah, I guess not worried." Ciara's head flopped against the pillows, short brown hair flying. "I have nothing to do but think."

The flowers had gone home after her first stay. Other than the photo of Moxie, the stark and impersonal space held nothing to distract her.

"If your concussion won't let you read or watch videos on your phone, what about an audiobook? Or podcasts?"

"Everything hurts and I can't concentrate. Except on sad things."

"Have you talked to the nurses? It's normal to feel vulnerable after a trauma. They might have a counsellor on staff."

"I can get through this by myself."

Landon pressed her fingers against Ciara's forearm. "It's okay to need help. Nobody's strong all the time."

Ciara's phone buzzed on the bedside table, and she did a slow-motion reach for the sparkly case. She squinted at the screen before answering. "Tait? Is Orran okay?"

"Far as I know and no thanks to you. Why shouldn't he be?" His anger punched through the phone for Landon to hear.

Ciara flinched and drew the phone away from her ear. Ashen-faced, she clutched at Landon's hand. "I—he was talking about dying. Why no thanks to me? What did I do?"

"You bragged all over the internet about the trinket he gave you. Did you learn nothing from that local theft—criminals tracking keywords? Tagging Orran means they'll be watching both of you. Did you even think?"

"I forgot about the thief." Ciara's eyes had gone wide, her lips a perfect circle. "Jade's pricey, but are you sure the bracelet's *that* valuable?"

"He didn't get it at the dollar store." His contempt dragged guilt across Landon's skin.

"I'll take it down. Right away."

"Do that. And hope it's not too late."

Ciara jabbed repeatedly at the phone screen, then dropped the jewelled case in her lap. Tears matted her lashes. "Orran's gift made me feel special. I didn't think about how much it could be worth, and I've ruined everything. Again."

She yanked the jade bangle from her wrist and thrust it at Landon. "Keep it for me? It's not safe here."

Landon frowned. "If—*if*—a thief saw your post, how would they find you now?"

Ciara's chin dipped, and her gaze cut upward. "I said I was in the hospital. If the thief Orran was talking about saw that picture and wants the bracelet, it's an open invitation. Take it—please." A hunted look twisted her features, usually so pretty and poised, and taut lines stood out against her pale skin.

Solid green with streaks of brown, the polished circle was surprisingly heavy. Landon zipped it into her purse. "You need to rest so you can get out of here."

"Ken, Kimi, and Shaun all admired it last night. That should be okay, right? I mean, I trust Ken and Kimi, and Shaun returned my other bracelet instead of keeping it."

"I'm glad you had company."

"Shaun brought his guitar and played for me. Quiet stuff. It helped me settle for the night." Ciara adjusted her position on the bed, stifling a gasp at the motion. "Ken and Kimi came after Orran. I don't know... Ken says he's built and sold a number of businesses and the next one's right around the corner. But he's hanging around here instead of going home. I'm worried about him."

"Maybe they stayed because they're worried about you."

"Well, I hope he finds a fantastic job. Even better, an idea for a new company. He's not ready to retire yet." The quiet thrumming of the oxygen machine swallowed her exhale. "I should try to nap. Will you bring me a few things tomorrow from the apartment?"

Armed with Ciara's keys and a list, Landon found her way to the cafeteria. Bobby sat at a table in the half-empty room, his back to the wall. He held up a finger as she approached, gaze never leaving the screen, and kept typing.

She plunked into the moulded plastic seat across from him. Instead of the goofy geek, here was the writer at work. His straw-straight hair stuck out like he'd been mashing it again, and his mouth pinched tight on one side. As she watched, his eyes narrowed behind the gunmetal-framed glasses as if he saw deeper than the text on his laptop.

A spurt of frenzied keystrokes. Then a relieved exhale. "Thanks. I didn't dare lose that." He snapped the laptop shut and tucked it into his grey leather shoulder bag. "Ready to go?"

"Can we stop at her apartment?"

"Sure."

When they walked outside, the sunlight left Landon blinking. She inhaled the fresh air. "Wow, I wasn't expecting it to get this mild."

"Hospitals always feel like it's cloudy out. And maybe rainy." Bobby jingled his car keys. "I blame the serious atmosphere. The waiting and the hush, even with all the machines and activity."

The sun's warmth wrapped her, slowing her steps. "I feel bad Ciara's stuck in there."

Bobby matched her pace. "You've had a rough time lately too."

As they descended the steps to the parking lot, he dipped his hand into the laptop case. "This might help when the school work gets too heavy and you need something mindless." He held out a paperback. "Travers's first adventure."

Landon's fingers closed around the crisp pocket-sized book. With her focus on the stairs underfoot, her peripheral vision caught a rocket-shaped spaceship. When they reached level ground, she took a proper look. "Thank you." He had no idea what a struggle reading was. If she told him now, he'd feel terrible.

She hefted the book in her palm, then opened the front cover. "You signed it!" It took a moment's concentration to master the cursive letters. "'To Landon, a real-life hero. Love, Bobby.' That's so sweet."

His cheeks had flushed as if he thought her slow response meant she didn't like his gift. But her smile drew a matching one, and some of the anxiety left his expression. "Gramp and I wanted to vet Zander. It's only fair I give you the chance to form an opinion of Travers."

Her thumb riffled the edges of the pages, sending a soft puff of air into her face. "He sounds so perfect. I'm a little intimidated."

"He's an action hero. We expect him to be over-the-top amazing. It's not real life."

She tapped the book against his chest. "Then it's okay for you and me to be ordinary mortals?"

"Kind of part of the human condition." He started toward the car.

Quick steps brought her level with him again. "So... Robert J. Hawke. James? John?"

"Jules. You're sworn to secrecy."

"What's wrong with that?"

"Nothing. It's kind of cool. Jules Verne wrote amazing science fiction in his day. But"—his fingers carved exaggerated air quotes—"Julie. It gets old fast."

After a brief stop at Ciara's apartment, they arrived at the inn shortly past noon. Landon said goodbye to Bobby and started for her room, but Zander called her name from the doorway to the common room. She bypassed the stairs and joined him. The weekend guests who'd checked in yesterday were still out, so they had the place to themselves.

Zander stood by the bookcase, one elbow resting against a shelf.

She tapped Bobby's book against her thigh. "Did they tell you anything?"

"Not much, but between the lines, my impression was that the investigation hasn't uncovered any solid leads. For this attacker or for the Bridgewater shooter."

"I'd be surprised if they could give details on an active case anyway." Although Dylan had slipped Landon a hint or two in the past.

"My background in corrections affords me a bit of an in. Plus, Constable Tremblay is grateful to have me here on-site with you. He'll feed me whatever he thinks will keep you safe."

Landon's fingernails dug into the book cover. "Protective friends are a blessing." Except when they took it too far and made her feel like an injured bird that could never be returned to the wild.

His narrow lips shaped a wry smile. Somehow he could always read her thoughts. "You do your part and support Ciara. I'll be the civilian liaison with the police."

## Chapter 14

*Sunday*

"This is all your fault!" Through the phone, Ciara wailed like an abandoned child.

Clutching the inn's cordless landline handset, Landon darted across the hall from the kitchen to Anna's private sitting room and shut the door behind her. She paced to the window and stared out at the rain. "Ciara, what are you talking about? What's wrong?"

"The police are here at the hospital. He broke into my apartment. Because you didn't stop when he told you to."

*He*—the attacker? It must be. They'd both agreed to keep hunting for answers, but Ciara didn't have the strength right now to fight. It *was* Landon's fault.

She blew out a heated sigh. To make matters worse, Ciara had been calling Landon's cell, upstairs on the night table while Landon was busy helping with breakfast cleanup before church. She pressed her forehead against the cool windowpane, closing her eyes. "I'm sorry. Is there anything I can do?"

"I can't cope with this alone. Will you come?"

Landon had never heard such fragility from Ciara. If the initial attack shattered her confidence, this new violation had ground the pieces to powder.

"I'll be there as soon as I can."

She returned to the kitchen to Anna's and Meaghan's curious stares. Zander waited in the pass-through opening to the breakfast room, one of the swinging white doors propped open with his hip. They'd all heard Ciara's plaintive cry. At least the weekend guests had already finished eating and gone upstairs.

"Now he's broken into her apartment." Landon banged the handset into its charger. "This has to end."

Anna's lips twisted downward. "Poor lamb. This is too much at once."

Zander stepped into the kitchen. The door swung closed behind him. "I'll drive you."

"No, I'll take her. We need to talk." Anna tossed her apron on its hook and bustled toward her quarters.

A corner of his mouth tightened. "Text me if you need a ride back. Meanwhile, I'll see if I can shake any clues loose from her coworkers. Somebody must know something."

Meaghan's red braid bobbed against her spine as she scrubbed the countertop. Landon had said no to investigating Gord's death, and now everyone was jumping to find Ciara's attacker. That had to hurt.

Landon paused at her side. "Did Zander tell you he's still asking around about your dad?"

"I don't have much hope."

"He has good contacts. And don't give up on the police."

Meaghan sniffed. "Like they're motivated."

"Actually, I think they are."

Landon raced upstairs for her purse and a jacket. Five minutes later, Anna was driving them along the coast road, windshield wipers batting the rain away.

Passing the site of their accident gave Landon a queasy stomach. Gord had sent them toppling into the ocean, and now he was dead. Saying good riddance was easier when you didn't see the grief left behind. "I feel sorry for Meaghan."

Anna focused forward. "Me too. And for Ciara. We have twenty-five minutes. Tell me why you're so invested in this."

"Ciara's so broken by it all. I want to help. Like others helped me."

"I'm picking up a real mama-bear vibe here."

Landon's breath rushed out in a hot throaty rumble. "Standing up for her meant rebounding from that creep grabbing me. Using it as fuel and not backing down. But all I've done is provoke him."

"Fuel. That's an interesting word. Can you describe what's burning?"

"Protection. Defence. Okay, anger. I want to make him pay." Her fingers hooked into her thighs.

"We have a Good Shepherd, remember?" A soothing lilt softened Anna's words. "He's the strong one. We weren't intended to fight on our own."

"But I want to." The truth seared her lips. Raged in her heart, a roaring fire, clawing for destruction. "He hurt her. They hurt me. It has to end."

*A Good Shepherd.* Landon's eyes misted. Discovering that Jesus valued her, that He saw her hopeless, ruined state as something to heal and restore, not something that negated her worth...

Faith had given her hope. Confidence. But this trembling in her chest, rattling her ribs and hardening her lungs, was pure rage. A hunger for retribution. For the vengeance that belonged to God alone.

The truth terrified her. Left her numb. Limp. Somehow cut free from her violent emotion. Without the hate to enlarge her, she felt like a tiny child, shaken and helpless after a nightmare.

"I thought I let go of the past." The whisper scraped her throat raw.

Zander had warned her that unforgiveness prevented wholeness. He'd coached her through the painful stages of releasing the trafficker and the others who'd abused her to

God's judgment. Free from the poison, she'd been rebuilding her life. Now she'd taken back the pain by identifying Ciara's hurt with her own.

A half-smile softened Anna's profile. "It's surprising the things that surface after we think we've dealt with them."

"So what do I do now?"

"What do you want to do?"

"Help Ciara and see justice done." And save herself from flashback emotions that would tear her apart.

~~~

At Ciara's doorway, Landon almost collided with a petite nurse in sky-blue scrubs. The nurse closed the door on Ciara's complaints and beckoned Landon to the side. "Are you the friend she's waiting for?"

When Landon agreed, the nurse's forehead puckered. "Try to talk her down? She's understandably distressed, but she's not doing herself any favours. The whole floor heard her response to the idea of a sedative."

"I'll see what I can do. Thank you." Landon smiled, but the woman deserved a salute. Supporting high-need patients all day? Hospital workers were heroes worthy of Bobby's Travers.

That brought a grimace. She'd have to tackle his book before he asked what she thought.

For now, make peace with Ciara—and offer what comfort she could. She palmed open the door.

Ciara sat propped up in the bed, Constable Ingerson in the visitor's chair at her side. At the faint squeak of the hinges, they broke off their conversation.

Of all the officers to be present—Landon repressed a sigh. Of course they'd send a woman if one was on duty. Set the female crime victim at ease.

Hands braced on her knees, slim legs tucked under the chair, Ingerson straightened as Landon entered.

Remembering the last time Landon meddled in an investigation?

Hefting the zippered overnight bag Ciara had asked for, Landon said, "I brought your things. I'm so sorry this happened."

Ciara's mouth dropped open, but instead of launching into blame, she started crying.

Ingerson stretched a uniformed arm to rest her hand on Ciara's. Her gaze caught Landon's. "While the break-in could be linked to the previous attack, I understand it also may be connected to a social media post about a valuable bracelet?"

Landon gasped. She propped Ciara's bag against the wall beneath the window and unzipped her purse. Fingers questing in the inner pocket, she located the jade bangle and held it high. "Here it is. I forgot to leave it at the apartment. As soon as I get to the inn, I'll ask Anna to put it in the safe."

Sniffling, Ciara reached forward, then yelped. "Ribs." She took the bracelet from Landon's outstretched hand and touched it to her lips before passing it to Ingerson. "Thank God it's not lost."

A corner of Ingerson's lips crept up. "Ms. Williams owns a surprising amount of art, mostly jade. Much of which appears to be missing. In her stead, we need you to do a walk-through and identify which pieces are gone."

"I'd never remember—"

Ciara tapped her sparkly phone case. "I have a list. For insurance purposes."

"Email it to me? I'll use the hospital Wi-Fi to grab it before I go."

"I've forwarded a copy to the officer on-site as well." Ingerson flattened her palms against the chair armrests, fingers spread. "Yes, Ms. Williams was recently attacked, and coincidences don't sit well. But we've had other local collectibles thefts."

Ciara's brown eyes filled again. "We were talking the other day about how one of the owners had bragged online about his cameo and it was stolen. Then I did the same thing." Most days, her round face with its small pointy nose reminded Landon of a cheerful rodent. Now it puckered like a dried apple doll. "I wanted to share happy news, not make myself more of a target."

Ingerson's expression didn't change. "In each theft, the items were different. That suggests it's someone stealing to sell, not for their own interests. If they went looking for the bracelet, they found other valuables instead." She focused on Ciara. "Aside from the social media post, how many people know about your collection?"

"My parents. A few friends like Landon. They all know about the bracelet, and I told most of them I'd sent it home. But they're people I trust."

Landon's lips squeezed into a tight line. Anna had trusted Gord right up to the end.

Ingerson produced a notebook and recorded all the names Ciara could think of. Then she fixed Ciara with a direct stare. "The other burglaries had no damage done, and none of the other people were harmed. So while the cases may be linked, they may not. How did you acquire your collection?"

Ciara resettled the thin plastic tube at her nose. Her mouth pinched. "They were gifts. Most came from my parents. The rest... I was in a relationship with a man who tried to buy my trust with expensive presents." She sniffed. "It worked. When the relationship ended, I kept the gifts."

"Would this man want the items back? I need a name."

Scowling, Ciara shook her head.

"Spencer Costain." Landon sent Ciara an apologetic look. "Dylan was going to check him out this week. One of the guests at the inn knows him—Ken Sanu. Ken's already on your list."

Brows tight, Ingerson scanned the page, then scratched another line. "I'll see what Dylan found."

Ciara's tears, coming off the hyper-emotional dramatics, seemed to have drained her. She lay against her pillows, pale and drawn and somehow small in the stark hospital bed. Did her parents know about the break-in? They must know she'd been readmitted since her stepfather was paying for the private room and security.

"Ciara, what about your parents? If it's not the same person as the other thefts, could it be someone trying to get to them through you?" Landon switched her focus to Constable Ingerson. "Maybe ask if they have any enemies?"

Ingerson's chin lifted. "That was a suggestion, correct? Not a statement of intent?"

"My questions only made things worse." Worse for her own mental health as well as for Ciara. Landon's breath shook. "My investigating days are done."

"Glad to hear it. Ms. Williams needs a friend. You do that part, and we'll locate the person behind these crimes. Now how soon can you do a walk-through of her apartment?"

"I need to wait for a ride, so maybe an hour?"

Ingerson checked her watch. "What if I drive you and your ride meets you there? Zerkowsky's still on-site, and he'd like to wrap up."

"Is that okay, Ciara?"

Her friend didn't meet her eyes.

"Could we have a couple minutes alone first, Constable?"

"Make it quick. I'll pull the car around." Long strides carried the officer into the hallway.

Landon dropped into the warm, just-vacated seat. "Ciara, you said you came home to figure some things out. Is there anything you can tell them to help find this guy?"

Staring straight ahead, Ciara passed back the jade bangle, then twined her fingers together. "I have nothing to say."

"We're on your side. We want to help you."

"So go see what damage he did."

## Chapter 15

LANDON HAD PREPARED herself for signs of an intruder in Ciara's apartment, but what she saw when she opened the door stopped her on the threshold.

A sickly grey sludge oozed from the galley kitchen. Scattered puddles and bits of trash littered the living area. An industrial-sized dehumidifier hulked where the living room met the short hall to bed and bathrooms, growling as it chewed through the damp air.

Despite the box fan in the open window, it felt like breathing inside a cloud. A warm, muggy cloud of jumbled odours she tasted more than smelled.

"Hello?" Ignoring the kitchen and stepping over a soggy microwave popcorn bag, she picked a dry route across the grey laminate toward the hall.

She found Constable Zerkowsky in the bathroom trying to lift fingerprints from the sink faucets.

"What a mess, isn't it?" His dark brows bunched. "Good thing Ciara doesn't have to see it this way. Has she calmed down any?"

"A bit."

He stood on a stack of wet newspaper. The contents of every bottle of hair product Ciara owned glopped the bathroom walls. Thick pinks, yellows, greens—a stomach-turning kaleidoscope with a cloying scent.

Eyes streaming, Landon put her fingers to her nose. "How hasn't this killed you yet?"

One bushy brow crawled higher on his forehead. "I'd take this over a week-old body any day."

The mental image, mixed with the sensory onslaught, raised the taste of bile. Good thing he couldn't see her mouth squirm behind her hand. She swallowed hard. Zerkowsky was too professional to unbend this way around civilians at a crime scene. On some level, he'd accepted her investigating.

He took one more sample and began packing up his kit. "I don't expect to get a clear print, but we can hope. He left the water running here and in the kitchen. Downstairs tenants called the super when it started raining inside."

Landon backed up to let him pass. "I'll be forever cleaning this up."

"If I hear you're tackling this on your own, I'll lock you up as an accessory." He peeled blue protective gloves from his hands. "You want your friend coming home from the hospital to see this? Nope? Then bring in helpers. Or get Ciara's stepfather to pay a restoration company." His brows lowered in an exaggerated scowl.

She giggled. "Yes, sir."

"Good. One thing more before I'm done—did you get a copy of Ciara's valuables list?"

"It's on my phone."

"Great. I haven't found any of the jade or the jewellery, but keep an eye out."

With his departure, the apartment walls shrank around her. Noisy fan and dehumidifier, sinus-searing air, squishy residue. Landon bolted into the hallway to phone for backup. Then she found the building superintendent, who supplied a couple of hefty rubber trash cans with thick black bags.

Back inside, she headed for the bedroom. Like party streamers after a whirlwind, bright-coloured garments coiled over every surface. Perfumes clashed for dominance. She darted to the sliding window and shot it wide, rattling the frame.

She'd been holding her breath. Now her lungs shook too badly for more than shallow sips of fresh air. With the trembling came a loosening of the heat in her core. Fear tumbled into the mix, and she clenched her hands. She couldn't go back to the broken mess she'd been.

Gasping a prayer, she spun to the bed and grasped Ciara's upended wastebasket from the floral duvet. Picking up bits of trash, she worked her way to the elegant cherrywood dresser. Murky gels smeared profanity across the mirror.

Seeing this would devastate Ciara. It wasn't random theft and vandalism—hatred hung in the air.

Landon slammed empty drawers into place one by one, her movements fast and jerky. How could he? How dare he? One of the bottom drawers stuck. Grunting, almost crying, she pushed it with all her strength. It didn't budge. She yanked it out and rammed it full force. The drawer closed so fast she fell against it.

A line of fire in her palm stole her breath. She pulled her hand free and stood staring at the angry red stripe. She traced the edge of her palm. No blood. But the forced stop had cut through her mental rant and given her the barest sliver of control.

Emotional vertigo churning, she backed from the dresser until her legs butted the mattress. If she gave in to this, chose vengeance over God, she'd end up like Elva. Bitter and hard-edged. Driving everyone away.

"Jesus, I need Your help." But this guy, whoever he was, deserved what was coming to him. The thought stirred a response deep in her heart. Drew her back to the precipice.

Her teeth clenched. She had to set her mind on better things. Fast. As she picked up the next drawer, she began to pray for Ciara, out loud. For her friend's protection, for healing, and for God to bring justice His way and in His time.

As the words poured out, she sorted the jumbled mound of clothing on the bed. Lacy lingerie, socks, and other small articles went into a clean garbage bag. Anna's washing machine could deal with all but the dry-clean-onlies. The larger garments she hung in the closet. She'd have to bring something from the inn to transport them for cleaning. The task became an offering, an act of service to her friend.

Zander texted as she shut the closet door. Since the buzzer linked to Ciara's phone, they'd agreed not to disturb her rest. Going downstairs to let him in was a sweet reprieve.

A dull pressure pulsed in her forehead, and each blink sandpapered her eyes. The sight of Zander reporting for cleanup duty in his dress shirt and pants comforted her. Zander was who he was. He wouldn't change for anyone, but he'd wade into anything with a passion to serve.

Still, as she unlatched the glass security doors, she gave him a rueful smile. "You'll ruin your clothes."

He dipped the nested rubber totes toward her, revealing two pairs of boots and some work gloves. "Anna's idea. She stayed behind waiting for the new guests."

"Anna's an angel." Landon hadn't wanted to step her sneakers into the mystery goo in the kitchen. "I hoped Bobby could come with you. We could use more help." His off-the-wall humour would lighten the atmosphere.

Zander wrestled the bulky totes across the foyer to the elevator. "Too many bodies in a small space. We'd be tripping over one another. I asked Anna not to call anyone else."

When he walked into the apartment, he froze. Then he growled a string of words Landon couldn't make out, ending with "...terrorize young women."

He'd be thinking of his daughter. How had she not realized? Yes, Zander had already been out investigating and could divert back to the inn for cleaning supplies. Yes, Bobby and Roy would have still been in church. But she should have waited. Texted Bobby afterward. Left Zander out of this. Except he'd have found out and insisted he help.

Stern-faced, he stuffed his pant legs into what must have been Murdoch's old boots and left his shoes at the door.

"The building super said he'd try to find a plastic shovel we could use in the kitchen. Zander, I so appreciate you coming. Maybe start in the living room. I'll finish in the bedroom."

She warned him to watch for the jade figurines and took one of the totes to Ciara's room for the bedding and pillows.

With the basics done, she went looking for Zander. "No sign of her collectibles?"

"Not one." He'd righted the loveseat and armchair and folded the tangerine throw to drape over the chair.

The rolled-up doggy bed stuck out of a trash can next to the coffee table. Landon tugged at the faux sheepskin. "Can't we wash this? She'll be sad to lose it."

Zander's thin features sharpened to a hatchet-like edge. "Broken glass. I shook out what I could, but it's not safe." He pointed at the curio cabinet, upright in the corner, but missing the glass panes and shelving. "Anything he wanted to break, he put in the pet bed first to muffle the sound."

The skin pebbled on Landon's neck. "Can we not tell her that part?"

"She needs to know she has an enemy. This was personal. You can see the edge of his boot heel in one of the paintings."

"It's another attack. But for all the destruction, he didn't slash the furniture or carve up her tables or anything."

Despite what Zander had picked up, bits of debris lay everywhere. He crunched across the floor to the closet, rummaged inside, and produced a broom and dustpan.

"By leaving the furniture intact and stealing or destroying everything she cares about, he created a scenario where she'll come home to what's familiar, lock herself in, and be surrounded by reminders of all she's lost." As he began herding the pieces of Ciara's life into manageable piles, he spat a bitter laugh. "I may be wrong about the psychology, but that's what it looks like to me."

Knuckles white on the broom handle, he stopped. "We will find this person. And stop him."

His cold certainty set her spine a little straighter. Could she leave it with him? Trust him to make it right while she kept her interfering fingers out of it?

She exhaled long and slow, pushing away the desire to fight. The worst of the ache faded from her bones. "You find him. You and the police. All I've done is provoke him." She studied the stained toes of her rubber boots. "I made Ciara's attacker a surrogate for my past, and it's undone the work we did. It's killing me to let go, but it's the right thing to do."

She risked a glance at him.

His laser-sharp scrutiny felt like a thousand tiny black probes into her consciousness. At last, he gave a crisp nod. "I'm proud of you, girl. It can be almost impossible to step away from vengeance and leave justice to God."

"I had a good teacher."

Her phone buzzed in her back pocket. When she unlocked the screen, the reminder notification flashed. "How'd it get to be this late? Anna's expecting us for supper with her guests. She won't let us near the table like this."

Zander brushed debris from his pants. "Indeed."

With an overflowing tote of Ciara's laundry filling the SUV, they made a chilly return trip to the inn with the windows down. As soon as Landon had Ciara's sheets in the washer, she tried to shower the residual scents from her hair.

She dressed in a butter-yellow top and her favourite skirt, a kaleidoscopic swirl of colours. Anna had reassured her that most guest speakers she hosted for the church were down-to-earth people, but the uncertainty had her nerves humming.

At the foot of the stairs, she headed for the common room. Zander sat closest to the door in one of the straight-backed chairs by the puzzle table, facing into the room. Torso at a slight forward tilt, fingers curved into his knees, he was as stiff as Landon had ever seen him.

She took a half-step back. Yet the quiet chatter from within seemed normal. Beyond Zander, Anna appeared unconcerned. He must still be on edge over the destruction at Ciara's. Two quick paces brought her to the doorway.

In the club chair by the bookcase, a sandy-haired man somewhere around Anna's age nudged his glasses into place above his short groomed beard. Casually dressed in lightweight pants and a tee shirt, he nodded slowly as his wife spoke.

His wife reflected Zander's pose, except she radiated engagement. Legs crossed, she leaned in with her hands clasped over the top knee. Her curly brown hair bobbed as she rocked forward and back, too involved in the discussion to sit still. "You have a vital ministry, leading these young people into hope and healing."

Anna's smile drew Landon into the room. "Landon, meet Ruth and Tony Warner. Zander's been telling them about his work."

Standing felt like being on display as Zander's Exhibit A even though this couple wouldn't know her past. Landon claimed the vacant chair beside Ruth. "It's good to meet you both."

"Tony and I are so grateful for Anna's hospitality. We could have driven out from Halifax for tomorrow night, but this gives us the day to play tourist. I'm glad it worked out for us to come."

The event had originally been planned for May—before Landon had any thought of returning to Nova Scotia—but a sprinkler malfunction had flooded the church and disrupted a month's worth of activities.

Her conversation with Zander diverted, Ruth settled back in her chair. Her tanned fingers linked loosely in her lap, unadorned except for a simple gold wedding ring set. Her only other accent was a pair of small hoop earrings. No dressing to impress here. Her ordinariness put Landon at ease.

Landon gathered her still-wet hair into a ponytail and let it fall loose on her shoulders. "Anna said you're speaking on forgiveness Monday night?"

"It's more of a testimony than actual teaching." Ruth reached for her husband's hand. "I spent a lot of time in therapy. With the healing came a... *call,* for lack of a better word, to share how I experienced God's faithfulness when I was abducted."

Ice pierced Landon's heart. She shot a panicked glance at Zander, his sallow features dark and tight. He must have known. Thought she'd known too.

She choked on a squeak. "Wait, what?"

Zander sat taller, shoulders military-sharp. Focused on Anna. "You didn't tell her."

"It was in the church events emails, but... no."

School readings took enough effort. Nonessential emails received a skim at best. And they'd missed church this morning when Pastor Vern would have given more details.

Anna's chin trembled. "When we rescheduled, all I could think was how much I needed help with forgiveness. I knew Landon might need it too, and she'd be encouraged by the redemption story. With Gord dying and everything else, I didn't think about trigger elements. Landon, I'm so sorry."

"'She'd be encouraged by the redemption story.'" Still the flat enunciation from Zander.

A warning would have helped, but at least she'd found out in time to avoid Monday night's event. Being blindsided in the middle of a crowded church would have sparked a full-on panic attack. A slow, deliberate breath lifted Landon's ribs and helped her raise a stiff shoulder. "It's okay."

Ruth had turned toward her husband as if trying to give the others space. The toe of one beige-sandalled foot scuffed the floorboards.

Zander caught Landon's attention with an up-tipped brow and a chin motion toward the door.

She shook her head. Her reaction had already made Anna's guests uncomfortable. She wouldn't walk out on them. "Ruth, Tony, some background: I'm one of Zander's clients. I was taken and human trafficked at fifteen."

"Oh." Ruth's eyes widened, the brown deepening. Her mouth bunched as she seemed to consider her response. "The inn would be a safe place for us to talk if you like. But you might want to skip tomorrow night."

Her warmth, the gentle way she bent nearer, drew Landon's heart. A hollow ache deep inside weakened the steel wall her anger had forged. Could this woman's experience help her regain what she'd lost? "Thank you for understanding."

She needed to shift the subject to safer ground. "So God helped you forgive?"

"Forgiveness and prayer got me into the ordeal. Then they got me through it." Ruth gripped her chair's wooden armrests as if bracing herself. "My story's not about me. It's about the redemption of a serial rapist-murderer. About the love of God being strong enough—audacious enough—to forgive the worst of the worst."

"'The vilest offender who truly believes...'" Anna's words came out low, half-sung.

"Landon will not have to experience that situation." Zander's lips pinched like he'd taken a mouthful of coffee dregs. "The trafficker died unsaved."

Tony fingered his short beard. "The concept of God redeeming certain individuals offends our natural reasoning. Believe me, I know."

A chill spread across Landon's shoulders to the back of her neck. She rubbed the spot. If her trafficker hadn't been killed... if he'd surrendered to Jesus... What would it mean for her if he escaped God's wrath? If he didn't pay?

"The scandalous grace of God that forgives the unforgivable." Zander sniffed. One foot tapped before he stilled it. "It's difficult to convince my survivors to release these criminals to God's judgment when He then forgives them. Can you imagine what that does to the victims? And their families?"

Ruth's mouth flattened, and the softness left her pose. "Harry Silver killed our niece. I've lived that fury. But God saves. It's not that He doesn't care about pain or justice. It's about His love and power being greater than even this magnitude of evil."

She studied Landon, her expression warm and non-judging. "You may not be ready to hear that, and I've been there. Please don't think I'm pushing you." A tight smile curved her lips. "I was furious when my pastor told me to pray for Harry."

Tony whistled. "*You* were furious. I wanted to clobber him."

Zander's head flicked a rapid side-to-side negative. "High-profile conversions, celebrity or criminal, rarely last."

"Sadly, I agree." His resistance didn't shake Ruth's calm. "But in Harry's case, it was genuine. I saw God wreck him. I've seen the change. And the rebuilding."

The chill had seeped from Landon's skin into her heart, numbing her emotions to the frozen ground they'd become during her captivity. In terms of theology, Zander was probably the most educated person in this room. Yet Anna, Ruth, and Tony affirmed this—what had Zander called it?—*scandalous* grace of God to forgive even the ones Landon had counted on Him punishing.

Her gaze sought his. "What about 'Vengeance is Mine, says the Lord'?"

Ruth rested a light touch on Landon's arm. "So is the authority to forgive. He paid the price Himself." The lines at her eyes and mouth proved she'd fought her battles to reach this place. "On the cross, Jesus said 'Father, forgive them.' He didn't say 'Father, condemn them.' And He had the right."

If the fires of justice burned hot in Zander, the blaze of love burned stronger in this quiet middle-aged woman. The same warmth that drew Landon to Anna.

But Ruth was wrong. She had to be.

~~~

"Are you sure about waiting around?" Landon stuck her head back into Zander's SUV. "Anna did say she'd come now that the Warners are settled in, and Bobby would too. I doubt he's working tonight."

Zander's thin lips compressed. He tapped his phone. "I'm fine. I'll send a few emails and do some reading."

"If I take too long, text me."

She walked across the parking lot, filling her senses with cool evening air to brace for the hospital's antiseptic atmosphere. The basics of Ruth's story, shared over their meal, jostled in her brain like ice cubes dumped into a pitcher of water, each chunk trying to reach the surface. If it could settle into order, she could inspect it piece by piece. But first, she had to give Ciara an update on the apartment.

With a light rap at her friend's door, she pushed it open. Phil Kirkwood stood at the foot of the bed. By Ciara's mutinous scowl, her stepfather was not welcome.

Landon stopped short. "Sorry to intrude. I can come back."

Ciara's fingers clutched air as if to stop her. "Please stay. I need to hear about the apartment."

"I'll duck into your washroom, then." Landon headed for the blond wooden door. Let them finish their conversation in private.

"No!" Ciara's squeal pulled Landon's focus to the bed. Colour high in her cheeks, she gave a pained, helpless shrug, lifting empty palms. "The toilet overflowed. I'm waiting for someone from maintenance. There's a visitors' washroom in the hallway."

Phil's shoulders twitched. "I'll go hurry them up."

"No. Please. You've interfered enough. You don't want me around, fine. It goes both ways. Just leave."

Spine straight, he pivoted. Without another word, he left. A minute later, the elevator chimed.

Landon dropped into the visitor's chair. "What did he do?"

"Just because he's paying for the security guard, he thinks he can decide who visits me. Lucky the guard's on my side."

Behind Landon, the bathroom door squeaked.

"You are a terror." Shaun emerged, wearing a soft-sided black guitar case like a backpack. He put a finger to his lips and cut an upward glance through his long bangs. "Just like college days, smuggling a boy into the girls' dorm."

Ciara sniffed. "You smuggled yourself in. And are about to leave."

"What, you want to obey Daddy after all?" He hiked a brow at Landon. "He tracked me down at the campsite to warn me off. Come on, do I look like trouble?"

Landon retreated toward the window, out of the line of fire. Ciara's lips clamped tight as if there were too many words to unleash at once. Her glare should have incinerated him. Then she let out a long sigh. "Zero interest in obeying Phil. And I appreciate you playing for me. Not the bedroom innuendo."

"My bad. Hitting on a woman in your condition would be low, even for me. The situation brought back fond memories." He winked and tipped an imaginary hat. "Want me to get lost for good or stroll by in an hour or so to do the minstrel thing?"

"It does help me sleep."

"Then I'll see you around."

Once he left, Ciara flopped her head onto the pillow. "I have no idea why Phil would care if Shaun was visiting. Or why Shaun would bother to keep helping a stranger."

"What's Shaun even doing in Lunenburg? He doesn't seem like a tourist."

"No idea." Ciara lifted a tee-shirt-clad shoulder.

Landon dragged the chair nearer and sat to relate a mild version of the apartment's condition. Ciara might well need lullaby music after this.

Other than deepening pools in her brown eyes, Ciara took the news well. "I'm glad my landlord isn't blaming me for the flood downstairs." Her fingertips touched the oxygen tube where it draped down from her head. "They want to discharge me soon, but now I'm afraid to go home. I need a security system. But Orran's away again, and Tait's probably still furious with me. At least he's keeping Moxie."

A fat tear tracked down her cheek. "All I have left is a little dog to love on, and he adores me—but only because I feed and coddle him." Another sniffle, this one wetter. "No matter how I try, I don't meet expectations. Or if I do, it's not enough, and people get distracted and move on. Nobody stays and likes me. Nobody cares."

"Hey, if you cry too much, it'll hurt your ribs."

"And my head. But I'm so sad." Wailing, she dropped her face to her hands.

Landon wedged a clump of tissues between Ciara's palm and cheek and plunked the rest of the box on top of her blanket. Shaun's guitar might help now, but Ciara wouldn't want him to see her like this. Letting her guard down in front of Landon revealed the depth of her heartbreak. Or it showed how non-threatening she considered Landon's opinion.

Ciara pulled the oxygen feed away, blew her nose, then wiped at the tube before replacing it. "Gross." Tears glistened on her lashes until she mopped the moisture away. Residual sobs rocked her shoulders. "You're a good friend to stay. And not to prattle stupid words."

She lobbed the wad of tissues into the wastebasket. "I just want to feel special. Is that so wrong?"

"It's a pretty universal need."

Ciara rearranged the light blanket across her chest. "You were awkward in junior high. How'd you learn to be so secure? So strong?"

A sharp retort came to mind. Landon pushed it aside. They'd both changed since childhood, and she wouldn't act now like Ciara had done then. This woman, now her friend, had asked a question from a place of pain. She deserved an answer.

Landon passed Ciara the foam water cup from the bedside table. *God, after what I heard at supper, do I have to share this now?* She drew a rueful breath. "Remember when we reconnected this summer? You said you were glad the rumours about me weren't true. What had you heard?"

The cup jerked in Ciara's grasp. She stared at it like it was all she could see. She pinched the paper straw, folding it down on itself. Repeated the motion. Not looking at Landon. The question weighted the air until she shivered. "That you were... working the streets somewhere."

Landon released the breath she'd been holding. Not on the streets. It'd been hotel rooms. "I was human trafficked. You have no idea. And you don't want to know."

She waited, watching Ciara's rigid profile until she thought the words had been processed. "I have hope and security today because God can handle this kind of pain and build me back to wholeness. As a friend and fellow broken soul, Ciara, I promise—Jesus loves you. In His eyes, you *are* special. We both are."

Ciara sniffled, her glossy pink lips shaping a mutinous pout. "If He loves me, why'd He let all this happen?"

"I don't know." Landon inhaled, rolling her neck to ease the tension. Zander and Anna had helped her see that a more helpful question was what does He want to do now? Ciara wasn't ready to hear that.

As if in agreement, Ciara scowled. "I need to be safe when I go home. If Orran isn't back by tomorrow, I'll have to grovel to Tait. He said he could set up a security system for me, but he's been taking his own sweet time."

"Does he know you had a break-in? That might speed things up."

"I texted Orran and told him the jade bangle was safe. I need to get it appraised for my insurance. If that's what the thief was after, he might try again."

## Chapter 16

*Monday*

"There's no need to drag Bobby into this. I can drop you at the hospital this afternoon."

"It's already arranged, Zander." Landon's ribs were shaking, but she refused to back down.

They sat with Anna at the inn's kitchen table, comforting steam rising from bowls of green lentil soup swimming with carrot chunks and pale shrimp. Rain streamed down the windowpane. Since she'd expressed her fear that Ciara's break-in was retaliation for her investigating, Zander had become extra-protective—a knight in shining armour turned prison guard.

Landon scooped a spoonful of the savoury soup, grateful for the warmth. The rain fed her growing sense of claustrophobia. She tore a warm crusty roll in two and slathered it with butter. "This soup is fantastic. Zander, we worked so hard on cleanup this morning that I didn't want to add anything else to your day."

His spoon clinked the rim of his bowl. "I can still run circles around you twentysomethings."

Chewing a hefty bite of roll gave her time to regroup. "Have you seen any updates about that gallery theft in Halifax?"

"No."

News had broken too late for the morning paper—Anna kept a print subscription for her guests—but it had popped up in Zander's feeds. A ruby pendant had vanished overnight. No alarms. No sign of an intruder. No pendant. The gallery site described it as a Burmese pigeon's blood ruby, so named because of its deep red shade. Worth millions and on loan from a private European collector. Stolen on the exhibit's final night. Online, the large red teardrop glowed with an inner fire. Bobby might call it a dragon's heart.

"Orran told Ciara and me about the pendant last week. He was going to take her to see it, but then she got readmitted. I wonder if the thief's the same guy who's been taking collectibles here. It makes sense he'd be hitting targets all around the province."

"It wasn't Orran's security company, was it?" asked Anna.

"I don't think so. But I'm sure they hired top of the line."

Since the apartment break-in, they'd been assuming Ciara's enemy was behind the other local thefts. If he wasn't local, it'd be even more challenging to track him down. Spoon to her lips, Landon glanced at Zander. "With everything yesterday, I forgot to ask—did you learn anything from Ciara's coworkers?"

Was it only yesterday Zander had missed church to interview the store employees before their day got too busy?

"They don't think much of her, but they couldn't see her having an enemy who'd try to kill her."

Anna took a drink and set her water glass on the glossy pine table. "You might catch the manager if you went on a weekday."

"Her stepfather too." Landon caught his gaze. "Even if I hadn't stopped asking questions, he's too polished and intimidating for me one-on-one. Could you cover that angle too?"

He folded his arms. "She's been here for months. Why wait this long to attack her—an attack that's allegedly a mistake—and why steal from her?"

Anna propped an arm on the table. "If this is about collectibles and Ciara's at least knowledgeable about jade, what if she noticed something incriminating about someone... say her boss or even her stepfather? Not that I have any reason to suspect either of them."

Zander was nodding, eyes narrowed. "It could be. You said Meaghan worked at the Treasure Stop before Ciara? I'll check in with the police for updates on the shooting if I haven't worn out my welcome, and that will give me a reason to touch base with Meaghan. I can ask about her former boss."

Landon would text Dylan too. He was off today, but he'd said to keep in touch. Maybe Constable Ingerson would check with Ciara's mother. If the focused cop could gentle down enough to convince Whitney to talk.

"Very well." Zander sopped the last of his soup with a chunk of roll. "You should be safe between here and the hospital in broad daylight. Make him watch the speed limit in that car."

"Why, Zander." Anna put on a lighthearted drawl. "Are you jealous of another man's wheels?"

"Of course not."

Landon could almost hear his vertebrae clicking into ramrod position. She gulped her water to hide a smile.

~~~

Landon tolerated Bobby's silence for about ten minutes before her patience ran out. Driving in the rain didn't require this much concentration. He'd offered to go, so it wasn't like she'd dragged him away from work.

"What's up?"

His jaw tightened. "When you texted that Ciara's place had been trashed, I assumed she had professionals cleaning it up. You could have asked for help."

"You could have asked if I needed it." She bit her lip. "I'm sorry. That was unfair. Zander said too many of us would get in one another's way. We finished this morning." The ache in her muscles testified it had been more than a two-person job.

"He doesn't want me around."

"Zander?"

"How did he react when he heard you were coming with me this afternoon?" He flexed his hands on the steering wheel.

Landon snickered. "Don't speed." She told him what Anna had said. "It's who he is. He takes life—and his responsibilities—too seriously."

"I get that he's wound super tight. And he blames me for not keeping you safe from Gord." One hand left the steering wheel to scuff through his hair, leaving a straw-thatch mess. "But, man, you'd think he was your father."

The familiar ache hollowed Landon's chest until her ribs felt like they'd cave in. She turned to the side window. Raindrops pummelled the waves into hunched grey-blue swells. A lone gull bobbed on the surface as if lacking strength to find shelter. The car swept on, abandoning the coast to cut cross-country. Leaving the gull behind.

Life swept on, unstoppable as the tide, increasing the distance between Landon's present and the fixed point of past loss. Trees flanked the road now. Solemn, dripping sentinels.

"My father's dead." Facing the window, she let the tears fall. "He tried to find me. The trafficker killed him."

Bobby's breath escaped in a slow hiss. He drove in silence until the trees gave way to private homes and cottages overlooking the LaHave River. Finally he coughed. "I'm sorry. For your loss and for saying something stupid. Again. Maybe Zander's right to steer you away."

Landon found a tattered tissue in her raincoat pocket and blotted her cheeks dry. "I know God is my capital-F Father, but if Zander wants to act like a surrogate dad, I need one."

"Gramp would adopt you in a heartbeat."

Warmth spread like honey. "He kind of has. For the record, Zander's dead wrong about you."

Some of the tension left Bobby's features, but the corners of his eyes remained pinched. "I'm used to not living up to expectations." His sideways grin wobbled. "My parents have always wanted to shape me to fit their vision. Jessie tried to renovate me too."

Landon fiddled with the snap on her raincoat pocket. Why couldn't the people closest to him see his strengths? "Your outside-the-box thinking this summer told us Anna was being poisoned. You may be the one who'll come up with a breakthrough for Ciara. Or even Meaghan."

"Reading between the lines, Gord's death sounds like a gangland execution. We never did know who he'd been affiliated with. That one needs the experts. But it's good you're fighting for Ciara, and I'll do whatever I can."

"About that." How could she explain so it wouldn't sound weird? She gazed past his profile to the river, flowing broad and blue. Bobby had seen her in full meltdown. More than once. Weird wouldn't faze him.

"I can't fight that way anymore." Her jumbled explanation of self-discovery left her shaken again by the fury lodged in her heart. Letting go had been near impossible when she thought she could rely on God's vengeance. Now Ruth—and Anna—claimed God would trade judgment for mercy for even the worst offender.

Unease rippled. "I'll help Ciara as a friend. For her sake, not for personal retaliation. Any clues I—or my brilliant getaway driver—find go straight to the police."

"That'll relieve the local constabulary." His deadpan delivery implied a mental eye roll.

"Yeah, I texted Dylan a few questions, and when I said I was backing off, he replied with starburst icons and a sound clip of the 'Hallelujah Chorus.' Zander's going to continue investigating, for both Ciara and Meaghan. He can keep up with some of his casework remotely too."

By the time they arrived at the hospital, the rain had paused. Low-hanging clouds warned them to hurry. In the elevator, Bobby braced an elbow against the wall. "I won't stay long. She'll open up more with you one-on-one."

They found Ciara propped up in bed, her violet sweatshirt accenting the drabness of her surroundings. The tube still ran below her nose. But her cheeks had almost regained their regular curve, and her eyes were less sunken. She set her phone aside and waved them in. "I'm not supposed to be on screens, but it's so boring."

Landon plunked a paper bag of Anna's blueberry muffins on the bedside table and dropped into the visitor's chair. "You could stream some music."

"I tried. Puts me to sleep."

At the foot of her bed, Bobby wagged a finger with mock severity. "Sleep is what you need, young lady. Concussion headaches are nothing to be trifled with, even without a side order of pneumonia."

She giggled. "Yes, Doctor."

He kept her smiling with a handful of what he called Roy's "irascible moments" before excusing himself. "I'll let you two visit while I try to make my word count."

Ciara squinted after him as he left. "How can he sit in front of a laptop day after day and turn words into a story?"

"Beats me. Have you read them?"

Her perfectly shaped brows puckered, and her lips curled down as if she'd stepped in something squishy. "Sci-fi's too out-there for me. How about you?"

"He gave me a book the other day. Now I need to find a break in school work."

"I think he likes you." The teasing singsong didn't match the bitter twist to her mouth. But where the Ciara of old would have shifted into competition mode—even though they both knew Bobby wasn't her type—today, she squirmed into a more comfortable position against her pillows. She fluffed her short brown hair, the bracelet Shaun had found glinting at her wrist.

"We're just friends."

"So says you. One day I'll get him alone and ask him."

He'd been so uncomfortable when Ciara flirted with him this summer. Landon could imagine the ruddy cheeks and downcast eyes if Ciara made good on her threat. What if it made him think Landon might be interested in him? He'd retreat, and she'd lose a friend. "Please don't. You know he's self-conscious."

Ciara cut her an unreadable look. "Have it your way. In other news, still on the theme of men who are not interested in me, Constable Ingerson was in this morning. Vancouver police had a little chat with Spencer. My ex."

"And?"

"His smooth denials don't mean he's not involved. The man's an eel. But this feels kind of... beneath him. He's power-hungry. Not petty." Ciara twined a finger into the chain at her wrist. "He treated me like a princess. Expensive gifts, romantic dinners, everything I'd dreamed of. Except he was using me to get to my boss."

Her features puckered. "The morning of the corporate takeover, he breezed into the office in an expensive Italian suit, thanked me for my help, and said, as my new boss, he couldn't maintain a relationship with me. And poor Ken standing there with this betrayed expression."

"That must have been awful."

"I believed his lies, and a good man paid for it. So I ran back here where I'd be safe and found a dead-end job that's sucking the life out of me because I'm so bad at it." Ciara's lips quivered, then firmed. "I didn't know Phil and Ken were friends, but that's why Ken hired me. So when I ruined the company, it reflected on Phil. No wonder he hates me."

"Hey." Landon reached to touch Ciara's arm. "Spencer is the bad guy here. Not you. Trusting someone's not a crime."

"He saw the real me, the one I didn't see myself. A gullible, foolish pawn. That's not who I want to be."

"It's not who you are. Don't accept someone else's label. This is a setback, but it doesn't have to define you."

Ciara's mutinous huff disagreed. She sank lower into the bed, head slumped down on the crisp pillowcase. Not making eye contact. The night they met Orran and Tait, she'd said she came home to figure things out. Landon had wondered if the issue was local, perhaps from her past. But after a disaster like this, of course she'd want a safe place to regroup.

She'd been home since at least June. It didn't make sense for the attack and theft to be a delayed response unless this Spencer guy considered Ciara a non-priority loose end. When had her stepfather discovered her role in the company takeover? Not until Ken came to visit? And had Ken and Kimi sought her out to show there were no hard feelings—or for payback?

~~~

"The grief and anger were killing me, and what did my pastor say?" Ruth Warner wasn't a dynamic, polished speaker, but she didn't need to be. Her simple account wove an emotional web that drew them all into the story.

Landon angled forward, the church pew's padded cover shifting beneath her thighs. Coming here tonight was one more act of defiance against those who'd crushed her innocence, but a God-directed one this time. The shiver in her breastbone said He wanted her here—and that she wouldn't like it.

She ached for relief from the anger, but the last time she let it go, she'd trusted God to pick it up. The idea of God putting aside His wrath to redeem evil men made her want to scream at the sky.

"'Forgive him. Pray for him.' The man who butchered our niece." Ruth jerked her chin, brown curls lifting. "As if that was going to happen."

Brief conversations with Ruth at the inn had prepared Landon for the trigger points, but the full story left her jittery inside. Only God could have kept Ruth praying for her abductor in her terror. And only God could have given her the desire and the privilege to lead him to salvation. It sure wasn't a natural response.

At the end of Ruth's account, the crowd murmured, divided as she'd warned they'd be. Light, rapid notes of praise met deeper, resistant chords of unrest.

Zander sat stiff and upright to Landon's left, jaw forward and eyes hooded. Forgiveness was a key part of his counselling for the victims' sake, but Landon had never heard him mention the offenders' spiritual need. For broken, traumatized victims, that would have been too much too soon. She focused on a brown hardcover Bible in the pew rack, worn and dented at the corners. Her trafficker was dead. But his partners and the nameless men who'd used her—what if God forgave them? Her stomach heaved.

Anna's arm circled her shoulders. "And they say faith is soft and fluffy."

The unexpected quip made Landon snicker. The woman in front of her turned with a squint-eyed glare. Landon mouthed an apology and leaned sideways into Anna's hold. She had to forgive for her own healing. And allow God to do the same. Ruth's testimony reinforced that truth. The shiver in her chest was a pressure now, a knowing, a call to take it further. God loved the worst like He loved the rest, and He wanted to save them all.

Trembling, she strained to breathe. Her gaze darted around the sanctuary.

Bobby flashed a fingertip salute from where he and Roy sat across the aisle. A brimmed camouflage hat at the end of a row near the rear—Nigel. Anna had invited Maria, but the inn's former owner had retorted that "Some of the lost need to stay lost."

Landon couldn't argue. The thought of redemption for the predators raked her heart raw again, filling her mouth with a metallic taste. She wanted them to suffer. Needed them to pay.

After Pastor Vern's closing remarks, she followed Anna on stiff legs toward Ruth and Tony. This would be goodbye before the couple headed home to Halifax. A loose ring of people stood near Ruth. Most held themselves a little apart as if to guard their privacy and that of others. A few folded-armed individuals gravitated together.

Tony had positioned his broad frame resolutely at his wife's side. When he caught Landon's gaze, a smile split his sandy beard. He bent his mouth to Ruth's ear, and she looked past the waiting folks to Anna and Landon. "Thank you for everything."

"Thank *you*." Anna waved. To Landon, she said, "If you want to stay, I can wait."

Landon pressed her fingertips to the pit of her stomach. "I'm good."

Anna's brown eyes seemed to measure her. "Okay, let's find Zander."

He stood near the exit, head together with Nigel. Two protective men, discussing tonight's topic or strategizing to find the one who'd attacked Ciara? Zander broke off and stepped toward them. Nigel nodded twice and touched the brim of his camouflage cap. He melted out into the night.

Before they reached Anna's car, his bicycle cruised past. They caught up to him on the next block. With his headlight and the reflective tape on his helmet and safety vest, he'd be visible to motorists even on the unlit road from town to the inn. To Elva's. Instinct told Landon he'd check in before cycling home.

The butter-yellow glow of the inn's outside light welcomed them as Anna followed the driveway to park beside Zander's dark SUV. Lamps shone through the windows. Anna maintained that, guests or no guests, the inn should be an inviting haven.

As they walked along the slate path, a shadow at the base of the stairs unfolded into a lean, ragged marmalade cat. Without glancing their way, he strolled toward the forest, crooked tail held high.

Anna snorted. "Hello to you too."

"Thanks for waiting up, Mister." He'd never be tame. He did seem to trust Landon now, although she was careful to let him make the first move. Soon he blended into the shadows. "That's the closest I've seen him come to the building."

With the door unlocked, Anna stepped toward the kitchen. "I'll put the kettle on."

Zander sidled past. "If you'll both excuse me, I have emails to attend to. For the local investigation and my day job."

Landon followed him along the hallway, calling over her shoulder to Anna that she'd be back. "Zander, your clients need you. It's been great to have your support here, but maybe it's time to go home."

He surged up the stairs on silent shoes. "First, we put an end to this threat. He's not going to stop on his own."

"The police will find him. You don't have to take this so personally."

Zander spun with the grace of a dancer and closed the distance between them. "When he involved you, he made it personal." His tight-lipped attempt at a smile couldn't hide his emotion. "Go down and unwind with Anna. I may join you if I get my work done."

She was pulling on a pair of red and black plaid pyjama pants when Anna called from the stairwell.

"Landon, Zander—we have a problem."

Leaving her skirt flung on the bed, Landon stuffed her phone into her pocket and raced for the stairs, fingers fumbling with the pants' woven drawstring. Zander's door clicked open behind her.

On the main level, Anna stood in the hallway, her arms clamped tight, her lips a hard line. Her chest rose and fell, rapid breaths shaking the thin gold chain at her throat. "Come and see." She strode back down the hall, shoes thumping against the hardwood floor.

"In here." In the private sitting room, Anna bypassed the twin teal recliners for the desktop computer.

Landon's pulse spiked and her feet slowed. Not again. Their online trouble, the fake reviews, and the hacked website—that was Gord. It was finished. No way could this be starting over.

Then she saw the wall above the monitor. The jagged hole in the front of the safe. The flap of metal peeled away like a tab to expose the interior. The air left her lungs.

One hand clapped to her mouth. "Ciara's jade bangle."

Eyes narrowed, Anna nodded. "Gone. I've already phoned. There'll be an officer here shortly."

Zander had activated the flashlight on his phone and elbowed the chair away from the desk. Now he crouched, peering underneath. "He left his saw."

"That's Murdoch's jigsaw." Anna's cheeks flamed. "Of all the—" Breath burst from her nostrils like a shot of steam.

Straightening, Zander pocketed his phone. "This tells us two things. He didn't come expecting to break into a safe. And he knew he'd have time to find any tools he'd need."

"Adding insult to injury is what it says to me." Anna dug her fingers into her hair, pushing the grey-streaked brown bob away from her cheeks. "We should wait somewhere else. I just wanted you to see this."

A firm rap on the rear door sent her scurrying from the room. Hinges creaked, and Dylan's deep voice washed some of the tension from Landon's spine.

He stepped into the sitting room, his focus first on her. A lingering look, a flicker of sympathetic headshake, before acknowledging Zander too. Long strides took him to the ruined safe. "Not the first time I've seen this. Fire safes are often too thin to deter a determined thief."

Anna stood with arms wrapped around her ribs. "I needed fire-retardant for our guests. International travellers often want a secure spot for their passports. I never thought it wouldn't be strong enough."

Dylan leaned a hip against the desk corner. "He could've cut a thicker one out of the wall and smashed it open somewhere else. If you want to replace it with a higher-end version, I'm sure Ciara's friend Tait can advise you."

He opened his notebook. "Let's start with what's missing."

While Landon explained about Ciara's missing bracelet, Anna tapped at her phone. Scowling, she passed it to Dylan. "The cameras didn't catch anything. He must have come in the front. It's locked. I checked."

"Who knew you'd all be out?"

A sick feeling rippled in Landon's stomach. "And who knew Ciara's bangle was here?"

Anna tugged her blouse cuffs down over her hands as if the temperature had dropped. "That poor girl. Can we wait for morning to tell her? I'll need to get the valuation details for my insurance."

"Sounds fair to me. It's late and she's still recovering." Dylan returned Anna's phone. "I know you already did it, but I want to have a look at the front entrance and the ground-floor windows. Landon, do you still have Ciara's keys? It might be wise to check her apartment too."

"I'll get them."

As Landon stepped into the hall, her phone buzzed a text alert. She tugged it from her pyjama pocket. *Please, not*

Ciara, not now. How could she tell her friend the bracelet was gone? Seeing Bobby's name was a relief.

*Are you okay?*

How did he know? She typed that question back at him.

*Just thought tonight might have stirred up some stuff.*

Tonight? Her brain caught up. Church. Offenders escaping wrath. Crisis of belief. That was tonight.

More words lit her phone. *Need to talk?*

Not telling him about the break-in until later would be worse than Zander excluding him from Ciara's apartment disaster. *Come over? We've been robbed. Let yourself in. Dylan's here.*

He replied with an open-mouthed text image. *On my way.*

Landon jogged upstairs while the others spread out on the ground floor to test the locks. Her purse dangled by its thin blue strap from the hook behind her bedroom door. She fished out Ciara's accessory-heavy key ring, then spun to give the space a slow once-over.

A locked door didn't mean the thief hadn't been in here. The realization stirred the tiny hairs on the back of her neck. As far as she could remember, the sage duvet had been smooth and untouched before she threw her skirt on it. The laptop on the bedside table was undisturbed. So were her hairbrush and the trinkets on the mirrored dresser.

He had no reason to come upstairs. But if he had, it wouldn't have been hard to figure out which room was hers. The front two, empty tonight, were open for airflow. That left the rear-facing rooms. If he used the passkey from Anna's desk, he wouldn't even have to breach the locks.

Staring at the stretched-canvas image of the yellow swallowtail with its stark black stripes, she counted ten slow breaths. There weren't many places he could have searched. A glance at the orange monarch print—bright colours for courage—and she took four swift steps to the dresser. Its satin-smooth, aged-honey finish matched the four-poster bed. Grasping the curved wooden handles, she tugged open the top drawer. If the thief had pawed through the familiar jumble of socks and underwear in search of Ciara's bracelet, she'd never know.

In the next drawer, her shirts lay neatly folded. Given the mess he'd made at Ciara's place, he hadn't been here.

She opened the third. A knife lay on top of her pink sweater, wooden handle dark against the knit fabric, wicked-looking serrations lining the blade.

Her gasp crescendoed to a scream.

A deadly cold spread from her core, numbing her mind. She forced herself to blink, but the image stayed. Threatening.

She retreated on frozen legs.

~~~

"Landon."

Her name penetrated the dead zone that held her.

Brown eyes. Arm's length in front of her. Dylan.

She blinked. Realized she was sitting. Somewhere soft.

Crouched before her, Dylan nodded in slow motion. "You're safe. Breathe with me."

Vision tunnelled on his gaze, she obeyed. Her lungs unlocked. Feeling returned. Warmth in her extremities, but still ice at her core.

"Good. Take my hands?"

She did, registering her surroundings. Anna's sitting room. Anna's arm around her waist, holding her close. She must have walked on her own. Or had they found her wandering lost and led her here?

Dylan gave her fingers a gentle squeeze. "Talk to me. What is it?"

Unsticking her tongue from the roof of her mouth took an eternity. She worked up enough saliva to swallow. "My dresser. Knife."

Anna gasped.

Landon's mind flashed back to the steel blade gleaming against her sweater. Her breath faltered. She tried to anchor on Dylan's face and the steadiness of his grip. On the warmth of Anna's hip pressed into hers.

"I need to see this." Dylan's uniform rustled as he stood.

"Is everyone okay?" Bobby skidded into the room, gasping for breath.

"Someone broke into the safe while we were at church and stole Ciara's bracelet." Anna's fingers curved tighter around Landon's ribs. "And—"

"A weapon was found on the premises." Dylan finished for her. "Since you're here, will you stay with Landon? Anna, if you could check your room while Zander and I go upstairs?"

Zander's caged-panther pacing ceased. He scowled. "My door was locked."

"So was mine." How could she sound so stiff when her nerves were jumping out of her skin?

Bobby rushed forward, smacking his shin on the coffee table. "He left a weapon in your bedroom?"

"A knife." The word tasted metallic. Cold.

Anna slid away from her, then stood. "I'll see if our thief left me any presents."

Bobby eased onto the pastel floral couch cushion as if it supported something fragile. Or a brimming cup. Or a girl he'd seen fall apart more than once. He offered his hand, palm up.

When she took it, his fingers curled around hers, a pressure barely felt yet comforting. "I hadn't found the knife when I asked you to come."

Anna returned and dropped into the space beside Landon. "Nothing out of line."

"It'll only be me. For defending Ciara and keeping her bracelet. I stopped asking questions, but he doesn't care."

"You don't know that. Zander's been investigating too." Anna didn't say what Landon thought—that Zander had a better chance of finding the culprit.

The stark red and black plaid of her pyjama pants blurred. "He's only helping because of me. Take me out, and he'll stop."

Bobby snorted. "Take you out, and Zander will move heaven and earth to bring the guy down. Perhaps our perp needs to know that."

Zander and Dylan returned with matching grim expressions. Once through the door, Zander stalked to the window. "Your forces are spread too thin."

Dylan stopped, feet apart, opposite the couch. With a pointed look at Landon's and Bobby's joined hands, he let one eyebrow drift upward.

Landon reached her other hand to clasp Anna's. Friendship and solidarity. Dylan could forget his imagined romance.

A faint smile said he caught her meaning. "Zander's room was clean. As was yours, Anna?"

"Yes."

"So this threat targets Landon alone." Dylan rocked on his heels. "He wants to show he can reach you through a locked door, but he hasn't tried to harm you. Yet."

Bobby stirred, shifting the cushions beneath them. "Stay at Gramp's tonight. In case he comes back."

"No." Zander clamped his arms across his chest. "If he tried anything there, you'd have no protection."

Bobby's exhale carried a growl.

She squeezed his hand. "Elva's the sharpshooter. But I'm not going there either—even if she'd have me. Dylan's right. This is a scare tactic."

Dylan tipped an index finger in her direction. "It *looks* like that's what it is. You need to be careful."

## Chapter 17

*Tuesday*

"BUT ANNA NEEDS to know for her insurance." Phone to her ear, Landon used her free hand to gather the clothes she'd need for school. Her sweater drawer remained shut even though Dylan had removed the knife last night.

She and Anna had slept in the front guest rooms at Zander's insistence while he camped out in the ground-floor hallway. For some reason, she felt braver to venture in for her things today while she was on the phone. Or maybe agitation at telling Ciara the bangle was gone had forced her into mindless motion.

Ciara sighed, heavy and hopeless. "This is all because I shared my gift online. Whoever this collectibles thief is, he's ruining my life. And hurting my friends."

"Anna feels terrible that her safe wasn't good enough."

"Tell her I feel worse because it's my fault. Come see me later?"

"After classes. Gotta go."

A hot shower soothed the gummy feeling in her eyes, and a couple of painkillers pushed back the throb behind them. Today would be brutal. Helping with trouble at the inn had cost her one course already this year. She didn't regret that choice, but she couldn't fail again.

Downstairs, a warm cinnamon scent from the kitchen said Anna's coping strategies were in full swing. Sugar-topped muffins rested on a cooling rack. Anna left the sink and wiped her palms on her apron, streaking soapsuds across the printed red and blue sailboats. She covered a yawn with her forearm. "Is she okay? I should have gone in to tell her in person."

The phone call had been a compromise. Landon felt responsible to give her friend the bad news since Ciara had asked her to keep the jade bangle. And Anna wanted to start the insurance claim as soon as possible.

Landon pulled a lighthouse mug from the cupboard and went straight for the coffee pot. "Orran's away and not responding to messages, but Tait should be able to reach him. I have his number." She dumped extra sugar into her cup and poured a hefty dose of cream. "You know how Ciara gets, but she didn't this time. She sounded more confused than anything. She's blaming herself for talking about the gift online and getting the thief's attention."

"That's a determined thief, to track it down when it wasn't at her apartment."

"It has to be someone she knows. Bobby's taking me to the hospital after school. I want to go through everything with her again. We've missed something."

"My thoughts exactly." Zander spoke from behind her.

Whirling, Landon sloshed hot coffee over her hand. "Yow!" She set the mug on the counter and grabbed a towel. Crouching to wipe up the spill, she looked up at Zander. "Did you get any sleep?"

"Some." His white shirt appeared freshly ironed, and a solid grey tie matched his darker grey dress pants. Despite a smooth shave, a heavy beard shadow clung to his jaw. The faint heaviness to his eyelids wouldn't register with anyone who didn't know him well. The eyes themselves glittered like a falcon's.

Landon stood, shaking her head. "How do you do it? Anna and I are stumbling around like zombies, and you could conduct a board meeting." She sniffed. "You're even wearing cologne."

"Looking alert helps me feel alert. Although I won't say no to a shot of caffeine."

Anna rummaged in the cupboard and drew out a tall pinstriped mug. "Help yourself. Breakfast's almost ready."

Muffin in hand, Landon carried her mug to the square farmhouse table. Elbows on the polished pine surface, she nestled the cup between her palms, inhaling the sharp aroma. It had been midnight before Dylan wrapped up his search. Fingerprint kits, bright lights, examination of every lock in the building, all for nothing. Which reaffirmed his initial read that this was a professional—one who'd now stolen their sleep as well.

Anna whisked a bowl of eggs for scrambling. No special orders this morning, just quick and easy one-size-fits-all. Sausages sizzled on the grill. Anna couldn't put on as good a front as Zander, even with the jaunty apron covering a flowered blouse and khakis. Her head and shoulders drooped, and her steps scuffed the floor. If Landon knew her friend, the problem wasn't lack of sleep. It was another violation of the inn. Yes, the theft, but most of all, the message in the knife's serrated blade—a message aimed at Landon.

Zander took the seat across from Landon. Positioning his elegant mug in easy reach, he steepled his fingers. "Before you leave, I want to go over it all again."

"After breakfast." Landon tipped her chin toward Anna pouring frothy eggs into the frying pan. "I think we need a respite while we eat." She downed half of her drink and set the mug on the table, then rose to put out the place mats and cutlery. By the time she'd filled water glasses, Anna was plating the food.

Anna took their hands to pray for the meal, with a long squeeze before she let go. "The Bible says a cord of three strands is not easily broken." Instead of picking up her fork, she stared at her plate, palms flat on the table. "I can't believe this is happening again, and this time it's worse. That knife was a threat."

Landon didn't dare think about it. She had to get through the day first. Rehash with Zander upstairs. Attend classes. See Ciara. Tonight, when she needed to sleep, her fears would have space to be heard.

Leaving Anna so distressed hurt, but staying wouldn't help. A diversion might. "You were right about not fighting from anger or in our own strength. If we win, we get the credit. And if we lose, people think God either couldn't or wouldn't help."

"I guess you do listen to me once in a while." Anna's attempt at a smile wobbled.

"We looked out for one another this summer, and we can do it again. Help me learn to fight in God's strength."

"It starts by believing He's got this, no matter how He allows it to unfold." Anna's shoulders lifted, a tiny bit. Enough courage for the day? "Committing ourselves into His care. Praying for strength, insight, and courage to follow His lead in trust instead of cowering behind locked doors."

Zander coughed. "Letting me and the local authorities ask questions and rattle chains while you two—and Ciara—stay out of harm's way. Let us draw the fire."

"The girls are already in harm's way." Anna's glass rattled against the tabletop.

Calm blanketed his intensity, the way it did in his counselling sessions. He was a soldier standing down from duty, still ready, but not poised to react. "Anna, will you be all right alone today, or would it be better to shelter with a friend?"

"He's not chasing me out of my home. But I don't want anything else to happen to Landon."

"Then, while you handle the insurance calls and Landon is surrounded by witnesses at university, I'll make more of a nuisance of myself. Do you know if Ken and Kimi are still in Bridgewater? They're on my list, as is the biker who rescued her."

"Ciara said they were in to see her yesterday." Landon stifled another yawn. Time to get moving before she fell asleep at the table.

Zander rose. "I also plan to visit the police. They could be doing more."

"They have Gord's death too," Landon protested. "Plus their regular duties."

"Which is why I may have to find this person myself."

Steel-cold certainty. If only it was that simple.

~~~

Landon sank into the Corvette's soft leather seat and leaned her head back. She'd made it through the day's classes. With the persistent ache behind her eyes, whether she'd learned anything was another story.

The commuter van wouldn't leave for another hour. Bobby's offer to pick her up this afternoon had been a literal godsend. "Thanks for this. And for checking Ciara's apartment last night."

"Dylan couldn't go in without permission, and Zander wouldn't trust anyone but himself to guard you." Bobby navigated the university's sloped driveway to the traffic lights. "I'm glad the thief hadn't gone back to Ciara's for round two."

Still the terse edge. So he wasn't just steamed at Zander. "Everything okay?"

He glanced sideways as the light changed. "You're asking me? I'm not the one whose personal space was invaded by a knife-happy cockroach."

She'd take that as a no. "I'm okay. I mean, I'm mad and I'm scared, but I'm not going to let him mess with my head."

Tight-lipped, Bobby hissed a slow exhale. "Having a little trouble with that today."

Landon nodded. Maybe he wouldn't catch the motion in his side vision, but it was all she had to give. That and a silent prayer.

Finally he spoke. "It sounds silly, me being more bothered by this than you are, but Tony said family and friends have their own stuff to deal with when someone's hurt. Or in this case, threatened."

Ruth's husband hadn't participated when she shared her story at church last night. "You guys talked after?"

"Yeah, this whole forgiveness thing. It's tough to let go of what happens to ourselves. It's a whole other level when the damage is to someone else."

"Like when it's your friend tossed over the cliff. Or the knife turns up in another friend's bedroom."

"That's why you were so fierce to defend Ciara. I get it now."

The iron lump of resistance lingered in Landon's will. "Anna had to push hard to make me see I was retaliating instead of acting God's way." Which did not mean she was ready to surrender. She forced a laugh. "The worst part of the battle can be inside ourselves. So did Tony have any advice?"

"Just that sometimes God has to break you before you can see things His way. Not the most comforting thing I've ever heard."

"No, but that was me in Ontario after they rescued me—broken. And counselling wasn't getting through."

Her eyes filled. "It was Zander. Something about his intensity, his passion—it reached me in that horrible black place. When he told me about the light of God, I believed him." Memory clogged her throat. "That's why I love him. Even though he can be over the top."

Bobby switched lanes and zoomed past a transport truck labouring up the steep incline. "I'm surprised he let you out of his sight today."

"He's going to revisit every possible suspect and source to shake out more clues."

"He won't win any friends, but I hope it works."

Landon tucked a fingertip under the simple bracelet she'd chosen this morning, thumbnail flicking the smooth pink beads around her wrist. "The break-ins were about Ciara's jade bangle. Even if it's the same person who's been stealing local collectibles, it must be linked with the original attack at The Ovens."

"Hence the threat he left you."

The beads stilled beneath her fingers. "But why try to kill her in the first place? She didn't have the bracelet then, and if he wanted her other things, he could have stolen them any time. Without violence."

"He told you the attack was a mistake."

Landon shivered. The knife in her drawer suggested he'd changed his mind. "Maybe she saw someone she knew with one of the stolen items, or they thought she did?"

"If so, she couldn't have realized it. But that's a good question to ask her."

In a rural area like Lunenburg County, word would spread quickly if someone had suspicious collectibles lying around. He'd have to dispose of it. "What about online sales sites? It might be too soon for him to post Ciara's bracelet, but we could search for the older thefts."

"He'd use the dark net, not places honest people can find. But it's worth a try. Have a look now."

"My phone doesn't have data."

He reached inside his jacket and held out his cell. "Here." He coached her through the swipe sequence to unlock the device.

At the first online auction site, *jade bangle* produced too many results. Landon added the word *green* and scrolled through a stream of pictures. Would she even recognize it?

At least the photos helped. Reading was hard enough on the full laptop screen. Mobile sites were not made for people with learning disabilities. "There's so many."

"Can you filter by posting date? Or location, although he might lie about that."

"Thanks." She spoke through clenched teeth. A four-year-old would know to sort by date. She found the filter and toggled the date. Two bracelets, neither a match.

Five sites later with no luck, she decided to try one of the previous thefts. Then the other. "This is never going to work. You're right. It was a dumb idea."

"That's not what I said. I said it was worth a try. Dumb would be having an idea and not trying it—and missing a clue."

"Maybe." She navigated back to the browser search box and typed *Burmese ruby pendant*.

Bypassing the retail sites, she found a link titled "Stolen Goods Database." Maybe that could point them somewhere useful, or at least suggest different search terms.

The page loaded an unexpected assortment of entries. Jewellery, paintings, stamps, but also figurines, firearms, furniture... "Here's a comic book."

"What?"

"It's an international stolen goods website. You wouldn't believe all this stuff. Like I said, a comic book." She scrolled further. "An ancient human skull. A sword. A meteorite. And normal things like coins and art."

"Have they added our items yet?"

"This is the ugliest lamp I have ever seen." She zoomed in on the next image, but it remained a blur. "Honestly, if it didn't say these things were valuable I'd think they were junk. Wait. Here's—I'm not making this up—a taxidermy squirrel in little clothes, teeing off with a miniature golf club."

Bobby snorted. "Bookmark that so I can show Gramp."

Roy's broken leg this spring came from a mishap with a squirrel, and the good-natured rodent humour showed no sign of dying down.

"A cast iron cannon. How'd they haul that away?" A flash of gold and red caught Landon's eye. Her scrolling slowed. Backed up.

Rich oval rubies ringed an ornate goblet, tucked below the rim where they wouldn't interfere with a drink. Smaller ruby chips outlined the tapered stem's base. Now this was beautiful. The colours had stopped her, but an idea was trying to form in her mind. "A golden goblet..."

"I'll stick with the squirrel, thanks. Can you imagine Gramp unwrapping that for Christmas?"

"Bobby, hush. Gold and rubies. Ciara—" The thoughts broke free in a clump, and she tried to sort them. "Ciara saw a ruby-studded goblet at Orran's as a child. She remembered because it was out of character for him. He claimed it was a prop for a play."

"And..."

"And what if it was real? Stolen?" Maybe that was the true reason he'd broken contact with the young Ciara before she found any other "props."

"A security pro whose side hustle is theft."

Heat washed Landon's cheeks, and she tipped her face to catch cool air from the dashboard vents. Bobby had left the convertible's top closed for highway driving. "Forget it."

"Hey, I'm not mocking you. It could happen."

"Forget it anyway. Orran's not in any shape to be the attacker." The jewelled image on the phone screen looked like it belonged in an old-time castle. Or a play. "I'm reading too much into this. It was probably a theatre prop after all."

Driving one-handed, Bobby drew thumb and fingers along his beard stubble from jaw to chin like a cartoon villain. "Was Tait around back then?"

"No, why?"

"If Orran was—or still is—a thief or in possession of stolen goods, he can't let his partner hear what Ciara saw. So he hires someone to scare her, but the guy takes it too far."

"Why do you think Tait isn't involved?"

"Long-term business partners aren't going to have a miscommunication of that magnitude."

Landon dropped the phone into her lap and pressed fingers like claws against the sides of her head. The tires' whoosh against the pavement swelled in her ears, churning her thoughts until nothing made sense. "We can't take this to the police."

"It's pure conjecture. First, let's see what Ciara says about that goblet. Maybe she'll laugh and admit it was plastic."

"It fooled her at the time." Landon leaned back in her seat and eased the shoulder strap away from a building heaviness in her chest. "She looks up to Orran. I don't know how to ask her if he's a thief. And if he is, it'll crush her."

## Chapter 18

"You have to come to her room with me." Parked in the hospital lot, Landon wasn't leaving the car until Bobby agreed.

He shook his head slowly. "Two on one looks like we're ganging up on her."

"You said you'd help."

Groaning, he shoved his fingers through his hair. "I did."

Tension crackled between them as they crossed the pavement. Or maybe it was all in her imagination. What was real was the heavy, quivering lump filling her stomach. Thin conjecture it might be, but if Orran was responsible for any part of what happened, the truth would hurt worse than the physical assault.

And how would they know for sure?

No matter what Ciara thought she'd seen, they couldn't prove or disprove Orran's past possession of stolen goods. Landon stopped in the middle of the hospital entrance. "Let's just go. Even if we convinced the authorities to search, she'd never allow her name connected to a warrant. Orran might see it."

Bobby held her gaze, a sad curve to his lips. "What if we don't ask and this is the clue we needed? If there's another attack we could have prevented?"

Tiny hairs lifted on the back of Landon's neck.

Leaving the elevator on Ciara's floor, they found Tait loitering in the hallway outside her room. He raised a hand in a half-wave. "Doctor's in with her now. He said to wait."

Landon's heart jolted. "What's wrong?"

Tait angled his head to the side, lips mocking. "Paranoid much? It's routine rounds."

Facing a possible suspect, was it any wonder she was jumpy? Landon hitched her purse strap more securely onto her shoulder. "Enough has happened this past week to make anyone expect the worst. Did Anna reach you today?"

"Yeah, that's too bad about the bracelet. Poor girl can't catch a break. I'll head over to Orran's tonight and check his files. The man's obsessed with paperwork. There'll be a receipt there somewhere."

"Ciara's afraid he'll be angry."

The outside corners of Tait's eyes pinched. "It was a mistake to post the pic online. But he won't blame her." He slouched against the wall, shoulder butting into the bulletin board with its health and safety notices. "That doctor's taking forever."

Landon made a show of looking at the round white wall clock. "Bobby, can we come back tonight? I have too much homework to wait around."

As true as that was, she wouldn't be able to concentrate until they'd talked with Ciara. But not in Tait's presence.

~~~

That evening, the hospital corridors were quieter. The daytime bustle had given way to the soft buzz of occasional conversation and monitor beeps from patients' rooms.

After she and Bobby had a few quiet words with the security guard, Landon knocked softly on Ciara's door and peeked into the room. The visitor's chair was empty. Good.

Ciara stood at the window, fingers tapping the side of her satiny pyjama pants. The oxygen tube stretched a thin line to the pole by her bed. She whirled toward the door, then grimaced and pressed her palm to her forehead. Her other hand tugged white-wired earbuds free.

"Hi, guys. Thanks for coming. Tait said you'd been here." She motioned them in and climbed to sit cross-legged on the bed. "Landon, you can sit with me and let Bobby have the chair."

Up close, her colour was almost normal except for the bruising on her cheek, which had ebbed to a sickly yellow. Her hair had a freshly blown-dry sheen, and her coral lipstick matched the rosebuds on her pyjamas.

Landon tucked a foot beneath her other leg and asked what the doctor had said. "Are they releasing you soon?"

"Any day now." Ciara rocked forward and back, jostling the mattress. "I'm dying for puppy cuddles. But Tait's still waiting for the security system he said he'd install."

Ignoring Bobby, she fixed Landon with a wide-eyed stare. "I'm afraid to go home."

Landon reached for her hand. Zander would go ballistic if she offered to sleep on Ciara's couch for backup. "You could stay with us if the inn doesn't feel too vulnerable after the robbery." Anna had rebooked most of this week's guests into other accommodations.

The worried motion ceased. "Would Anna be okay with that?"

Landon grinned. "Have you met her?"

"The inn would be perfect." Ciara squeezed Landon's hand tight enough to compress the bones before letting go. "Ken and Kimi offered to put me up, but they have a one-bedroom suite. I'd be in the way."

"It's sweet the way they've stayed around longer in case you needed them. He must have been a fantastic boss."

"I can't believe how kind they've been. Especially with the way things ended." Ciara cut her gaze sideways toward Bobby as if to ask Landon to keep the job disaster between them.

Ken seemed like a peaceful man, apart from that one glimpse of anger. He said he didn't blame Ciara for her ex's scheme. But the attack came after he and Kimi arrived. Their rental car had covered some dirt roads that day—like the one to The Ovens. He recognized the value of the jade bangle too.

How vengeful would a man—or his wife—have to be, to travel clear across the country after a broken-hearted girl? It didn't matter. Landon had a sick feeling the villain was much closer to home.

She gave her head a mental shake. Time to quit stalling. "Ciara, remember the ruby goblet you saw at Orran's, the theatre prop?"

"Why?" The word came out small. Quiet.

"What if it was real? If it was stolen and you remembered... you'd be a threat."

Bobby held out his phone. "Did it look like this?"

Ciara's hands pulled tight to her body. "I don't—no." Her chin tipped up, and her arms unlocked to glide her palms over her pyjama pants.

He tapped the screen. "What about this one? Or this?" He shrugged at Landon. "I was bored after supper."

Shaky fingers reaching for the phone, Ciara let out a sound like a strangled hiccup. "Let me see."

She scrolled the images, then expanded one and peered at every bit, her round cheeks hollowed. The tip of her chin shook. She thrust the phone at Bobby. "That one. There's a nick in the rim the same as I saw."

Her knees drew in to her chest and she locked her arms around them, puckering the satiny fabric. "It was heavy for a prop. I told myself it was lead."

A weight lodged in Landon's gut. "I wanted us to be wrong."

"Sunday, after I had to give the insurance people the details on what was stolen, I looked online to see if any of my things had been posted for sale." With a gulp of air, Ciara leaned her forehead on her upraised knees. "I found a goblet that sent me looking for other ones. Orran played it calm back then, but I knew he hadn't wanted me to see the one at his house."

Bobby scraped his chair closer. "If you knew..."

"I wanted it to go away!" She sniffed. "So he had a stolen object when I was a kid. That has nothing to do with what's happening now."

Straightening, she pinned Landon with a tear-filled gaze. "You've met Orran. He's physically incapable of throwing me over that cliff—or making a getaway on foot."

"We think he hired someone, maybe to keep Tait from finding out." Landon had vowed to help Ciara. How did she end up in a position to cause more pain?

"If I hadn't told anyone yet, why try to kill me now to keep me quiet? And trash my place?" Ciara's head whipped back and forth between them. "Would Orran give me a gift and then steal it back?"

Landon glanced at the door. Had the nurses heard Ciara's cry? "Bobby, would you get her a glass of water?"

As he picked up the foam cup from the bedside table, Landon shifted sideways to put her arm around Ciara.

The girl's entire frame shook. "I can't believe this."

Landon's fingers moved in a slow circle over Ciara's shoulder. "The other collectibles thefts, remember how Orran said the one guy deserved to be robbed?"

When Ciara didn't answer, she added more. "That priceless Burmese ruby pendant he was talking about here in the hospital, the one that vanished Sunday overnight? We have to report this."

"I have to see him first. Maybe he can explain."

Bobby returned with the water. When Ciara shook her head, lips shut, he set it on the table in easy reach and flopped back into his chair. "Ciara, he's been away. Could well have been in the city when the pendant was stolen. They're saying it was an expert job."

Her lips clamped tighter. "One whisper of this would ruin his business. I refuse to take that chance. What if we're wrong? I saw that goblet for seconds. Years ago. The rest is pure speculation."

Landon squeezed Ciara's shoulder. "The police know how to be discreet. They won't say anything without proof."

"Things leak." Then her spine straightened, and she gave a brisk nod. "I know. You two sneak into his house. If you find anything, I'll admit what I saw. Tait often works out there, so I'll ask him to visit me."

"Wait, no." Landon flailed her arms, bouncing the bed and pulling a creak from the frame. "No breaking in. Tell them what you know, and they'll do a legal search."

"If you really cared, you'd help me." Sucking air through her teeth, Ciara clasped her ribs. "Fine. They're releasing me any day now. If Orran's not back, I'll go myself. Right from here, before he can get home."

Bobby curled forward in the chair. Elbows on his legs, he addressed the floor. "Ask Tait to show you around."

"Orran won't have left anything in plain sight." Her mouth shaped a mutinous pout. "Without my memory of the goblet, you have nothing to give the police for a warrant, so it's you or it's me."

Landon left the bed and walked to the window. Orran might be the one person Ciara had left to look up to. Ken still fit, but her part in the corporate takeover had cut that tie, at least in her mind. The assault, the thefts... she'd been through so much. Of course she'd hold out against believing her faith in Orran was a lie.

Wouldn't Landon feel the same about the people she respected in her own life? She stepped to the foot of the bed. Tears trickled down Ciara's cheeks as if she'd abandoned the dramatics and settled for victimhood. Bobby's entire countenance was a flat no.

Watching him, Landon folded her arms. "We can't let her go alone."

Scowling, he slouched low in the chair.

Before he could speak, Ciara said, "I'll tell you where he hides the key. And my code for the alarm."

Shivers prickled Landon's shoulders. An alarm. This was their way out. "He's bound to have changed it since you were a kid."

"Each user's is unique. Mine might still be active." Ciara's gaze shifted from Landon to the doorway. "Hi, Shaun."

Shaun took a few steps into the room and leaned his soft-sided guitar case against the wall. "So this is where the party is."

His slim-cut black leather jacket hung open over a black tee shirt and black jeans. A silver chain gleamed at his throat. A motorcyclist would travel light, and he certainly hadn't bothered with variety.

He eyed Landon and Bobby. "Her stepfather asks, I was never here."

"He has no business running my life." Somewhere in the distraction of greetings, Ciara had wiped her tears and found a confident posture. "Thanks for coming, guys. Landon, I'll text you that information later."

Bobby pushed up from the chair and motioned Landon ahead of him toward the exit.

He didn't speak until they reached the parking lot. Then he planted his feet on the pavement. "This is insane. I'm going back in there to tell her no."

"She played us like a pro, didn't she?"

His stubble-framed lips turned down. "We could get arrested."

The evening sky still held the light, but clouds of little flies roamed the predusk air. Landon waved them away. Breaking into Orran's place... If they were caught, what would that do to Bobby's reputation? She kept forgetting this quiet, unassuming guy was an author with a public following. Her fingertips twisted the thin purse strap dangling from her shoulder. "Just because I've been talked into this doesn't mean you have to do it. I'll ask Roy."

"He'd do it too." He glanced upward, shaking his head. "Man Breaks into Private Home to Save Grandfather Jail Time."

"I wasn't trying to manipulate you—honest. Roy'd think it was fun."

"My parents would dump on us both like the proverbial ton of bricks. Ton and a half. No, I'm in. It won't be the most asinine thing I've ever done for a girl. And don't ask."

He'd be thinking of the girl from his past. The one he'd said could be Landon's evil twin. She met his eyes. "Thank you. I feel a little safer going with you."

Bobby shoved his fingers through his hair. "You said no more fighting for answers—support and simple questions. How can you think this is a good idea?"

"I don't. But it's a worse idea for Ciara to go, and you know she would."

She pressed her palm to her breastbone, fingers fanned. "I don't feel like I'm pushing this time. More like helping. But if the key's not there or the code doesn't work first try, we get out of there fast."

## Chapter 19

*Wednesday*

"Ciara says Tait's on his way, and he confirmed Orran's still not home." A flurry of nerves constricted Landon's chest.

They were really going through with this.

"Right." Bobby tugged the brim of his faded ball cap lower on his forehead and eased Roy's pickup truck onto the gravel road from the small park where they'd been waiting. The truck would be less visible than a white Corvette, and with a fresh layer of dirt-road dust on its body and licence plate, maybe it wouldn't be easy to trace. Not that they planned on being seen.

Landon had chosen the most colourless clothing she owned and tucked her hair up inside a navy knitted hat. A pair of disposable latex gloves from a box at the inn padded her rear pocket.

Bobby had gloves too. He didn't seem to own a tee shirt that didn't have a strange graphic or slogan, but he'd turned a black one inside out.

Fifteen minutes from the park, they jostled to a stop in front of Orran's home. Bobby slewed the truck around to point back down the narrow lane. "I don't like this. If we meet someone on the way out, we're blocked in."

"Tait's in Bridgewater with Ciara. If Orran comes home, we can say we were checking on him." That didn't keep Landon from sharing his nerves. She hopped from the truck and hurried toward the trees. "Peek in the garage and make sure his van's not there?"

"Gotcha."

Ciara's first landmark was a slender white birch at the edge of the grass. Easy to spot. Landon passed it to the left and counted five paces forward. Ahead stood four grey tree trunks, arm's length apart in a rough diamond shape. With a notch in the farthest one where a branch had split off on the right.

Bobby called an all-clear.

Cringing, Landon stuck her fingers into the decaying leaves that filled the spot where the branch met the trunk. Amid the damp matter, she touched metal.

She seized the key and ran for the front of the house.

When no one answered her knock after what felt like an hour of nervous twitching on the deck, she tucked her hands into her gloves. With a deep breath and a glance at Bobby beside her, she inserted the key in the deadbolt. "If this doesn't work, we can say we tried."

The key turned and the handle twisted. Inside, the door alarm beeped its warning countdown. Her heart jolted. "Here we go."

Bobby reached the security panel in two long strides, muttering the code as he punched it in.

She hadn't dared leave that to her dyslexic brain. Not when they had one chance to get it right.

The beeps continued, matching the pulse of a red light on the screen.

"Get out!" Bobby launched toward her as she ducked outside.

Landon risked valuable seconds to lock the door, then flung the key toward the trees. She bolted for the truck.

Bobby had the engine running. She'd barely shut her door when they rocketed into the lane.

Wild, whistling gasps shook her ribs, and her heart thudded fast and heavy. "Cannot... believe... we... did that."

Bobby grunted, white-knuckling the wheel. However fast his pulse rate, he stared ahead without wavering.

The truck fishtailed around a bend, and Landon screamed. The tires held, and their mad flight continued.

Her phone buzzed in her pocket. Clutching the door armrest in a desperate attempt to keep her seat, she didn't even try reaching for the phone. It buzzed again.

With her free hand, she hauled the seat belt across her body. The buckle clicked shut seconds before the truck tire nearest her dropped into a hole. The jolt snapped her teeth together.

"Sorry." Bobby kept driving.

Good thing he'd had the wheel to hang onto.

The insistent phone buzzed. Now she tugged it free and unlocked it. Three texts from Ciara. "Tait's on the move. She says he left in a hurry. Do you think Orran has an alert set up? Forwarded to Tait when he's away?"

"Almost there."

Ahead, the trees opened up. At the end of the lane, Bobby cut a tight turn onto the narrow paved road. Stones spat from beneath the tires. Their pace slowed as he one-handed his seat belt into position.

Landon's scalp itched under the knit hat, but she kept her hair covered. They could yet meet Tait. She peeled off the gloves and stuffed them out of sight.

She texted Ciara a quick update, that they'd failed but had escaped. When a response buzzed, she ignored it. She had no strength for more right now. Not with her nerves still rattling.

Bobby navigated to the park where they'd started this crazy escapade. "Gonna clean the licence plate. Not too much, but I don't want a ticket for driving with it obscured."

When he returned, his shirt was right-side-out again, a pale moon stark against the midnight fabric. He tucked Roy's old ball cap into the door pocket.

Landon freed her hair from the tight hat and shook it out. Her fingernails tackled the itchy spots. "Where to now?"

"Home, but not directly. When's the last time you were on the LaHave River ferry?"

"Maybe as a kid?"

"Then it's overdue. We need to decompress—at least I do—and I want us to take longer getting home than if we'd driven straight from Orran's."

"Hey, you're good at this sneaky stuff. Travers would be proud."

"Travers would have had nothing to do with this from the start. But if he did, he'd have some fantastic tech to bypass the security. I wonder what Reyton would come up with..." His words had gone soft, almost crooning. One hand on the gearshift, he simply... paused. The truck idled in place.

"Bobby?"

The faraway look fled. "Sorry, plot idea. Occupational hazard."

"So who's Reyton?"

He eased the truck into gear. "Guess you haven't got very far in the book yet. He's the ship's engineering whiz."

Oops. "I've been saving it for when I can relax, not cram it in while my brain's exhausted with school."

Bobby rapped his knuckles against his forehead. "I remember university reading lists. What was I thinking, dumping another book on you right now?"

"That I don't have proper respect for Travers despite your glowing praise? You want me to see the hero in action." It might take her until Christmas break, but she did want a peek inside Bobby's imaginary world. And at the larger-than-life character he felt he'd never measure up to.

Bobby's long way home led them farther away from town. A network of back roads looped around to the river, and they followed it to the ferry landing. Parked in the gravel lot, they watched the boxy navy and white vessel approach. When it reached the dock, the ramp lowered, and a handful of vehicles trundled off.

The safety-vest-clad attendant directed Bobby into the left-hand lane behind a van that had been waiting before them. Five more cars joined them in the single-deck holding area before the ramp raised and the winches started hauling them along the submerged cable to the other shore.

Landon and Bobby left the truck and stood with their elbows on the ferry's white metal railing. Sun sparkled on blue-green wavelets below. Wisps of soft cloud streaked a deep-blue sky. Out here in the wide-open space, with green trees softening the rock-edged water, the air tasted free. Landon filled her lungs again and again. "Thank you."

"For what, exactly?"

"Helping when you knew it was a bad idea. For this chance to calm down. And for not going all man-hero and trying to make me stay in the truck at Orran's."

He snorted. "Like that would've worked. Now we have to convince Ciara to talk to the police."

"She answered my text. I should see what she said." The bright day made it difficult to read a phone screen outdoors, so she waited until they returned to the truck. Then her heart rate spiked again. "If we report the stolen goblet, she'll deny it—and she'll tell them we tried to break in."

"Because she pushed us." With the window down, his shout turned the ferry attendant's head, a car-length away.

Dylan would be furious. Worse, Ingerson might well find a way to prosecute them. Landon couldn't breathe against her racing heart. "What do we do?"

"Turn around and head for Bridgewater to talk some sense into her."

He nosed the truck along the ferry ramp to exit, then pulled over to the edge of the lot. He cut the engine and twisted in his seat, light reflecting from his glasses. "She's not thinking straight. But after what we just did to keep her happy, she's not going to blackmail us."

Blackmail? Landon stretched out a hand. "She wants to ask Orran first. He'll have to come home soon."

"Unless he knows she's suspicious and he's taken off. Not answering his messages is odd."

"She said Tait expected him any day. Can we wait? Theft is bad, but it's not like lives are at stake."

"Ciara's better not be. If he feels threatened, who knows what he might do?"

Landon's teeth caught her lower lip. "I need to talk to Zander. He's not obligated to report anything, and he knows more about things like this than we do."

"Landon, he'll nail me to the wall." Bobby winced. "You won't get off much better."

"If we keep quiet and Orran does hurt her again, what then?"

Bobby started the truck and swung around to join the ferry queue. "First, let's try to talk to Ciara."

~~~

"You don't have to be part of this." Landon's mouth felt clogged with sand.

Ciara had insisted on waiting to confront Orran privately before speaking to the police. And that she'd report Landon and Bobby's break-in attempt if they spoke out. When Bobby countered that her texts would prove she'd been the instigator, she wailed about a headache and called a nurse to throw them out.

Without her account of the goblet, the more recent thefts pointed nowhere near Orran. So here they sat, Roy's truck nose-in to the grey barn behind the inn. While Landon tried to grow enough of a spine to confess to Zander.

Bobby had turned off the engine, but she'd meant what she said. It might be easier one-on-one with Zander, without a witness to his fury. She unlatched her seat belt and turned toward him. "Please, go home. I'll tell you if there's anything we can do."

Instead, he slid the key from the ignition and opened his door. "Travers taught me better than that. Always own your actions. And never let a teammate face the fire alone. Let's go." The truck door closed behind him.

With a groan, she plucked her navy knit hat from the truck console. Together they walked the paving stones to the deck.

Anna called a greeting from her sitting room as they passed. Landon flipped a casual wave and answered without stopping. "Looking for Zander." At the top of the stairs, she marched to his door and knocked.

"Behind you." He spoke from the other side of the stairwell. She whirled, bumping Bobby with the hand clutching her hat.

Zander sat in the windowed alcove over the main entrance. He snapped his laptop shut and placed it on the round wooden coffee table. "Trouble?"

"Any luck yet?" Landon skirted the stair rail and perched in an empty chair, hands squeezing her knees.

Bobby dropped into the third seat.

"I've arranged to meet Ken Sanu tomorrow afternoon. He may know more about Ciara than he lets on." Zander's watchful gaze flicked between them. Waiting.

When Landon opened her mouth, Bobby cut her off. "We've done something stupid."

His account was brief, almost stark.

Zander surged to his feet and rounded the coffee table, stopping toe to toe with Bobby. Both fists gripped Bobby's tee shirt and jerked him from the chair. Stitches popped as a seam let go.

"What were you thinking?" Each word rocked them both.

Landon launched at him, dodging a floor lamp that crashed down. She hooked her fingers into Zander's shoulders and tried to pull him back. "Stop!"

"What's going on?" Anna's cry froze them all. Pale and breathless, she advanced on Zander, phone in hand. "Do I call in a domestic disturbance, or do we sit like civilized people while you explain yourself?"

Landon stepped to his other side, leaving him space to retreat.

Zander remained immobile. Then a shudder swept him, and he drew a heavy breath. His fingers uncurled from Bobby's crumpled moon shirt. He took a precise step back, brushing his hands against his pant legs. "I apologize for my actions. There's no excuse for either of us."

Bobby wagged his head as if collecting his scattered wits. Sweat trickled from beneath the hair on his forehead. One hand adjusted his gunmetal-framed glasses. "I should have come to you and let you stop her." Shoulders back, he straightened his shirt and passed his palms down the front. The wrinkles held. "Landon thinks you may be able to help. Is her trust misplaced?"

Anna stood with one hand fisted on her hip. "I'm waiting for an explanation."

Landon righted the floor lamp and flicked the switch. Nothing. The inn was meant to be a welcoming haven for travellers. Not the scene of a brawl. Why had she allowed Ciara to manipulate her into such a ridiculous scheme? More than ridiculous—illegal. Bobby might have tried to do the noble thing and take responsibility. But it'd been her decision, and they both knew it.

She plucked her hat from the floor. "We think Orran may be behind the attack. I asked Bobby to drive me out there to break in and look for clues."

Anna's chest rose in a slow breath that she blew out through thin lips. "I see."

She strode into the open Schooner Room and returned, dragging a wide-armed wooden rocker. Claiming it like a queen—or a judge—she motioned the rest of them into the blue fabric club chairs. "I thought I'd heard the last of the harebrained schemes when my kids hit adulthood. Tell me how this ever seemed like an even remotely intelligent plan."

The story left her shaking her head in a slow, wide arc. Then she stilled, aiming serious brown eyes at Landon. "Just Sunday, you said you weren't going to fight this battle. You were going to support Ciara and leave the detecting to the police."

Inside, Landon shrank to a little girl, tiny in this grown-up-sized chair. "It didn't feel like fighting. I did pray about it. God didn't say no."

One corner of Anna's mouth tucked in. "Before you decided or after?"

Landon stared at the hat, twisting the navy knit. "Bobby would have been right to tell on me." As angry as the idea made her.

"So until Orran comes home and Ciara can have this conversation, the investigation is stalled." Anna spread her fingers on the wooden armrest. "At least he can't cause trouble here while he's away."

"If he's actually away and not hiding somewhere close." Zander's foot tapped a slow beat.

"There's still the issue of why you attacked a guest in my home."

"I have done all I could to support Landon after her trauma." He lasered Bobby with a glare. "Only for a weak-willed jellyfish to endanger her safety. And not for the first time."

Landon's nails dug into her palms. "Zander, you've made a huge difference in my life, but you have no right to judge my friends. I'm an adult, and I take responsibility for my own choices. Even bad ones like this."

The tendons in his neck corded. With a harsh exhale, he pressed his hands, fingers wide, against the creases of his dress pants. "You know I lost Gabriella."

"Yes." He'd never shared his daughter's story, and out of respect, she hadn't searched for details online. But it was tragic and he'd never recovered.

Zander drew Anna and Bobby into the tale with the point of his chin. "My wife died when our daughter was six. Gabriella was my life. When she disappeared, I nearly lost my mind."

The cramp of his mouth released for a brief smile. "Like Landon, she was rescued from the clutches of human traffickers. She vowed to testify against them in court."

His eyes closed briefly, and his throat convulsed. "I found the threats later—anonymous, but I knew the source—what he'd do if she talked. My baby girl took her own life."

Landon's heart tore. "Zander, I'm so sorry."

Tears sheened his eyes, the iron set of his jaw defying them to fall. "I experienced a breakdown, and my faith was shaken for a time. When I returned to work, I could no longer face the vilest of the vile, so I switched to victim services. Perhaps God could use my pain to help others. I made it my mission to bring hope to trauma survivors, offering the light of Christ in their darkness. Teaching them to forgive and to leave their abusers to God's judgment. I have not, perhaps, done so well forgiving myself."

He steepled his fingers, elbows braced against his armrests, and angled toward Anna. "I regret my loss of control here. I'll leave if you wish."

Anna's chair rocked back and forth, then stilled. "Bobby? Landon? What do you think?"

Landon deferred to Bobby to speak first. His lips flattened into a faint but grim smile. "Lesson learned. Let's move on together and end this threat."

Zander's pain had defused the last of Landon's rebellion. "Your help means a lot, Zander. Stay, if your work can spare you."

"Well, then." Anna set the rocker in motion again. "We won't let one bad moment ruin the good you've been doing here, for Landon and Ciara and Meaghan."

Zander dipped his chin to his chest. "Thank you."

Landon tucked a foot underneath her in the chair. "What about asking Tait for a tour of Orran's house? Say we've heard rumours and we don't want to involve the police if we don't have to?"

"Even if Tait is innocent, Orran will hear about the request and be warned. Assuming he has anything to hide." Zander's index finger tapped a matter-of-fact beat on his thigh.

Right. Foolish idea. And still supposition, as Ciara had said. If Orran wasn't the culprit, they needed to keep looking. Every day they waited for him to come home would give the real villain time to do more harm.

She rubbed her forehead. "Tait probably went there from the hospital. What if we go knock on the door? Say we have some questions. Maybe ask for a tour once we're in?" It sounded so inane that she cringed before anyone had the chance to reply.

But Zander said, "I've been rattling everyone else's chain. A visit there is overdue."

"You distract him in conversation, and I'll excuse myself to the bathroom and prowl around."

Zander's breath hissed between his teeth. "A quick surface snoop won't find the evidence we need."

Landon caught Bobby's sympathetic shrug. Why couldn't they have thought this through before she dragged him out there and into trouble?

Zander stood, tugging the cuffs of his sleeves into place. He brushed his palms together. "I'll go see what I can stir up."

## Chapter 20

LANDON COULDN'T STOP thinking about Zander facing Tait alone. In their scenario, Tait was innocent, but logic wasn't proof. If he knew about Orran's crimes and if Zander approached the subject too directly—

She glared at the carrot in her hand and attacked it with the peeler. Supper prep as a way to calm down wasn't working. Especially with Anna on the phone with Ciara.

When they'd confronted Ciara earlier today, the oxygen tube had been gone. Still, Landon had expected she'd have at least one more night to be monitored. The one-sided conversation sounded like the hospital was discharging her.

Anna replaced the phone in the countertop base. "Funny she called me instead of you."

"She's afraid I'd say she couldn't have a room after all."

"Would you have?" Anna retrieved a bright orange carrot peel from the floor and dropped it on the pile of curls in the sink.

"Of course not. But I'd have told her to drop the blackmail about Orran's place." Landon rolled her shoulders and tried to lose the tension. "It's good there's a spot for her here."

Not that a full inn would have denied Ciara a bed. Landon could have slept on the sitting room couch for a night or two. She'd done that before.

Anna looped her apron over the hook in the pantry cupboard. "It's late in the afternoon to let her go, but the doctor was in surgery all day. I'll collect her while you finish here."

Motion outside the window drew Landon's attention. She hadn't heard Zander's SUV, but now he crossed the slate path toward the deck. With a brisk knock, he opened the door.

Anna poked her head into the hallway. "In here, Zander. I'm just leaving."

"You may want to defer that." Footsteps sharp, he stepped into the kitchen, his mouth a grim line. "Orran's dead."

"What?" Landon shared a horrified glance with Anna, who stood with her shoulders pressed against the cleaning cupboard.

"Tait was contacted this afternoon. They found Orran's body in his van in a Halifax parking garage. It'd been there for days. He'd been shot."

Landon couldn't breathe. Poor Orran. And Tait. And Ciara. Her brain spun, connecting other dots. "So..."

Zander pocketed his keys. "So Orran did not break in here Monday night. Or steal the Burmese ruby on the weekend. Tait is devastated. He asked us to tell Ciara."

Anna pressed her palms together. "She'll be staying with us for a few days. I was on my way to pick her up from the hospital. I won't say anything until we get back."

He inclined his head in a slow movement. "One other point."

The air seemed to chill. Landon braced a palm against the countertop.

"Tait said there'd been an attempted break-in at Orran's today. With a key. None were found on the body." He lifted an eyebrow at Landon. "His cameras malfunctioned, so he had no images for police. They're linking this to the murder."

Cameras. Of course a security pro would have cameras, discreet ones.

Shivers swept her, and she clung to the counter's support. "We have to tell him. We can't mess up their investigation."

Anna's rueful smile confirmed Landon's words. "It might be easier to talk to one of the officers. Tait's grieving."

Landon remembered Tait yelling at Ciara on the phone. This would be brutal. But— "An officer might have to charge us. Tait may want to anyway, but I'll try to explain."

How on earth could she say they'd suspected his dead partner of assault and theft? By the time she'd finished chunking up the vegetables and set them in the oven to roast, she still had no answer.

It was spitting rain when Anna shepherded Ciara through the back door. The girl's features, pale after days in the hospital, looked pinched from damp and exhaustion. If the doctor could see her now, he'd rethink releasing her.

The last of Landon's frustration evaporated. In this fragile state, Ciara wasn't at her best. And they were about to add another layer of pain. First, they helped her settle in the room across from Landon's. Ciara tried to exclaim over the decor and Anna's kindness, but she sounded near tears.

Landon hugged her. "Why don't you lie down? I'll come for you when the food's ready."

"I can't believe they threw me out. I couldn't reach Phil to stop them."

They ate in the kitchen, the square pine farmhouse table drawn out from the wall to seat a fourth person. The pink-tinted walls and homey rose and grey flagstone-patterned floor drew warmth from the overhead lighting on such an overcast day, making the space a refuge.

Quiet and subdued, Ciara picked at her meal. The others kept up a light conversation, by unspoken agreement saving Orran's death until the food was gone.

That conversation would be difficult enough. Telling Tait they'd been at Orran's—that storm loomed heavier than the one building outside. Landon didn't eat much more than Ciara.

She and Anna did a hurried cleanup while the coffee dripped and the tea steeped. Then Anna piled slices of cinnamon-apple coffee cake onto an oval serving dish and set it in the middle of the table. "Ciara, how do you take your coffee?"

Once they each had a steaming china mug, Anna folded her arms on the pine tabletop. She'd chosen her prettiest flowered mugs tonight, building Ciara up even in small ways. Now she gazed across the table with sad brown eyes. "We have bad news."

Landon reached for her friend's hand, offering a warm pressure while Anna relayed what they'd heard from Zander.

The kitchen fell silent except for the spatter of rain against the window. Ciara's hiccupping breath unleashed a thin keening like a child lost in the night.

Landon reached to embrace her friend, but Ciara shrunk in on herself, a tight knot resisting comfort's touch.

Ciara's chair scraped away from the table and bumped the wall. "I need to be alone." She dodged Zander and fled into the hallway. Her feet thudded heavy and slow on the stairs.

The sound resonated in Landon's mind like an ominous, slow-ticking clock. She took a thick slice of coffee cake from the plate and broke off a corner. "I have to phone Tait."

Zander lifted his mug and studied her over the rim. "I'll drive you if you'd rather talk in person."

The cake, so sweet in her mouth, felt like pebbles in her throat. She washed it down with a sip of tea. "He's going to be so mad. I'll phone and see if we can go over."

She found Tait's number in her contacts. "Jesus, help me with the right words."

Tait answered, gravel-voiced.

She should have texted. "Um, Tait. I'm so sorry about Orran."

"Yeah."

"I need to talk to you. It'd be better in person. But if you'd rather not see anyone right now, I understand."

"I'll come to you. You're at the inn?"

"Oh no, you don't have to do that—Zander will bring me."

A ragged breath filled the receiver. "I have to get out of here. The silence is making me crazy."

"Ciara's here at the inn too. We told her."

"Thank you. Trying to get the story out for Zander nearly broke me, and he had no emotional investment in Orr."

"Orran was a special man. It's a huge loss. A tragedy."

"Someone will pay."

Landon caught the shadowed sympathy in Zander's hooded expression. She ended the call and laid her phone on the table. "Don't leave me alone with him when he comes?"

Zander splayed his fingers on the tabletop. "Not a chance. What about your partners in crime? They should wear the fallout too."

She'd planned to tell Bobby about Orran after confessing to Tait. Take the blame before Bobby's noble streak tried to shield her.

He would be furious. Hurt. Somehow that frightened her more than Tait's wrath.

She swallowed the last of her tea. "I'll call Bobby. Ciara may be too fragile tonight."

~~~

Landon pleated her skirt between her fingers. Smoothed it flat. Folded it again. She sat in one of the hard-backed chairs beside the puzzle table, facing the rest of the group. Bobby had the other wooden chair. Sharing her penance?

Anna and Zander had taken the upholstered seats, leaving the leather club chair for Tait. Ciara had not joined them.

Positioned by the window, Landon saw Tait's vehicle arrive. When he rang the bell, she glanced at the others. "I hope this doesn't look like we've united against him."

Anna went to meet him at the door, and a shrill bark interrupted her welcome.

He'd brought Moxie. In his grief, he'd thought to comfort Ciara in hers.

Tait shushed the Chihuahua. "I know dogs are against the rules, but can she have a few minutes tonight? Even if they have to go to the basement? It's too wet outside."

"Let me take him up to her room where we can contain him. This is so sweet, Tait. The poor girl."

He stepped into the common room, shedding a mist-beaded wool coat. Features stiff, he curved an eyebrow at Landon. "I said I couldn't handle the silence, but that didn't mean throw a party."

She winced. "Bobby's part of this too. Zander and Anna are moral support, but they don't have to stay."

Tait's brow hiked higher as his head tipped left. "Now you've got me curious." He flopped into the empty chair and dropped his coat on the floor beside it. "This is the worst day of my life."

When Ciara's shriek and Moxie's barks cut through their condolences, Tait glanced upward with a tight smile. "She taking it hard?"

Landon nodded. "I know she wasn't as close to Orran as you, but she's been through so much these last few weeks."

"So, what gives? Or do you have to wait for Anna?"

"Here I am." Anna stopped in the doorway. "Tea, coffee, anyone?"

At the sudden pinch around Tait's eyes, Landon launched into the story. "Tait, the attempted break-in this morning at Orran's—it was us. Me and Bobby. We don't want to mess up the search for the killer."

Chest lifting in a slow breath, he flattened his fingers on the chair's armrests. After a beat, one finger lifted, tapped. Lifted, tapped. "What was worth invading his privacy instead of talking to him? Or to me?"

"We couldn't talk to him. That's the problem." She shot a helpless glance at Bobby. "We were afraid Orran was behind the collectibles thefts, Ciara's and the others. And behind the attack."

Tait's expression froze, the grief etching deeper. He studied them each in turn as if hoping someone would tell him this was all a bad joke.

Bobby cleared his throat. "There's a ruby goblet in an online database of stolen goods that Ciara thinks she saw at Orran's when she was young. She couldn't reach him to ask for the truth, and it happened before you came—you wouldn't have seen it."

Tait slid lower in his seat as if the accusation weighed more than he could bear. "How could you even think such a thing? It's the polar opposite of his life's work. And where did you get a key?"

Fingers twisting in her lap, Landon said, "She told us about the one in the tree. She guessed Orran hadn't bothered to delete her security code. She was going to drive out by herself as soon as she got out of the hospital, and she's too weak for that."

She forced herself to hold Tait's gaze. "It's my fault. If Bobby hadn't taken me, I'd have found another way. I'm sorry. Especially since Orran—"

"We're both sorry." Bobby raked his hair into a squashed haystack. "As Orran's partner, you'd be within your rights to press charges."

Lips tight, Tait sniffed. "For what? You didn't get past the threshold. I'll tell the investigators a friend was worried about Orr. The killer has his keys, so that was our first thought. I was going to stay there tonight and guard the place. Now I can sleep in my own bed and leave it to the security system."

Landon rested her forearm on the puzzle table, palm pressed against the smooth oak. Her ribs loosened to allow a full breath.

Tait's hands clenched in his lap. He rocked in his seat, a vibration as if his body held too much energy to be still. "If you suspected Orran, you suspected me. We know"—his mouth spasmed—"*knew* one another too well."

She looked down at her wrinkled skirt. "We thought he might be trying to silence Ciara so you wouldn't learn his secret. If it's true, he's been at this since before you met."

He blew out a harsh breath. "We talked about that goblet in the hospital. It was a prop for a play. Why did she think he'd still have it?"

"She thought he'd have newer things, stolen, but not disposed of."

Tait slapped his knees. "Come to the house. Right now. Before I could hide anything. This ends tonight."

~~~

The tour of Orran's house was every bit as uncomfortable as Landon had feared. Radiating outrage and wounded pride, Tait insisted she, Bobby, and Zander inspect every corner of the building and the garage. Then they repeated the process at his apartment.

When they returned to the inn, Landon said good night to Anna and left Zander to report the details. It wasn't even nine thirty, but she was running on fumes.

Upstairs, she tapped on the wooden schooner plaque on Ciara's door. "Are you awake?"

"Come in."

Ciara sat propped against snowy pillows, under a sea-blue duvet. She waved toward the mound of clothes in the rocking chair. "Just throw those on the floor. I'll unpack tomorrow."

As Landon transferred the pile to the age-darkened hardwood, Ciara asked, "How's Tait?"

"Gutted. Finding out we'd suspected Orran was one hurt too many today." Landon eased the rocker into a gentle motion. Enough to keep her blood flowing and her eyes open. "You need to talk to him. Apologize."

"I will." Perfect teeth caught Ciara's bottom lip. "I'm sorry I pushed you and Bobby to go out there."

"We should have had the brains to refuse. How are you feeling? Did Moxie help?"

"More than you know. Precious little guy. And Tait, still keeping him when he has to be angry at me. I'm just... drained. The drive from the hospital exhausted me, and then hearing about Orran..."

Tears slid onto her cheeks. "I mean, I'm relieved to know for sure he wasn't behind the attack and he didn't steal my things. That was a terrible feeling. But—" She covered her face with her hands. "He was always so kind to me. We were beginning to reconnect, and now this."

Landon rocked, the floor cool under her feet. "Tait showed us everything in the house, plus his apartment. Even inside Orran's big wall safe. We didn't see anything remotely suspicious." She snickered. "But you should have seen Bobby drooling over the man cave in Orran's basement. He says it's a gamer's dream."

"Tait must be his heir. Do you think he'll move into the house?"

"At least for now. He says there's a place he's wanted to buy but the owner's not ready. Oh, and he dug through Orran's files and found the paperwork on your bracelet. It came from a dealer in Chicago. He scanned it for Anna's insurance." Landon hadn't seen the valuation certificate, but Zander's brows had shot up. Not a cheap trinket, for sure.

Ciara peeked up over her fingertips. "I'm so glad Orran was innocent, but you know what this means. We don't have a clue who's out to get me."

Landon had been thinking the same thing. "At least we know Tait's safe to trust. Orran wouldn't have let him near you otherwise." She smothered a yawn. "I'm toast, and I have classes in the morning. Zander's heading to the city later to meet a few people Meaghan thought might know about Gord's enemies. He'll bring me home, and then he has an appointment with Ken and Kimi. He's been trying to catch up with them all week."

"He doesn't think they're behind this?"

"He's talking to everyone again to see if it stirs any leads. It does look odd for your ex-boss to extend his vacation because of what's happened to you, but Ken and Kimi seem like that kind of people."

Hugging the duvet closer to her chest, Ciara drew her shoulders up to her ears. "This has made me doubt everyone I've ever trusted."

## Chapter 21

*Thursday*

"So Ciara finally had a ride in your car?" Landon lounged sideways in one of Anna's recliners, back against one armrest and legs draped over the other. She let her cheek rest against the plush teal upholstery. Between yesterday's high emotion and today's pop quiz in class, she had nothing left.

Bobby sat at Anna's desk, tapping keys and doing an update to the inn website. Anna had insisted it wasn't a rush job, but of course he'd arrived the same day she called. He swivelled the desk chair toward Landon. "It's not a long drive to her place but yeah, I think she liked it. She's glad to have her own wheels again, though."

Ciara had texted her at school to say she'd scored an opening at the spa this afternoon. Something about needing both a pampering and the courage to apologize to Tait.

The entrance chime sounded. Landon jumped up. "That'll be our guest at long last."

When Zander dropped Landon off before his meeting with Ken and Kimi, Anna had deputized her for welcome duty and dashed out for groceries. Landon scooped the pewter lighthouse key ring from the coffee table and hurried along the hall to the front door.

"Welcome to the Green Dory Inn. You must be Jessica."

About Landon's age, the slight newcomer wrestled an enormous red suitcase over the threshold. A matching carry-on leaned against the wall. She stared at Landon with a deer-in-headlights look, lips parted and cheeks drawn in. One hand flew to her light-brown pixie cut.

Landon offered a welcoming smile. "Did you have a rough trip?"

"Oh—no—well, two hours late landing, but—" Her mouth snapped shut.

But...? "If you've changed your mind about staying after the break-in we had, I can find you another spot. We understand."

The girl drew herself as tall as possible, shoulders back, jaw firm. "This is the most convenient place. I'm here to visit my boyfriend. Robert J. Hawke, the author? Your temporary neighbour."

"Oh." Landon felt her eyebrows crawling up.

Jessica. Jessie.

Bobby was in the sitting room.

Landon grasped the suitcase handle. "I'm sure you'll want to freshen up before you see him, so let's get you settled. I'll save the downstairs tour for later." Without waiting for an answer, she lugged the heavy case toward the stairs.

"I can carry it myself, really." Jessie's footsteps followed.

On the second floor, Landon heaved the case onto its wheels and steered it toward the Lighthouse Room. She opened the door, then passed the keys to Jessie. "This one's for your room, and the other's for the front door. We lock it after ten or if we go out ourselves. The Wi-Fi code is on a card on the night table."

The minute Jessie's door shut, Landon fled downstairs and through the hallway. She burst into the sitting room and hissed Bobby's name, a finger to her lips.

He looked up with a start.

"Shh—Jessie's here. Your Jessie. Upstairs."

He went statue-stiff except for his eyes, which pinched shut. When they opened, he shook himself. "You didn't tell her I'm here."

"No. Prepare to act surprised when she shows up at your door. Her room's in front. You're safe to sneak out the back."

He hit a few more buttons on the keyboard. "I'll have to end there for now."

In the middle of the room, he stopped. "How do you know it's her?"

"She's here to visit Robert J. Hawke. Know him? He's her boyfriend."

"He is not—I mean, I'm not." Both hands scrubbed through his hair. "She said that?"

"Could she have misunderstood?"

"I made it painfully clear." He let out a low groan. "I don't need this." His cheeks had gone a splotchy pink, and he didn't seem to realize he was shaking his head.

"We could pretend we're a couple to convince her it's over."

A shuddery breath rocked his frame, and the exhale seemed to drain him. Gaze resolute in a suddenly hollowed face, he reset his shoulders. Now when he shook his head, it was a deliberate movement. "I'm yours if you ever want me for real, but faking would kill me."

She fought for air. "But I remind you of—"

"She who will not be named?" An odd smile erased the strain from his features, softening his jawline and lighting his eyes. "Not anymore. The more I look at you, the less I see her. Even in other things. Gramp was watching football last weekend, and I walked past when the cheerleaders were on the field. Didn't even notice I hadn't reacted until it cut to a commercial."

"Does he know?"

Bobby shuddered. "No! He just thinks I hate football. Which I sort of do. Look, what I said—you deserve the truth.

But please don't let this ruin our friendship. We make a good team."

Without waiting for an answer, he peeked into the hallway and then dashed for the exit.

Landon followed him outside on autopilot. She reached the deck to see him disappear toward home along the path through the trees.

The marmalade stray strolled from behind the barn. He stared at her, crooked tail high, then walked with a swaying precision into Anna's flower garden. He dropped among the blue and white pansies and rolled on his back in the dirt. Still skinny and ragged, he wasn't the skeletal creature he'd been in July.

Landon snorted. "You're pushing your luck, Mister."

In the three months she'd known him, Bobby had been so kind to strays and wounded warriors. But today... this was more. She'd believed no decent man would ever want her, not with the horror in her past. His words warmed her, elevated her. She felt it in her spirit, her very core, even in her frame—a lifting as if freed from gravity.

In the garden, the cat stretched long, belly up to the sun.

Landon wanted to stretch too. To luxuriate in the experience. Instead, she had to send Jessie off to certain disappointment. From the little Bobby had said, the girl was not a good fit for him, nor he for her, but that didn't mean it wouldn't hurt.

She glanced toward the path. What she felt now... gratitude, deep affection. Hero worship, maybe. It wasn't the romantic love Bobby needed. Somehow she'd have to make sure he didn't misinterpret her affection. He deserved someone with less baggage anyway. But if she'd helped him get over the deep wounds from the toxic cheerleader-valedictorian high school nemesis in his past, then she'd given him something worth keeping too.

Back inside, she collected his half-full coffee cup from Anna's desk and poured the dark liquid down the kitchen sink. She was toying with the puzzle in the common room when Jessie's shoes rapped on the stairs.

Makeup refreshed, Jessie wore a snug plum top and curvy black jeans. A silver star swung on a thin chain at her throat. She brushed it with a fingertip. "Bobby gave me this, but he's so hopeless he won't recognize it."

"It's lovely." Standing in the doorway, Landon spread an arm toward the space behind her. "I'll give you the two-second tour before you go. This room is open to all guests, and you're free to browse the books or add to the puzzle." She stepped across the hall. "Breakfast will be in here between seven and nine, and the fixings for coffee and tea are available all the time. Anna often has a baked snack or two as well."

Jessie spared a glance for the yellow-clothed square tables. "Thank you. Am I the only one staying?"

"No, next to you upstairs is Ciara, who's about our age. Zander has the room across from you, and I'm in the fourth one. I'm sort of a cross between long-term guest and helper."

"I see." Jessie's plum-glossed lips pinched. "You must be the one who nearly got Bobby killed. He mentioned Anna having adult children. From his story, I assumed her friend was from her own era."

"We rescued one another." They did make a good team. And Landon would not inform fifty-six-year-old Anna that Jessie considered her to have an era.

"Well, don't presume anything from that. He's taken."

Zander's SUV purring along the driveway made a welcome end to the conversation.

Jessie dredged her rental key from the depths of her glossy shoulder bag and stepped past Landon to the door. "It's a beautiful day for a walk, but not in these heels."

Landon pushed the door shut behind her and rested her forehead against the cool metal before heading for the rear of the inn. She was halfway along the ivory-painted hallway when Zander opened the screen door from the deck. In mild weather and in the summer, Anna left the inner door open during the day.

"Any luck, Zander?"

"Not with the former boss, but I do have other information."

"Let's talk in the kitchen. I'm waiting to help Anna with the groceries."

"Pretty girl who just left. The new guest or a friend of yours?"

"Guest. Bobby's ex. It could get messy here tonight."

Zander's gaze drilled into her. "You're not falling for him, I hope."

She let the pause linger long enough to torment him, but not for him to speak. Then she pressed her palm to her heart. "He's not for me. Not that way. But you can bet Jessie sees me as the competition."

In the kitchen, Landon poured herself a glass of water. She grasped the white frame of the nearest chair and drew it out for a seat. He'd talk when he was ready.

He sat across from her and folded his hands on the table. A hum of satisfaction vibrated his lips. "Phil Kirkwood. Two things."

She sipped her water, waiting.

Zander nodded approval. "One—his wife, Whitney, hasn't been seen outside of the home in some time. I've had hints of health issues and perhaps expenses relating to them. Two—one of the recently stolen local collectibles was found in his office this morning, courtesy of an anonymous tip."

"Ciara's bracelet?" She'd be ecstatic to have it back.

"The eighteenth-century cameo." He tapped a forefinger against his knuckles. "He's resisting the police request to search his house—I expect because of his wife rather than guilt. Although who knows?"

That was the brooch whose owner Orran had accused of inviting a theft. Maybe they'd be wiser now.

Landon rotated her glass a half-turn on the pine tabletop. "He's quite protective of his wife, and she did seem frail when I met her."

"Or it could be a strategic move—plant one thing on himself for the sole purpose of deflecting suspicion. You saw no bare spots in the home where objets d'art might have been removed for sale?"

"Their house is like a museum."

"Which means if he does need cash he's not selling visible assets."

"But he's been paying for Ciara's private hospital room and trying to throw money at her to leave town."

Zander's squint deepened the lines at the corners of his eyes. "Inconclusive, I know. I'll see what I can glean from my police contacts once they've squeezed him a bit."

"Ciara'd like it to be Phil." Better the stepfather she fought with than the former boss she admired.

A car engine outside drew Landon to the window. "Anna's home. You said the leads Meaghan gave you didn't help. Anything else?"

He stood. "I put a few feelers out about Tait. He came back clean."

Good to have that confirmed.

Shaun was another unknown. Anna said he'd been in to visit Ciara last evening while the rest of them were out with Tait. If he kept up his nightly visits, there might be a chance for one or two well-placed questions.

~~~

"Ooh, chocolate gelato. Is this for tonight?" Landon removed the tub from the bag and nestled it into the freezer.

Anna passed her another tub—raspberry. "The mood around here needs a bit of a lift."

"More than you know." At Anna's indrawn breath, Landon told her about Jessie. Not to gossip, but to prepare her. "Did Bobby tell you he broke up with her when he and Roy did the road trip over Labour Day?"

Zander snickered. "Anna, are you running an inn or a college dorm? Drama, drama, everywhere."

"I'll take old-fashioned angst over murder any day."

Landon draped an arm around Anna's shoulders and squeezed.

They'd almost finished unpacking when Ciara arrived, glowing but quiet. "The spa felt so good. Then Tait let me have a little visit with Moxie." Her glossy lips formed a pout. "I wish I could go home, but Tait's still waiting on my security system order. I can't rush the poor man. Not now."

Zander's arms locked across his chest. "We need to solve this so you'll be safe."

"Yes, please." She covered a yawn. "I think I'll take a nap before dinner. My head's still wonky."

A couple of hours later, Shaun's motorcycle growled into the inn lot as they were polishing off the gelato.

Anna stood from the table. "Ciara, since we don't know when our other guest will be back, could you stay downstairs? Shaun's music isn't loud, but she may not be in the best space."

They hadn't told Ciara Jessie's connection with Bobby. Nor, for that matter, that Bobby was single.

When Ciara scooted off to let Shaun in the front door, Landon rose. "I'll see if I can join in. Maybe I can get him talking."

Zander snorted. "Good luck. He doesn't respond well to me."

A bad-boy rebel type not getting along with an intense authority type? Zander's counselling skills had gone out the window when he turned investigator. Landon kept her amusement to herself. "I know you'll be around if he tries anything."

Once the kitchen was cleaned up, Landon carried a plate of Anna's chocolate chip cookies and two tall glasses of water into the common room. Shaun perched at the edge of the club chair, knees wide to support his guitar. Ciara lounged in one of the oak-armed fabric chairs, her russet sweater a striking contrast to the mint upholstery behind her head.

Placing the tray on the table next to the puzzle frame, Landon listened as Shaun's fingers wandered over the guitar strings in a steady, soothing stream. "That's nice. Especially after the week we've had."

"Week?" Ciara extended her fingers one by one as if counting. "I make it ten days. Not including today. Today's been good."

Without looking up, Shaun muttered, "It's not over yet."

Taking his pessimism as an excuse to stay and join the conversation, Landon dropped into the chair beside Ciara. "What do you mean? The day or the trouble?"

He swiped strands of black hair from his forehead with his leather wristband. "Just how life goes."

Ciara took a glass from the tray and set it on the floor beside him, then positioned one of the hard-backed chairs in the space between them to hold the cookie plate. The other glass in hand, she eased into her chair.

Was Shaun lying low from trouble at the campground? Could that be why he stayed?

Landon was trying to form a polite way to ask when the front door opened. The chimes overpowered the guitar, their gentle notes jarring tonight because it had to be Jessie. Nobody else was expected.

A quick staccato of heels ended with a stomp. Jessie stood in the doorway, oversized purse clutched under one arm like a bagpipe, her cheeks blotched and her eyelids puffy.

"You"—one index finger jabbed the air, punctuating the word—"stole my boyfriend."

Landon wished she could vanish under the chair cushion.

Ciara whistled, long and low. "Are you Bobby's girl from away? Or I guess ex-girl from away?"

Jessie whirled on her, free hand fisting on her hip. "Who are you?"

"*I'm* the one who actually contemplated trying for him. Landon always respected he was taken." Ciara tossed a brittle laugh. "You're better off without him. Bobby's married to his books. And maybe to his car. You'd be third place."

"Huh." Jessie's glare swung to Landon. "He won't be what you want either."

"We're not a couple." Spine pressed into the seat back, Landon kept her head high. "But Bobby's been part of every worst moment I've experienced here. That should have sent him running in the opposite direction. Instead, he always finds time for Anna and me. He's a gentleman. And a hero."

His fictional Travers would be proud.

Jessie's lips trembled, but she fought them under control.

Ciara flipped a languid wave. "Honey, I've been there, and I'm sorry for you. Go on home and find another man. But don't settle. And if a guy seems too good to be true, he probably is." She cut a glance at Shaun. "No offence."

He plucked his water glass from the floor, fingers at the rim, and raised it in a dangling salute. "None taken. Too bad to be true, at your service. Temporarily reformed."

Jessie fled. Her steps hammered the stairs and across the floor above. A door slammed.

"Well, that was awkward." Ciara's smirk dismissed Jessie's pain. "I guess you got him after all."

"He's not a collector figure!" Landon drove her fingernails against the armrests' wooden undersides. "And not everyone wants a relationship."

"Oh. What you said about… yeah." Ciara scrubbed her palms on her lap, then reached for the cookie plate. She held it out to Shaun. "So… too bad to be true? Do tell."

He winked. "Not true means nothing to tell."

"Then why reform?"

He snatched a cookie as she started to withdraw the plate. "Dude throws some girl over a cliff and casts me in the role of good guy."

Ciara sniffed. "There's got to be more to it than that."

When he finished chewing, he brushed cookie crumbs from his hands and resumed his wandering melody. "We all have stories." Head tipped low, he focused on the guitar strings, fingerpicking a complicated sequence. Then he peered up through heavy black bangs. "I should've moved on by now, but I need to know you'll be okay. We're strangers. It shouldn't matter."

"Thank you. For saving me and for staying. Someone here hates me, and I feel like being a stranger makes you safe."

Odd logic, but it made sense in this context. Ciara and Shaun had no history. Unless he was working for someone—like her ex on the West Coast.

Landon was supposed to be asking questions. "California to Nova Scotia on a motorcycle. Why'd you choose here?"

"Choose?" His fingertips rapped a quick percussion on the front of the instrument. "More like something snapped. Or they started mixing the sound wrong. I didn't care anymore, so I took off. Then one day, the road spit me out on Prince Edward Island, at one of my exes'."

A wicked grin lit his features before morphing into an almost wistful nostalgia. "She was every bit as crazy as the rest of us. Now she's living on a hobby farm. Husband and a kid. Cows. Herbal remedies and goat soap. She's happy." Another riff of the strings. "Husband's a pastor, of all things. I stayed a few days, but it was creepy. She gave me this guitar and the backpack case for the road. Said to listen to the music."

Landon tapped her foot. "What music?"

"That's what I said. 'Whatever comes out,' she said." His fingers stilled. "So far, this is all I've got. I can't go home until I get my head in the game, but I should at least cross into Maine."

Where did a young guy like this get the money for such a long trip—with extra to splurge on fixing Ciara's overpriced bracelet? And with no apparent deadline to be back on the job. Landon's instinct was to trust him, that whatever his story was it didn't involve harming Ciara. But she'd trusted Gord too.

## Chapter 22

*Friday*

LANDON SNAPPED HER laptop shut. "There."

Jessie had departed first thing this morning. With Zander out unravelling more threads he'd found concerning Gord's death, she and Ciara were alone on the upper floor, nestled in two of the blue club chairs in the conversation nook. The extended dormer window space above the main entrance made an ideal spot to bask in the morning sun and watch any sailboats on the bay.

Today, Ciara had been basking and mostly succeeding in letting Landon read. Landon had pulled her chair out of direct sunlight and soldiered through another chapter in her reading assignments. She set the laptop on the chunky wooden coffee table and repositioned her chair to catch the sun's warmth. "Thanks. If I space the units out, they're not so bad."

Ciara yawned and stretched her arms high and wide. "I feel fine sitting here, but if I spend too long on a screen, my headache will flare up. Concussions are the worst."

"At least your boss is holding your job for you."

"Even though I'm not very good at it." Ciara sniffed. "I'm afraid to go back in case my enemy's someone there. I know Zander's been checking them out."

"Between him and the police, there has to be a break soon." Until then, Landon had to keep resisting the urge to get involved. No more pushing in her own strength. No more following leads and breaking into people's homes.

In front of the inn, a car slowed and navigated up the long driveway. Ciara glanced out the window. "Speaking of the police, that looks like one of them now."

Landon's feet hit the floor. "Coming?"

Ciara seemed to curl tighter in her chair. "Concussions are exhausting, and I don't have much stamina after the pneumonia."

"You rest, and I'll tell you if there's any update."

After stowing her laptop in her room, Landon headed downstairs. In the kitchen, she found Anna offering Dylan a cup of coffee.

"Yes, please." He angled his stance toward Landon. "How are you doing?"

Nothing in his expression suggested he'd heard about the break-in disaster. Landon relaxed. "It's been quite a week."

He accepted a blue porcelain mug from Anna and carried it to the table. Landon joined him, and Anna followed once she'd heaped a plate with blueberry muffins.

Dylan rescued the top muffin as it wobbled. "Some things about this job, I really like."

Anna beamed. "When we're done with this mystery, you need to come for a meal."

"I'll hold you to that. It'd be good to see you both outside of investigations. For now, to work." He took a big bite of muffin, washed it down with coffee, then leaned back in his chair. "I tried to catch up with Shaun Riggs this morning, but he's checked out of the campground. No wonder, with that hurricane on track for us. I thought he might be staying here."

"No, but he comes to see Ciara. So does Tait." Anna's warm gaze found Landon. "It's good to know she has friends who support her."

"You must have his number. Why not call?" Landon chose a muffin for herself.

"I wanted to surprise him. You get more honest answers that way."

"But he has no history with Ciara. And he rescued her." Or was interrupted trying to tip her off the ledge. Landon had thrown that one at him early on.

"Let me know if he comes in today?"

Anna tapped her left hand against her mug, rings clinking on the porcelain. "Can you tell us why?"

"Anonymous tip. I can't give you more than that."

She sniffed. "Well, I don't believe it."

"Then you won't spook him by acting suspicious." Dylan's empty coffee mug dangled from a curled finger. "Someone tried to point us to Ciara's stepfather yesterday. This may well be more of the same."

"Zander told us. So you don't think it's Phil blowing smoke to protect himself? If—" Oops. Zander may not have shared his other information about Phil and Whitney.

"If?" Dylan's gaze sharpened. "You're not holding out on me, I hope."

"Zander heard a rumour. I don't know from where."

"The wife's health?"

"Yes." Good. He already knew. "Health insurance covers most things, but there have to be gaps."

"There are." The tight line of his lips closed that line of conversation.

He eased his chair from the table and carried his mug to the sink. "Call me? If it's not till I'm off, I'll pass it on to the night crew."

~~~

Shaun arrived around four, minus his guitar. The roiling grey clouds overhead might have influenced that decision.

Zander had returned, retiring to his room for a video counselling session. His caseload must be piling up. Landon didn't know how much longer he could stay. Or if he'd go when he should.

Because of Zander's work call, Anna asked Shaun to stay downstairs again today.

Landon headed for the stairs. "I'll tell Ciara you're here." Once she did, she plopped into one of the chairs overlooking the bay to call Dylan.

"Thanks. If he tries to leave, ply him with Anna's cooking until I get there." He chuckled. "Seriously, I'd like to know where he's staying, but don't say or do anything to alert him."

Landon stayed in the conversation nook to slog through more homework while keeping watch for Dylan. Up here, she wouldn't be tempted to eavesdrop on the investigation. Much as she wanted to know what the tip had said.

Ciara could tell her later.

Instead, soon after Dylan arrived, Ciara reappeared. Her eyes wide and bright, she transferred her hand from the banister to the nearest wall as if her concussion headache was back and affecting her balance. She leaned there, taking slow shallow breaths. "Dylan has questions for Shaun, but he says he'll only talk to you."

"Me?" Landon uncurled from her seat. "Are you okay?"

"I need to lie down. Shaun can't be a risk. He just can't." Her sentence ended in a whisper.

Ciara's door clicked shut as Landon descended toward the main floor.

Dylan stepped into the hall to meet her, brows low and mouth tight. He led her into the breakfast room. "He answered our questions before. I don't know what's up now, but I don't have enough for a warrant. I hate to involve you."

She pointed toward the guest rooms above. "Don't tell Zander."

"Agreed." He cupped her elbow and steered her across the hall. "I'll ask my questions. Then I'll go to the kitchen. This door stays open. The first sign of trouble, I'll come."

Leaning into the leather club chair, black-jacketed arms stretched wide and knees bent, Shaun sneered. "Stand out front and watch through the window. If I touch her, you can shoot me."

Dylan's eyelid twitched. "Window it is." He stood with feet spread, arms loose at his sides. Once Landon settled in one of the mint chairs, he cleared his throat. "Shaun, we've had a tip to look into your reasons for being in Canada. Specifically, here in the Lunenburg area. I'd hoped for a casual chat, and I'd prefer not to invite you to the station for something more formal."

"This is a colossal waste of time."

"Then help me speed it up. It's Friday for me too. You're demanding to speak with Landon, a civilian. Why?"

"Because Ciara trusts her. So I'll trust her."

Dylan rocked back on his heels, his gaze locked on Shaun. "What I'm hearing here is that you may have secrets you want to keep from law enforcement agencies and which you believe are unconnected with Ciara's trouble."

Shaun tapped his temple with his index finger. "See, I actually like you, for a cop. Got it in one. Do you wanna do a pat-down before you go, or am I good?"

"Just don't let me catch you doing anything that I can make my business."

Dylan strode toward the exit. The front door chimed, and there he was outside the window.

Head shaking slowly, Landon gripped the chair's armrests. "What is your problem?"

His chest rose in a slow breath. "Listen and learn, babe."

The words. The name. The superior, confident drawl. Echoes of her past. She launched to her feet.

Part of her mind stayed in the present, aware of Dylan outside. She waved him an all-clear, then rounded on Shaun. "Don't take that tone with me. Ever."

Hands fisted on her hips and weight on the balls of her feet, she leaned into his space. The adrenaline rush felt good, fighting back for the terrorized child she'd been.

Was that respect in his stare? Or fear? After a long moment, he blinked. "I apologize. My reform slipped."

With a rib-stretching breath, Landon nodded. "Accepted."

She flashed Dylan a thumbs-up and reclaimed her seat, spine tall. She'd buried her defiance deep, thought it broken. Now somehow she had to give it to God for defusing. Like an unexploded bomb.

Massaging the ache in her forehead, she drew one more calming breath. "Okay, Shaun. For Ciara's sake, let's start again."

He sat forward, fingers spread over his knees. "I heard her scream. Saw her fall. I don't know why I'm still here, except she was so helpless. Nobody ever needed me before."

"So what is it you don't want Dylan to know? I'll have to tell him if it applies to this case—or anything else local."

"Not local. And I'm not wanted by the law or anything." He flipped his bangs out of his eyes. They fell back. "I'm in the country illegally. On my brother's passport."

"Why?"

"Like I said last night, it wasn't a planned thing. I had to get out, borrowed his bike, and we swapped IDs too. I thought he was crazy when he gave me his passport, but it turns out he was right."

"Would your ex on the Island vouch for you?"

"If you had to ask."

"What else would she tell me about you?"

His breath hissed through his teeth. "The sole illegal thing I've done in your country is to be here. She'd tell you I'm the front man for a chart-topping alt-rock band in LA. Known for bad behaviour and bizarre stunts." Muttering words she couldn't catch, he drew his phone from his jacket pocket. A few touches, and he passed it over. "That's me in the middle. You may not want to hear us. Or to read my press."

He'd muted the video's sound. Landon paused it, zoomed in on his image. Still the midnight garb, like it was his life uniform. Heavy silver neck chains. Longer, scraggly hair. Her gaze tracked between the image on the screen and Shaun here in real-time. The same exotic eyes met hers.

In person, they didn't hold hate. Just tension. He flexed his fingers against his jeans. "I fell out with the in crowd, and instead of pulling a scandal-worthy stunt to prove I still had my edge, I left. Haven't even looked to see if they replaced me."

"How can you afford to be gone so long?"

He sniffed. "I blew most of what I earned, but the royalties are still coming in. Living lean like this, I wouldn't have to go back for years."

"Are you going back?"

"To that life? I don't know. To the States? The sooner the better, if I can know Ciara's safe."

Landon took another look at the image before zooming out to read the band name in the video title. In case he was conning her. She returned his phone. "What are you afraid of? If the truth comes out, you'll be deported, maybe fined. Isn't that sort of notoriety good for you?"

"Not when it ties to my brother. He'd block the identity theft charge—tell them he gave me the documents and the bike."

"You said he did."

"It'd ruin his reputation." Shaun's hands linked, drooping between his knees. "Unlike mine, his is worth saving."

Landon tapped a fingernail against her jeans. "Sounds like your ex on the farm isn't the only one who believes in you. Are you going to tell Ciara who you really are?"

"She's already skittish. Why make it worse?"

"Because too many people have lied to her and you seem to care."

"I shouldn't care. And I've lied to her too."

"You've lied to us all. That may be different. But it's your secret, not mine. I won't tell her."

"What about him?" He rolled his eyes toward Dylan.

"Not one word. He'd have to act, and getting you deported would be one more strike at Ciara."

"You're a good person. Even if you terrify me."

She'd never be terrifying. Still, something inside her preened. Rising to her feet, she beckoned to Dylan. "Don't give up on being reformed. It might grow on you."

Shaun stood too. "I'll get out of here so you can debrief. Before the rain hits hard."

"Where are you staying? Dylan said you'd left the campground."

"Ciara offered me her place. Once her security system's set up, I'll go back to The Ovens or see if I can get her room here."

"I hope she told Tait. If he goes to do the install, he needs to know you have permission."

Dylan had taken position in the hall as if Shaun might try to run. "Everything okay?"

Landon nodded. "Shaun's reasons for being here are personal. Nothing to do with causing trouble—other than his attitude."

"Hey—ouch!" But Shaun winked at her.

Dylan's eyebrow lifted. "Wish I could have heard that exchange at the beginning."

"But she vouches for me. Am I free to go?"

"Provided I can find you if I need to."

Shaun stuffed his hands in his pockets. "Solve this, and I'll be out of your country and out of your hair."

Dylan gave a curt nod. "Deal."

When the door shut behind Shaun, they returned to the common room. Landon flopped into the chair she'd vacated. "I'm surprised Anna didn't come running when I yelled at him." Zander must have had headphones on for his call and not heard.

"I asked her to let me handle however it played out. She'll grill you later."

Shaun's motorcycle roared past the inn toward the road, then streaked off toward town.

Dylan sniffed. "Wish I'd had a radar gun on that."

He took the seat opposite Landon, but the set of his shoulders said he was still a cop on duty. "Now, why should I ignore the tip to dig deeper on him?"

"I promise you, he's not a threat to Ciara or anyone else. His story is—complicated—and you don't want to know."

"But do I need to know?"

"You and I have both seen more than our share of liars and cheats." She shrugged. "Shaun is not a nice person. But I believe him when he says he'll make this right. He's no danger to anyone. Except maybe slow drivers."

She gathered her hair in one hand and let it trickle through her fingers. "He'd be halfway home by now if he hadn't rescued Ciara. It sounds like the first kind thing he's done in a while, and I think this protective instinct shook him. It's like he's caught between who he was and who he might be. Like he needs space to find himself."

"A campground in the middle of nowhere, inky black sky at night... the vastness does have a way of putting things into perspective." Dylan's features almost relaxed. Then his focus sharpened. "What is it he claims he'll make right?"

"If you know what he's done, you'll have to tell someone."

"It's my job to ask."

Landon offered an apologetic smile. "I'm sorry, but I'm going to withhold information that is not pertinent to your investigation. Do you have to arrest me?"

His jaw bulged as if he were gritting his teeth. His exhale was almost a growl. "I do have other resources, you know."

"Dylan, please. He has nothing to do with this case. When it's resolved, give him a couple of days to cross the border. Then he won't be Canada's problem."

One eyelid twitched. "Look at me straight on. Now tell me—is Shaun exerting any influence over you?"

Landon sat taller. With her past conditioning to submit to harsh male commands, it was a fair question. She appreciated how Dylan kept his tone warm, safe, but strong to draw out the truth. In his gaze now, she saw concern, not mistrust. Maintaining the connection, she consciously dropped any barriers. "He is not. He's the type who could, but no." Then she giggled. "You saw me rip into him. Man, that was liberating. All those times—"

Her throat clogged, blocking her breath. Through sudden tears she saw him jerk forward, reaching out. She clapped both palms over her face. "It's okay. Healing—has to come out."

But did it have to come out now, embarrassing them both?

Dylan's hand fell awkwardly on her shoulder. "I'll get Anna."

"No, just—a minute." She counted her breaths, slowing each one, while scrabbling in her pocket for a tissue. With a mighty, sinus-burning snort, she regained control. Drying her tears allowed two more deep lungfuls of air. Then she peeked through tear-thickened lashes to find Dylan standing tall at her side, an awkward sentinel.

Her cheeks heated. "Sorry you were in the fallout zone. My counsellors tell me it's a good sign of progress, but it doesn't do much for my social life." Her attempt at a laugh didn't rise.

Dylan stepped back and squatted to eye level. "As a friend, I'd have held you, but as an officer on duty, alone in a room with you, it's not advised. I'm not afraid of tears."

She'd felt such sympathy and care from him in the past when teetering on the edge. That steadied her smile now. "We have enough of a history for me to be sure of that. Anyone who thinks you're cold is likely on the other end of your arrest warrant."

"There's a time and a place." He stood, retreating from her space. "This time and place are for me to say goodbye and get to work on my reports. I'll take Shaun at your word unless more comes to light. You might advise him to ease off on the throttle if he doesn't want more questions."

"Why, Dylan, Bobby would say that sounds delightfully like blackmail."

"I prefer to call it a warning. Say goodbye to Anna for me." With a mock salute, he was gone.

Landon sat in place, damp tissue fisted in her palm, thinking and praying over the encounter with Shaun. Growing peace wrapped her spirit for his connection with the mystery. For his personal state, not so much. But she knew the God who rescued the broken. For all his boisterous show, Shaun was a man in need of a healer.

After a few more minutes, she headed for the rear of the inn. Anna would be wondering about her—and about Shaun, although she pretended to keep aloof from the mystery.

Quiet conversation led her to the kitchen where Anna sat across the table from Nigel, a plate of muffins between them. Anna gave her a sharp glance. "Everything okay?"

Nigel's camouflage hat dipped. "You managed your conflict."

Please, let him have been inside when she yelled. She'd hate to think her shout carried through windows and exterior walls. "Shaun is not our villain. Dylan's not happy to be in the dark, but he's accepting it for now."

Landon washed her hands and poured herself a tall glass of water, then joined them at the table. "I'm fine. Shaun was just—rude. The counsellors warned me I had some repressed anger. There's less now." The base of her glass rapped the table like a gavel to close the subject.

Nigel blinked in rapid succession. "Stronger than you know."

Landon? Or the anger? Best not to ask. "How are you, Nigel? How's Elva?"

He blinked again. "All seems well. I understand the other young one is here. Ciara. Afraid to go home?"

"Do you blame her?"

"Those I blame deserve it."

*Oh, Nigel...* the man's sense of justice was strong and complex. Zander had reassured them he'd found no evidence of Nigel's presence at the site of Gord's murder. Landon prayed that would hold true.

"Shaun kept her from falling to her death. He seems to see himself as her protector." She squeezed her palms around her glass. "It's messing with his sense of identity, and he needs prayer."

Anna's fond look embraced them both. "Protector is a fine calling."

"Best way to protect this one is to find the source of her trouble." Nigel scowled into the bottom of his mug.

"You saw nothing around the inn Monday night when he broke in?"

"Anna has been catching me up on events. No."

"So you know about Ciara's parents, her former boss, the ex-boyfriend in BC." Landon tapped a fingernail on her glass for each one. "Her boss and coworkers, old friend Orran and his business partner. Shaun, who we've just ruled out."

"Plus any number of other people we haven't even thought of." Anna rubbed her forehead.

Nigel tipped his mug to his lips, catching the last drops. He set it on the table. "Good tea, Anna. As always. I hear things, but nothing about any of these."

Landon drained her water in a long gulp. "I should go reassure Ciara about Shaun."

At the top of the stairs, the only open door was to the Lighthouse Room, cleaned today after Jessie's abrupt departure. Low tones from the Forest Room suggested Zander was still on his call or on another. Landon tapped at the Schooner Room's door. "Are you awake?"

"It took you long enough."

That'd be a yes. She stepped inside and closed the door behind her.

Ciara lay on the bed under a light blanket, one arm tented over her forehead. "I heard you shouting, then lots of silence. People going in and out, but nobody remembering I was up here."

Landon settled in the rocker. "We knew you were resting."

"I've been listening to the rain against the window." Ciara peeked out from under her arm. "Did Shaun tell you he's at my place?"

"That was kind of you. He'd wash away in a tent."

"There's nothing between us. Not like that. He'll vacate when I go home."

"He told me." Ciara, not wanting to make a big production about relationships? "Um, he also told me his secret, and it's nothing for you to worry about."

"But he hasn't said anything to me." Her lower lip trembled.

Landon focused on the rocker's motion. "Have you shared your past with him?"

"No! But—"

When the silence stretched, Landon said, "I asked him to tell you, but don't push him. He presents strong, but he's struggling as much as we are."

"Really."

"Yes, really. He could have stayed to eat with us, but I think he wanted to get out of Dylan's sight."

She left Ciara and wandered to the conversation nook. It had grown so dim she'd need a light to read, but she curled up in a chair to watch the rain. And the waves. The wind had come up. Shaun's motorbike had better stay parked for the duration.

A faint aroma of onions and seasonings reached her from downstairs. She should go see if Anna needed help preparing the meal. Looking out at the grey rain and waves, she decided to phone Tait first. Whether he was at his apartment or at Orran's, he was alone in the storm with his grief. He didn't seem the sort to find much comfort in Ciara's yappy dog.

He picked up on the third ring.

Words of comfort failed her. "Hey. I thought I'd check in. I know this is rough."

"Tell Anna thanks for the food she sent yesterday. I have no interest in cooking right now."

"Do you have contract deadlines, or can you take time away from work?"

"Work's the one thing distracting me. I need that."

A seagull flew against the wind, its powerful wings making slow headway above the bay. "You're on the prevention end, but can any of your connections help find who did this to Orran?"

"I've made inquiries, but I'm not hopeful." His laugh was harsh, a burst of sound like ripping paper. "They've been no help in Ciara's case either."

"I feel so bad for her, afraid to go home. This person may not want to kill her, but he's attacked her and stolen everything she loves. All she has left for him to go after is her car and her dog."

"The Terror's safe with me for now. Currently hiding from the wind."

"Yes, but she has to be able to go home and get on with her life. She can't kennel him every time she goes to work, and we already know this guy can get into her apartment."

"The equipment I want is still back-ordered, but it should be in soon. I can add interior cams in case he breaches the alarm."

Landon curled her legs tighter into the chair. "Tait, you're being fantastic about all this with all you're going through. But if this guy wants to hurt her? She'll get the video feed of a masked intruder killing her dog, and he'll be gone before the police arrive. It won't stop until we find him."

"These things take time. Justice will be done."

"I want to help, but all I can do is be there for Ciara as a friend."

"Don't discount that. She appreciates it, I'm sure. I appreciate you thinking of me too."

Although this week felt like a month of strain and sorrow, nothing had been directed at Ciara since Monday's theft of her bangle. "It's been a few days. You don't think he's given up, do you?"

"You don't. Not with what you said about the dog."

A gust of wind threw rain against the window. Landon shivered. "No. I'm afraid for her."

## Chapter 23

*Saturday*

GALE-FORCE WINDS shrilled around the corners of the inn all night. Raindrops struck like pellets. Landon woke early after a troubled sleep, second-guessing her decision to trust Shaun. She clicked on her bedside lamp and bunched the pillows behind her against the four-poster's headboard. Sitting up, laptop on her knees, she typed the band's name into the search field.

So Shaun Riggs was his real name, but on stage, he went by Rigged. At The Ovens, he'd told Zerkowsky that Shaun was a nickname for whatever was on his passport.

Ignoring the videos, she skimmed news reports and gossip sites, grateful for her ad-blocker. What she saw didn't match the man who risked his life to save a stranger. Obnoxious as he still was, his "temporary reform" had made a difference. Not that she trusted everything she read. His behaviour was part of his star persona, calculated to drive publicity. The media would reflect that.

He'd never been arrested, but article after article spoke of wild house parties, domestic disturbance calls, drug allegations. This was who'd befriended Ciara. Landon shuffled her feet under the covers. How much had he changed and why? Change on a whim wouldn't stick.

She clasped her hands behind her head and leaned back, bouncing her knuckles against the satin-smooth headboard. Across the room, the butterfly prints caught her lamp's soft glow. Bright orange and soft yellow wings, black accents giving each a stained glass effect. God's specialty was bringing beauty to the broken. She prayed Shaun would experience that truth.

Stories of his past aside, the speculation about his present made her shake her head. Most thought he'd killed himself or checked into a substance abuse facility. Or he was living on the streets in Memphis. She skimmed past a video of a homeless man singing what the post claimed was one of Shaun's songs. As if that proved it was him. From the band itself, nothing official. Rumours claimed they were auditioning a replacement.

She closed the laptop and swung her legs over the side of her bed, feet landing on the braided mat. Ciara's insistence on maintaining boundaries with Shaun was a good thing. If only she didn't end up giving more trust than he could keep.

Downstairs, Ciara and Zander shared breakfast in the kitchen with Landon and Anna. Anna insisted the designated eating area was for "outside guests."

Anna had all the lights on against the storm, making the stainless steel appliances and white cabinets gleam. The oven added a cozy warmth, producing plump, golden-topped tea biscuits to go with their sausages and eggs.

None of them had slept well, and Ciara flinched whenever a gust slammed the house. When the lights flickered, her yelp sounded so much like Moxie that Landon pressed her napkin to her lips to stop a giggle.

Anna laughed, warm and comforting. "This old house was built to last. The power grid's fairly stable too, but if the lights do go out, we'll be fine."

Ciara shuddered. "The guy who's after me could be waiting for a chance like that. Everybody charge your cell, just in case."

Landon's phone app projected the hurricane's eye to bypass them to the east. For all its wind velocity, the storm's forward momentum lagged, leaving them in the grip of wet and nasty weather.

The day limped along. Halfway through the afternoon, engine revs outside drowned out the wind. In the common room, Ciara shrieked. Her chair shot back from the puzzle table where she and Landon had been half-heartedly piecing together Anna's latest choice.

She sprinted for the rear of the inn. Landon dropped a segment of bright red dory and ran after her.

Ciara had the door open. "Shaun, you crazy fool, get in here!"

His boots clomped across the deck. For once, he wasn't all in black. A bright yellow poncho, hood down, covered him from neck to knees. Rain cascaded from his shoulders like he'd emerged from a river. He stopped in the entrance and flipped up his helmet's visor, grinning like a kid with an unlimited carnival pass. He drew a pastel pink pastry box from beneath the poncho and held it out to Ciara by the string.

She took it, sputtering. "You are certifiably insane."

"Heard that before. You may be right."

When they stepped aside to let him in, he winked. "At least this time I'm sober. I'll remember every glorious second."

"You've done this before? Impaired?" Ciara retreated farther, pushing Landon along with her.

"Weather like this begs for it. And the higher you are, the better you hear it." He surveyed the puddles forming around him. "Can I come in, or are you sending me back out to play?"

Landon shook her head. "I'll get the mop." Turning, she dodged to avoid stepping on Anna. "We can't let him go anywhere in this."

Anna's fists anchored on her hips, elbows jutting to the sides like a barrier. "He's not staying if there's trouble."

Zander had crowded into the hallway, his expression sterner than Anna's. "What's going on here?"

At the same time, Ciara waggled the bakery box. "What's this?"

"A treat for an exhilarating day. Something you said you liked."

Landon shooed Ciara and Zander toward the kitchen with the mop, barring Shaun with a chest-height thrust. "Don't mess with her. Reformed, remember? Think about Dylan."

"Gotcha."

He dragged the helmet from his head, tossing his hair. Face alight, he spun toward Anna, palm up like a pledge. "Nothing unnatural in my system, I swear. Sorry for getting a bit... exuberant."

Ciara's squeal pierced the moment. "Shaun, it's perfect."

Landon left the mop by the door and joined the others in the kitchen where Ciara stood at the table unboxing a layer cake swirled with thick, creamy frosting.

Zander had backed Shaun against the counter. "You are an utter cliché. A leather-jacketed, guitar-playing rebel with a motorcycle—either a rich trust-fund brat or a refugee from an inner-city gang. There's not one original thing about you."

Landon held her breath. One punch from Shaun, and Dylan would drag everything into the light.

Shaun sniffed. "Guitar's acoustic. Not electric."

"You're a waste of oxygen."

"Or a sinner in need of a saviour. You preach a great gospel, Mr. Righteous. Bet you change a lot of lives."

The back of Zander's neck flushed. His shoulders rose.

Landon started forward to grab him.

Instead of lunging at Shaun, Zander wheeled around and stalked into the hallway, tugging his cuffs into place and brushing down his shirt front. "I'll be upstairs. I have calls to make."

Chin tucked, Shaun glanced around the kitchen. His eye contact came in short, upward peeks like a little boy afraid the adults would scold him. Standing free of the counter, he let his hands hang at his sides. "For all the ones who've seen me at my worst, I'm trying to show you people my best. Epic fail."

Feet planted wide, Anna crossed her arms. "And riding that bike in a hurricane?"

"It's this storm. I haven't felt so alive since—maybe ever." He flicked his hair from his forehead. "Best behaviour doesn't mean I'm any smarter."

"Or more likely to die of old age." Despite the barb, the lines softened around Anna's mouth. "Now tell us about this cake you brought. What's the occasion?"

"It's my birthday, and this extrovert needed attention."

Ciara squealed again. "Happy birthday!" She bounced as if she wanted to run and hug him but didn't dare.

Anna pulled dessert plates from the cupboard, and Shaun left Ciara to cut wedges of moist carrot cake. He eyed his piece. "For a small girl, you serve a decent-sized hunk of dessert."

"Birthday calories don't count."

When Ciara and Shaun moved to the common room, Landon trudged upstairs for the next round of reading. Breaking it into chunks made it manageable, but it felt like she was never done. Lights on, she settled into a comfy chair in the conversation nook. Between the dreary day and the beat of rain against the glass, she didn't even try the read-aloud setting on her laptop. Today, she'd be powering through the textbook's digital version with eyes on screen.

She'd been at it less than half an hour, a headache already building, when her phone buzzed a call.

Bobby? They hadn't spoken since Jessie arrived. Maybe he thought she needed space to process what he'd said. Something she'd been stalling on because, after the initial warm gratitude, she'd feel guilty for letting him down.

The phone buzzed again as she snatched it from the coffee table. Tait. Not Bobby after all. Disappointment melted into sympathy. "Hi, Tait." She caught herself before asking how he was.

"Is Ciara with you?" His words came fast, clipped.

"Want me to get her?"

"No. Listen, I need your help." Before she could ask for details, he pushed on. "I came out to Orran's. Wanted to check on the place. Plus, there's a generator in case the power goes down. Moxie got away from me when I opened the car. He's out there somewhere in the storm."

"Ciara—"

"Don't tell her. She'd freak out and trigger one of her concussion headaches. He likes you. Help me search?"

"But he'd come to her voice."

"Not if he's gone to ground. And she shouldn't be out in this kind of weather. She's barely over her pneumonia."

Landon exited the textbook and closed her laptop. Indistinct words filtered through Zander's closed door. He was on another call. "I'll get Anna to bring me."

"I'm almost there. I have you on hands-free. Figured you'd be home on a day like this."

"Okay, I'll be ready."

"Don't let Ciara suspect. I'll confess once the little guy is warm and dry."

"I'll come out the back. She won't see me."

Call ended, she hurried to her room for an extra sweater and warm socks. She'd seen heavy-duty raingear and rubber boots downstairs. She ducked into the sitting room to whisper the story to Anna. "Pray we find him fast? Ciara's lost so much."

Anna caught her hand and squeezed it. "Will do. Tell Tait to join us for supper, and since we don't have any outside guests, he can bring Moxie. Ciara will need time with the little fellow."

"Timkin will love that." The inn's cat was still giving them the silent treatment from the Chihuahua's visit earlier this week. Even today, when he wouldn't step a paw out into the wet weather, he snubbed them both, glaring from the shadows beneath Anna's desk.

Landon waited inside until Tait's SUV appeared. Then she ducked out into the storm. The wind drove rain like needles into her exposed face. She tugged her hood lower and ran toward the parking lot.

Her fingers slipped on the wet metal handle as Tait nudged the door open from inside. "Thanks." She scrambled in out of the rain. "Wow. Poor Moxie, out in this."

Tait whipped around and navigated down the driveway. "He'll be terrified. I had a rough drive getting here. Water's over the pavement in a few places."

On the other side of the road, huge grey waves tossed white streamers of foam. The ground here was elevated enough to be safe from a storm surge—she hoped—but it dropped to sea level nearer town. She clutched the seat belt, pushing down memories of her and Anna's crash this summer. Anyone in that water today wouldn't stand a chance.

Both hands on the wheel to steady the vehicle against the buffeting wind, Tait maintained a slow speed. They didn't meet many other drivers. A gust slammed them sideways toward the water. Grunting, Tait wrestled back into position.

His confident skill reassured Landon. "Anna's making a big pan of lasagna for tonight. Stay when you bring me home? Moxie's invited too."

He didn't look away from the road. "Thank you. Man, I feel terrible. He twisted out of my hold and took off for the trees. Every step I took toward him, he ran further. Instead of driving him deeper under cover, I came for you."

"Does he have a favourite squeaky toy?"

"Good idea. Most of his things are at my apartment, but there are a few toys at Orran's."

Tait worked through the side streets to the far side of the subdivision and along the rural road until he reached Orran's long private driveway. Here, out of the wind, he picked up speed. They bounced through puddles, tires throwing water high to the sides.

The trees swayed and bent as the storm whipped their crowns. A massive root plate had clawed free to their right, a huge sentinel pine felled whole.

A gnarled branch lay in their path, and Tait powered over it. "If anything big comes down once we're in, there's a chainsaw at the house to get us out."

"Good to know." Landon's hand ached from her hold on the door, but she couldn't let go. The uneven ground tossed the vehicle side to side.

He must have heard her tension. Their pace slowed. "Sorry. I'll get you there in one piece."

They emerged into the clearing, and the wind blasted with full force, howling around the vehicle. Leaves and branches littered the lawn. Tait cut a loop in the driveway and reversed up close to the garage. "I was going to get in touch with your friend Zander today. One of my contacts forwarded a tip about Ciara's stepfather. A past misdemeanour related to collectible baseball cards. It might be nothing, but it could be a clue."

"It's worth a look." Landon's seat belt clicked open, and she jumped from her seat. Turning to the trees, she called Moxie's name. No response. She called again.

Tait's door slammed. "Come into the house and help me pick the best toy? If he were a cat, we could just rattle treats for him."

He'd never met their orange-striped stray. Landon clomped up the stairs behind Tait, glad of the building's shelter while he unlocked the door. As soon as he shut them in, the wind's howl died to distant shrieks at the corners of the building.

"His toys are in the kitchen." As he spoke, he tapped the keypad to disarm the security system.

Washed with a sudden rush of shame for her and Bobby's fumbled break-in, Landon stepped out of her heavy boots. "Okay, let's see what we can find."

A metallic click whirled her on the spot.

Tait's stillness, his stance...

Her gaze dropped to the pistol in his hand.

Pointed at her.

Her heart kicked so fast she fought to breathe. She pulled her sight from the gun and locked on Tait's face. The focused stare, the hardened jaw.

"Anna knows I'm here."

"You won't be when you die."

She'd heard him angry, grieving, even playing the self-proclaimed ladies' man. But she'd never heard raw hatred. It pebbled her skin clear through to the bone.

"Tait, why?"

"You killed Orran."

"This is a mistake. I know you're angry—"

"You might as well have pulled the trigger." His mouth spasmed.

"No—I—"

"Shut it." He scuffed his feet on the entrance mat. "Through the kitchen and down the stairs."

The commanding tone meant compliance. Yet dread—and maybe anger—blocked its hold. If she dodged into the living room, could she break out through a window?

His fingers clamped her upper arm and thrust her toward the rear of the house. Down the stairs to the sumptuous man cave. Faint yips came from behind a closed door. She should be relieved Ciara's Chihuahua wasn't outside at the storm's mercy.

Tait propelled her past fitness equipment, a big-screen television, and oversized brown leather recliners to a heavy, dark-stained bookcase. His fingers dug into her arm while his other hand reached past her to a row of matching hardcover books.

The move positioned his body far too close to hers. He must have stashed the gun in his pocket, but she couldn't twist away.

He drew one volume from the line, shifted a few sideways to fill the gap, then slotted it into the new opening.

Unbalanced, she reached to steady herself on the bookcase but missed. It wasn't her sight after all. The whole unit was retreating. Gliding away from her without a sound.

"Zane Grey. Orr's father's favourite author. They were lucky to have castoffs and library copies when he was young. When he hit decent money, he bought the complete works to honour his dad."

The spines looked stiff and new. Unread. The bookcase stopped, then slid downward to reveal a panelled hallway lit with evenly spaced wall sconces. The bookcase top became part of the floor.

The way sloped down in a gentle incline. Further underground. Landon mashed a hand against her trembling lips.

Tait pushed her forward, but her legs had locked. A whimper escaped the pressure on her mouth.

He growled a curse. "You will not die on this property. I won't even hurt you here if I don't have to."

"I can't—"

"Move." A shove between her shoulder blades sent her stumbling forward, arms out to break her fall.

By the time she'd regained her footing, the bookcase had risen into place. The way was shut.

Her vision greyed. Tait's triumphant glare was the last thing she saw.

~~~

Landon woke in a warmly lit room, slumped in a soft chair in... a museum? Blinking, she searched her memory. She'd fainted in an underground passage—because Tait had a gun. A gasp jerked her upright.

Her wrists lay bound together across her stomach, hands curved around opposite forearms. A frantic flail of her feet revealed her ankles were tied as well.

Terror clawed her lungs.

"Those Fabergé eggs in the far unit are to honour his mother, legally acquired as his success grew. Everything else is his private obsession." Tait strolled into view from behind her chair. "Making this a fine place to wait until it's time for you to go."

Arms drawn into her belly, she fought the shakes. Anchor. Breathe. *God, help!*

Tait stopped in front of her, feet wide and hands loose at his sides. A gallery guide with a gun stashed out of sight.

Soft track lighting illuminated a lavish mix of treasures. Paintings, maps, and sketches lined the walls. The nearer glass cases held jewellery and carvings. A massive bronze sundial caught light from overhead.

All these collectibles. It had been Orran and Tait all along. "So you attacked Ciara."

He snarled. "Orran was furious. And you—I told you it was a mistake, but you couldn't let it go. You have no one to blame but yourself."

Heat surged through Landon's body, launching her to her feet. Unbalanced, she fell into the chair. She fought to breathe over her racing pulse. "You attacked my friend and left her broken. Somebody had to fight back."

"Your meddling is why she lost her jade pieces. I'll unload most of them." He selected a green circle from one of the displays and held it up between thumb and fingertips. "This, I'll keep. It should have been part of my inheritance all along."

Ciara would be relieved to know Orran hadn't betrayed her trust, though they were right about him being a thief.

Nobody would keep a collection hidden like this if it was legal.

"You said inheritance. This is all his?"

Tait swept the room in an expansive gesture. "Everything you see. I preferred to convert mine to cash, but for Orr, it was all about the trophies. Proof he could crack the tightest security nets."

"So the cameo—"

"He couldn't resist. That guy practically begged to lose it."

A dull ache throbbed behind her forehead. "The ruby pendant on the weekend. You must have stolen that. They say Orran was dead by then."

A faint smile touched his lips. "That was my tribute to him. He'd planned to claim it himself."

"But he couldn't because he was already dead." Landon's teeth pinched her lower lip. They hadn't found Orran until Wednesday. For Tait to know he was dead on the weekend—

Cold gripped her. "You killed him."

Tait's face contorted. "Orran should have lived his final years in peace. Enjoying his collection. Sending me out for the occasional new piece. But he started getting reckless. Stealing too close to home, too often."

He clutched the jade bangle, shaking it at her. "The night Ciara brought up his injury, he told me what happened—and how she'd seen the goblet. I wanted to get rid of her before she could remember more details and put them together with the local thefts."

He replaced the bracelet and moved to an oak cabinet, lit from within. Then he opened the door and lifted out a gold cup rimmed with rubies so polished they glowed.

"This is it. A kid might buy the lie about a theatre prop, but not an adult with her taste in valuables. It was a matter of time. Orran swore she'd never rat him out. But I couldn't chance it."

Head bowed, he returned the goblet to the cabinet. "Then he gave her the bangle. I misjudged him. Thought it was from a job before we met. If he was giving her stolen goods, it was over."

"But you gave Ciara and Anna copies of the valuation papers."

"Found after the fact. He may even have bought it with the intent to give it to her. Instead, it's my revenge for what she stirred up." He glared through slitted eyes. "Part of my revenge. I like what you suggested about the dog. I'll install the cameras next week. Once she sees that, her death will look like suicide."

"No! It's not her fault. And it's not mine. Why—"

His hand whistled toward her.

She flinched and tried to duck, but the chair held her in place.

Instead of a blow, fingers grabbed her hair and yanked sideways, fierce enough to bring tears. "Better if they fish you out of the water unbruised."

Tait's breath rasped. "You signed Orran's death warrant with your relentless digging. You wouldn't quit. You'd get Ciara remembering. If Orr softened, she'd have him confessing."

Another scalp-ripping pull at her hair. "He'd have died in prison. Ruined and cut off from everything he'd built here. I couldn't let it happen."

Swearing, he let go and stalked away. At the far side of the room, he pivoted, expression empty of heat. "He saved me at my first heist. I was way over my head, and he grabs me, hustles me out to his car, and lectures me on my clumsy technique. Then he sends me back in to do it right."

His shoulders sagged. "He'd been after a more valuable item in that museum, but he passed it up to help a worthless kid. He became my mentor. My friend. Everything a father should have been. I had to save him. Even when that meant ending his life."

The revelation was too much to process—a storm surge of grief and tortured reasoning. Compassion flickered in

Landon's heart, but fear thundered louder. She couldn't reason with him. He'd kill her, convinced it was payback for Orran. Justice in his mixed-up mind.

Tait prowled the displays, stopping to touch various items or to stare at others. At times, he murmured to himself.

She was melting in this heavy rainsuit. Moisture trickled down her spine. Tait had tied her around the coat and pant cuffs, maybe so the bristly nylon rope wouldn't leave marks.

He'd bound her wrists so each palm lay against the opposite forearm. Mouth dry, she watched him move around the room. When he stopped with his back to her, reaching for an object in another cabinet, she tried to turn her bottom wrist.

The line pulled tight. Stopped her motion. Sweat prickled her hairline as she strained to keep twisting her arm.

It shot around with such force that she grunted.

Tait spun toward her.

Screwing up her face, she wrinkled her nose as if fighting a sneeze. A second sneeze if she could fool him about the first sound. She held her arms with the repositioned hand underneath.

When he looked away, she worked her wrist into its original alignment. The movement was easier now, as if the sweater under the rubber coat was compressing.

Such a small motion. What was the use?

She drew a slow breath, praying with open eyes fixed on her captor. God saw her. He was here. She might die today, but He wouldn't leave her alone. He'd help her bear it. Or He'd help her escape. Her part was to notice any options. Right now, that meant a wrist that could turn.

Her pulse throbbed in her throat. Last time she'd confronted death, she'd had Bobby. God had given them what they needed to keep their heads and escape.

Bobby. If she died today, it'd break his heart.

A chime rang from somewhere behind her. Three quick dings, like a fasten-seat belt warning in a car.

Tait's head jerked toward the sound. With a swift but reverent motion, he returned the ebony elephant he'd been holding, then strode past her.

The sound repeated.

Tait swore. "Better and better. Anna was going to receive a text from your phone that you'd asked me to drop you in town to follow up on a clue. Before I dumped you in the water near the docks."

"Tait, please—"

"Now you and Zander will go together. Shot instead of drowned. Or maybe a car accident in the storm. I knew I'd have to deal with him before this ended."

"Zander's here?" Landon's heart jolted. Tears flooded her cheeks.

Somehow he'd get in. He'd find her. It'd be okay. She craned around in the chair until she saw a bank of monitors. Zander addressed one of the cameras. "Let me in. We need to talk. Or do I call in a 9-1-1 hostage situation?"

"On my way." Tait pulled his finger from the talk button before the scream left Landon's mouth. He whipped around. "Shut up."

Zander spoke again. "If you've harmed her, there is no mercy. No escape."

Tait gave her bonds a quick tug before snatching his gun from the monitor station and heading for the door.

She should give him time to reach the bookcase, in case he doubled back. Her thrumming pulse wouldn't let her. Zander had found her—somehow. He'd have a plan, but so would Tait.

Desperation twisted her wrist in the bonds, turning her hand out like a claw. Bent double, the bulky sweater digging into her stomach, she strained toward her ankles. Clutching her pant leg, she hauled the rubberized material upward. Nothing.

She stretched her arms longer, shoulders burning. Hooked the toe of her sock with her fingers. Tugged. Again. Again.

Until her sock slipped down and loosed the pressure on her ankles.

Now she could pull up the pant leg. She dragged her foot free, tender skin scraping against the rope, and kicked the loop off her other foot.

She stood, wobbled, and cast around for a weapon.

On the monitors, Tait strode through the house. Almost to the front door.

Scanning the display cases, she spotted a sharp-tipped hunting knife. She sprinted for it. The handle looked like ivory. Old, yellowed. It lay smooth and cool in her grip.

The screens showed Tait opening up to Zander. Not much time.

Back in her chair, she wedged the knife under her thigh, blade forward. With a deep breath, she inserted the point under the rope and dragged her wrists back and forth.

The yellow nylon cord parted and fell away.

The knife wouldn't work against Tait. She tucked it into her jacket pocket and seized a three-legged wooden stool. Too light.

On the monitors, the two men walked through the house, Zander in front. His rigid gait suggested Tait held him at gunpoint.

As soon as Zander stepped into the room, while his body blocked the sight of her empty chair, she'd hit Tait.

There. Against the far wall. A field hockey stick. Dark with age, smooth from use. Straight, with an umbrella-handle U-curve at one end. She grasped it in both fists and took a practice swing in the air.

Yes. She ran for the door and flattened herself against the wall, heart hammering.

Moments later, footsteps rang in the tunnel.

The door opened inward, and Zander stepped through. He paused, blocking the opening. "Someone's been busy."

Landon held her breath, poised to strike.

"Move." Tait's voice.

Zander jolted as if poked by Tait's gun. He walked forward with slow, measured steps.

Tait followed.

Lungs bursting, Landon sliced the stick downward at his head. It smacked the back of his neck, knocking him forward.

His arms flailed. The gun went off.

"Zander!"

Zander didn't need her warning. He'd spun and kicked the weapon out of reach. Flipped Tait onto his back and dropped a knee on his chest before pinning Tait's free arm.

"Get me the gun." The words barely penetrated the roaring in her ears.

The compact pistol grip would have fit her palm if she'd been willing to touch it with more than thumb and fingertips. A silencer extended the barrel. Keeping her feet away from Tait's clutching grasp, she pressed the awkward metal weapon into Zander's hand. "How did you know?"

"Shaun recognized the SUV leaving the inn. It was at The Ovens the day of the attack. When Tait claimed he was elsewhere."

The man on the floor cursed. His shoulders heaved as if to throw Zander clear.

The hate in his glare matched the fire in her veins. Safe. She was safe. Tremors swept her body, but her fists clenched, remembering the feel of the polished wood. The satisfaction of striking back.

If Zander hadn't been here, if she'd had the chance to make the same defensive move... Gaze locked on Tait's, she swallowed a sob. That first blow was necessary. But on her own, she wouldn't have stopped. Her hands knew and the sinews in her arms. She'd have kept pounding him where he lay, for herself and for Ciara. Maybe to death.

She choked back a sob.

Zander spoke without taking his eyes off his prisoner. "Landon, go to the main basement and free that supposedly missing dog. I'll finish here."

"There's rope for you to tie him up. I'll get it." Thank God Zander was handling this. She hurried back toward the chair.

Grunts erupted behind her. A scuffle. Another gunshot. She whirled with a scream.

Zander straightened to stand over Tait's bleeding torso.

Tait twitched twice. Then, with a wet rattling rasp, he sagged flatter against the floor tiles.

"No mercy. No escape." Zander stepped over the body and walked to the monitor station. He placed the gun on the shallow desk. "We may have to leave this room to get a cell signal."

Landon stared. He'd just ended a man's life.

Her stomach was a heaving mass.

The body on the floor drew her. She knelt at Tait's side, hesitant fingers stretching to touch his forehead. The vengeance she'd thought she wanted, feared she'd have taken... meaningless now that a man lay dead. "God—" Words of prayer wouldn't come, but He knew her heart.

Tait's hazel eyes had a glassy look. Landon gulped against rising bile.

Zander waited in the doorway. "Don't waste your effort. He's gone."

Dry-mouthed, she focused again on the body and the way it lay, remembering Zander's posture. If he'd been off-balance in a struggle for the weapon, he wouldn't have gained his footing so fast. And he'd have been breathing hard.

Muscle by muscle, she pushed to her feet. "You didn't have to kill him."

His thin lips set into the sorrowful expression reserved for his most hurting clients, and he spread his palms. "Self-defence. Unfortunate but necessary. He grabbed for the gun."

In this climate-controlled room, layered in heavy clothing, the sweat she'd built up turned to ice. Shaking, she backed against the nearest display case. To her questing fingers, the case seemed to rock to the same unsteady rhythm.

Zander beckoned, patience in his gaze and a sympathetic smile lifting the corners of his mouth. "The police won't thank us for delaying. You're safe now. Let's go."

Cold consumed her, froze her in place. "You... executed... him." As casually as flushing a toilet. With less emotion than swatting a fly.

He stiffened. Took a step toward her.

So her lips worked and her brain didn't. She needed to play dumb. Get out of here. Let him call the police. Get Dylan or Zerkowsky alone and tell him what she'd seen. "I'm sorry, Zander. You're right. I—I've never seen someone die before." She forced her feet to walk toward him. Toward the door.

He took her hand, and his head started a slow shake, a small motion back and forth. "Not until we agree on what happened here. We need to talk this through. You need to understand."

Her lips clamped against the words that wanted to attack him. She understood. One of the most trusted figures in her life had just killed a man in cold blood.

And she was alone with him in a room no one else knew existed.

## Chapter 24

"HEAR ME OUT. You owe me that much." Calm, almost hypnotic, Zander led her to the brown wingback chair where she'd been bound. He rotated it toward the underground passage before dragging its twin to face it. His chair. Between her and the door. "Sit, please."

She dropped into the seat and retrieved her cast-off sock. Dried sweat prickled against her body, but she didn't want to shed the coat now. Urgency thrummed in her veins. "Zander, we need to call the police. They won't believe self-defence if he lies there too long."

He steepled his fingers and raised them to his lips and chin. His forehead dipped, casting his eyes into shadow. "You don't believe it either. Therein lies the problem."

Landon worked moisture into her mouth. "Then help me believe. I didn't see what happened."

"The man intended to kill us both. We struggled for the gun. I shot him."

All true. But his flatline delivery sent an ocean of shivers across her skin.

To dismiss a life so easily... This couldn't be the first time he'd been in this position. "No mercy. No escape." His earlier words tumbled from her lips. She covered her mouth, but too late.

His sallow skin darkened. "You can't deny you want vengeance. In providing it, I've kept you clean and taken the curse upon myself. Now that you know my mission, you need to keep the secret."

"Mission?" Her ribs locked, trapping her lungs, reducing her air to frantic shallow gasps.

"I exact justice. Dispatch those who prey on the innocent to judgment."

He rose and circled the floor, maintaining position between her chair and the exit. "I once considered myself a type of Old Testament Avenger of Blood. Until that woman's serial killer accepted Christ and evaded eternal torment." Zander whirled on her, his cheeks an ugly red. "His salvation is the ultimate betrayal of his victims—a mockery of their pain."

God knew her struggle with this. How her heart agreed. And yet... "If vengeance belongs to God, then so does forgiveness." Landon's throat strained so tight that swallowing brought tears. "God is good. You taught me that. He knows what He's doing, even when we can't answer the questions."

"He goes too far." Zander resumed pacing, his heels ringing on the grey and white tiles. "My purpose is clear. If God won't cut these evildoers off, I will. When they stand before Him without repentance, He has no choice."

He circled back to his chair and eased into the upholstery. "When I met you... my heart wept at how terrified you were of your trafficker finding you again. And yet, like Gabriella, you intended to testify. In your voice, I heard my daughter's final anguish. I couldn't let it happen again."

He reached out as if cradling a gift. "You won't have to worry about meeting your trafficker. Gord. Tait."

Gord... Her trafficker... Landon's stomach lurched. "How many years have you been doing this?" How many lives?

"The one who took my daughter got off on a technicality. Because of her trauma, Gabriella's statements had inconsistencies. The defence lawyer claimed her suicide proved her evidence was unreliable."

His lips twisted. "Everyone knew he was guilty. I shadowed him for weeks, hoping to catch him in another crime. Then God put his life into my power. Instead of saving him from the river, I cracked his head and let him drown."

"What if God wanted you to show mercy?"

"Then He tapped the wrong person."

Where was the compassionate counsellor she'd trusted? This man was all sharp angles and cold tones. The fanatic light in his eyes...

She didn't know him at all.

Holding his gaze, she allowed her fear to leak out with her tears. Could she reach the real Zander—was there a real Zander? The man who cared and protected? "Zander, I'm frightened. Please take me home."

"I'm sorry." Fingers steepled, he inclined his head in a seated bow. "My mission can't end here. Others will need me."

The breath left her lungs, hollowing her to the core and stopping her tears. The moment stretched. "So what happens now?"

"You remain in this place until you understand. I'll close up the house as if we've never been here. Keep a key. Deal with the body, dump his vehicle. Bring you food and whatever else you'll need."

"Anna—"

"I'll think of something." His hands, flat in his lap, curled to clutch his thighs. "You can't ruin my life's work."

"Your life's work!" Landon shot to her feet. "Murder matters more than all the hurting souls you've helped?"

She couldn't dodge him for the door, so she sidestepped around her chair. Anything to put distance between them. "You want to trap me here? You'll chain me up? Put me in a cage again?" The shriek scraped her throat.

Zander stood too. "Landon, you need to see. Trust me once more."

She should be quiet. Pretend to submit. But he'd already seen through that attempt. "You killed my trust when you killed Tait. There's no way out of this. Let me go."

He clasped his hands at his waist and made a brief half-bow. "Then you force my decision." With measured steps, he retrieved the pistol from the monitor station. "It will be easiest if you let me put this to your heart."

The hunting knife weighted her pocket. Useless against a gun. She darted frantic glances around the room. Glass display cases, soft chair, nowhere to take cover. She stood her ground, chin high and fists clenched. "This is how you protect the ones you love?"

"Don't be afraid." His countenance softened as he approached, a trace of the Zander she knew. "Think about heaven. No more pain. Peace."

She backed away. Dodged a display case. Zander had introduced her to the love of God, to forgiveness and healing and hope in Jesus. But this time, he was wrong. If she didn't have his theological degree, she had the simple truth.

Chest heaving, she jabbed a finger toward his heart. "You've become the same as the ones you judge."

Tears poured onto her cheeks. Not a sign of weakness. A sign of life.

In her blurred vision, Zander wavered.

She braced her core, shoulders stiff. Praying.

The gun dipped toward the floor. "God could have stopped me. Taken me out whenever He wanted. Instead, He let me go. It's been worth it to take a few forsaken with me."

The emptiness in his expression wrenched Landon's soul.

Angling the gun away from her, he ran slow fingers along the matte black metal. "Go now. You shouldn't see this."

Arm shaking as if fighting an enormous weight, he bent his wrist toward himself.

A flood of horror, icy and relentless, swelled from her stomach to her mind. "Zander, no, please."

Hands outstretched, she walked toward him. Carefully, with no sudden moves. "What if God let you live to give you a chance to repent?"

"This is my choice." The gun shook in his grip. "Sweet child, let me spare you this one last thing. Go into the house. When you hear the shot, you'll know to call the authorities."

She continued her steady approach.

Eyes glittering, jaw a sharp line, he snapped his shoulders to military attention. "Very well. Remember me as a bloody corpse."

He raised the weapon.

Everything stopped. Landon's vision shrank to his stone expression and the gun jammed between his teeth.

Gazes locked, they stood trapped in time.

Zander's cheek twitched. Black terror filled his eyes.

His arm dropped. Gun in hand, he bolted for the door.

Landon choked on a sob. Then the shakes started. She tottered toward the security desk. One of the monitors showed him sprinting along the tunnel.

The second showed the area in front of the house. With another car. Anna's? If she met Zander coming out—

Bobby sprang from the vehicle.

Landon shrieked and dove for her phone. Would it even work in here?

One bar. She hit his number, praying, tracking Zander's progress on the screens. Inside the tunnel, he scrabbled for the bookcase latch.

Bobby stopped. Grabbed his phone. "Landon?"

"Get around the house. Or behind the car. Don't let Zander see you—he's coming out the front."

He stared at the house. "You're alive! What—"

"Bobby, move! Please. Once he's gone, come inside and lock the door."

Zander was running up the stairs.

Outside, Bobby hesitated, then darted from one monitor to the next as he rounded the building.

Landon wilted against the desk.

Zander reached his SUV, whipped it around, and sped out of view.

With shaking fingers, she keyed in 9-1-1. "God, don't let him hurt anyone else."

She spared Tait a regretful glance as she left the treasure room, giving the emergency dispatcher a description of Zander's vehicle. "He has a gun, and he might be suicidal, and—tell them to be careful."

She was still answering questions when she reached the main basement and a flurry of frantic yelps burst from the closed bathroom door. With an apology to the 9-1-1 operator, she freed the trapped Chihuahua.

If a dog could cry, the little fellow did, whimpering, yipping, and jumping at her knees. Landon scooped him into the crook of her arm and headed for the stairs.

Above her, a door slammed. Not Zander. Please.

"Landon?" Bobby's voice washed sweet relief through her bones.

She muffled the phone against her side and called, "Here."

At the top of the stairs, she set the dog on the floor. He dashed away, an amber and white blur, then sped back to circle her ankles.

Bobby stopped in the kitchen's arched entrance, his face haggard, stormy eyes huge behind rain-spattered glasses. His gaze seemed to drink her in, head to toe, as if reassuring himself she was real.

She spoke into the phone. "I'm safe and locked in, and I'm not alone now. I'll stay on the line until the police arrive, but I'm going to put the phone down."

The dispatcher's answer came as the phone clicked against the granite countertop. Landon left it behind. "You came."

"I didn't know what to do, but I couldn't stay away. I'd gone to the inn to finish the website upgrade Jessie interrupted the other day. Zander had told Anna, and she told me."

Moxie's pattering feet traced a figure eight around them. Bobby didn't move. His gaze never left hers. "Tait's SUV was at The Ovens that day. He nearly ran Shaun off the road. When Shaun found out that's who you'd gone with, he alerted Zander. What's up with him taking off? And your crazy warning?"

Landon drew a shuddering breath, but the words wouldn't come. She stepped toward him, reaching out.

He closed the space between them in a blink. Then his arms were around her, sheltering her close. He drew her head to his. "You're safe now. Did he go after Tait? I'm guessing Tait's gone too."

Tait was gone for good. Maybe that could have been funny, but it started her crying again.

Bobby held her with a soft rocking motion, one hand against the small of her back, the other stroking her hair. "I know you're not mine to hold. Just let me be here for you now."

His beard stubble poked her cheek as she leaned into his embrace. Held. Safe. Selfishly taking comfort from the one whose love she couldn't return. Yet he was trembling worse than she was. Maybe he needed this too. For this moment, she locked her arms tighter around his ribs and let her questions fall away.

When the sirens approached, she stirred and pulled free.

Bobby caught her hand and squeezed. "You can do this. I've got your back."

"Anna—will you tell her it's over? I'm supposed to keep my line open with 9-1-1." She scooped up her phone and started for the front of the house.

The sirens hadn't sounded close, but they'd stopped. A check through the living room window showed Anna's vehicle and Tait's in front of the garage. No police cruisers.

Bobby joined her, tucking his phone into his jacket pocket. "She had way more questions than I had answers, but she said come home when you can. Where are the cops?"

"I don't know."

Landon shed her rainwear and draped everything over one of the cream leather loveseats. The interview process wouldn't be quick. Tugging at the thick knit of her sweater waistband, she flapped air underneath to dry off. Peeling down to a thin, sweaty tee shirt would be too drastic a change.

A bulky police SUV rocketed into the yard, jolting to a stop with lights flashing. The driver's door opened, and Zerkowsky sprinted toward them through the rain.

Landon and Bobby raced to let him in. Moxie threw high-pitched barks from Landon's heels.

Zerkowsky stopped in the entryway, dripping on the ceramic tiles. "Sorry for the delay. Accident on the road out. You're okay?" He looked first at Landon, his gaze searching, then to Bobby. "We thought she was alone."

"I just arrived."

"Good of you to call us." Zerkowsky's heavy eyebrows crowded low.

"Zander phoned 9-1-1 on his way. I couldn't believe you weren't already here."

"Zander who's now our fugitive?"

Landon gulped. "He's—be careful."

"He won't be a danger to anyone for a while. Broken tree branch speared through his windshield, and he rammed the nose of his vehicle into a rock. Dylan's there with him waiting for the ambulance."

"Is he alive?" Her hands clenched.

"Unconscious but breathing. You want to tell me how he fits into this? And what exactly *this* is?"

She scrubbed her palms against her scratchy sweater. "Tait brought me here to kill me. Zander killed him. Zander also killed Gord, but Tait killed Orran. Clear?"

Zerkowsky shed his wet overcoat and scuffed the worst of the mud from his boots. "It will be. Is Tait's body on the premises?"

"I'll show you."

Turning, she caught Bobby in an open-mouthed stare. He snapped his lips closed.

"Hold one minute." Zerkowsky keyed his radio and updated the others.

Dylan's voice carried across the connection. "Ambulance is here. Ingerson's going to meet them at the hospital. I'll see you soon."

"Let yourself in."

Landon coaxed Moxie into her arms and led the constable to the basement stairs. "There's an open passageway to a hidden art collection Orran and Tait have stolen over the years. He's in there, on the floor. Could I stay up here?"

"For now. Point Dylan my way when he comes."

She'd have to experience the scene again, describe the movements in the underground room. Show them how to work the secret door. But not yet.

Back in the living room, she set the dog on the claret accent rug. Mouth wide and tongue lolling, he seemed to laugh at them as he wove in and out under the coffee table.

Landon curled up in a corner of a loveseat, throw pillow clutched to her stomach. Bobby took the other end, his body angled toward her. She squeezed the pillow tighter. "You have a million questions, and you're being so patient."

"Two million. But I'm trying not to make you tell the story more than once."

"Until I get home. They'll want to hear it all again."

The front door opened, and heavy boots sounded on the tiles. Landon jumped up. "Dylan?"

His head poked around the edge of the wall. "Both of you. Landon, you need to put this guy on salary if you're going to keep dragging him into places like this."

Bobby stood beside her. "I'm paid in ice cream. And Anna's baked goods."

"Man, winter's coming. Hold out for burgers." Dylan focused on Landon. "You don't need medical attention?"

"No. Zerkowsky's downstairs. He said I could wait up here."

"I'll check in with him. One of us will come for your story. You can walk us through the crime scene after that."

By the time Landon arrived at the inn, she'd answered Bobby's two million questions and more. Zerkowsky, Dylan, plus two more officers who arrived later, wanted details on top of details. Nuances, inklings.

The art expert who drove out from the city had all but swooned over the vault's contents. Landon extracted a promise from Dylan that they'd bring Nigel in to consult on the hidden room. She pitched it as the possibility of finding yet another hiding place, but they both knew it was a perk for the one local resident with a bunker of his own.

They'd taken the dog carrier from Tait's SUV to transport Moxie. Landon hoped Shaun would take him to Ciara's apartment tonight. Or maybe Ciara would want to sleep in her own bed now that the danger was past. Unfastening him now in the inn parking lot, Landon crooned, "Good boy. It's over now."

Despite the rain, Anna, Ciara, Shaun, and Roy crowded onto the deck to welcome them home, Ciara squealing at the sight of her pet. Anna herded them into the kitchen to two heaping plates of lasagna and salad and shooed everyone else out. "Eat fast—before they explode."

As Landon sank into her chair, exhaustion fell like a weighted blanket. Her head drooped. "Will you say grace?"

"Jesus. Thank You. For everything." The words dropped like rocks into sand, landing heavy and inert.

"Amen."

The spicy tomato-cheese scent and the vibrant colours hit like a carnival of overload. Landon's brain had no space for this. Her stomach, empty though it must be, felt numb. When she'd forced down as much as she could, Bobby's plate was empty. He tipped a half-smile. "Nobody does comfort food like Anna. Ready?"

In the common room, Bobby waved Landon toward the empty club chair. She groaned. "If I sit there, I'll be asleep."

Shaun transferred to the soft leather embrace in one fluid movement. He gave a cheeky wink. "Taking one for the team."

Lowering into the seat beside Ciara, Landon couldn't help a smile. Thank God Shaun had recognized Tait's vehicle to know he'd been at the park that day. If not... Her gaze flicked to the oval clock on the bookshelf. She could be dead by now. Drowned, submerged wherever Tait chose to dump her for an innocent local to find.

Gulping air, she clasped her palms to her elbows, pressing into her sweater's rough weave. Anchoring on the physical sensations. The firm upholstery beneath her. The people around her.

Ciara clapped her hands. "Don't keep us in suspense. Spill it." In her lap, Moxie sat up with a little yip.

Somehow the sight of the tiny amber and white dog, who couldn't tell his story of imprisonment, released Landon's words.

When Landon finished, Ciara's cheeks were parchment white. Biting her lips, she cradled her dog close.

Shaun reached out and bumped his fist against her arm. "Happy ending, remember? Landon's safe, and your menace is over."

She shuddered. "Ken lost his business because of me. Now Landon nearly died. It's all my fault."

"You're not responsible for the actions of others—Ken or Tait or Zander." The grim cast of Roy's jaw dared anyone to argue.

Sniffling, Ciara pressed quivering lips into the top of Moxie's head.

"And it's not about you." Bobby's scowl matched his grandfather's.

Roy coughed. "We almost lost Landon today. Twice. Betrayed by one of the people she trusted most."

Shaun bounced his palm against the leather armrest. "Zander thinking he can fast-track people to hell—or to heaven—man, that's twisted."

Zander's resolute stare, the pistol pointed dead at her. Landon's heart lurched. "I'm so glad the tree branch stopped him." He couldn't pull the trigger on himself. Desperate as he was, would he have tried to force the police to shoot him?

Blinking away tears, she focused on each person here, absorbing the unspoken. Love and concern from Anna, Bobby, and Roy. Confusion from Ciara. Curiosity from Shaun. Silently, she blessed each one. "Thank God for His care today. And that this is over."

"Amen." Roy's voice rang the loudest, but even Shaun joined in.

Anna stood and took Landon's hand. "Let me help you upstairs. You look like a puff of air could blow you over."

She could have walked alone. Maybe. Although her hands didn't have much strength to grip the banister as she trudged upward.

As she climbed into bed and drew the sage duvet up to her chin, she whispered, "Thank you, Anna. You don't have to stay. I'll be all right."

"I know you will. But something else is troubling you." Anna's chair rocked slowly beside the bed. "It's hovering right over your head like a heavy grey cloud about to dump."

Groaning, Landon rolled onto her side. "I don't know how to say it."

"Then let it dump."

Landon folded an arm and tucked it beneath her head. "It's Zander." Tears roughened her throat. "He taught me to drop my grudges and let God into my hurts. To forgive. But he was killing people at the same time. He also connected the dots for me to find Jesus. If he was that off-base, what does it mean for my faith? Was it all a lie?"

Anna's chair creaked as she leaned forward. "God can speak through someone who's seriously off the rails. It doesn't mean He's blessing or affirming their current situation. He even spoke through a donkey in the Bible."

"I guess."

"This blindsided us all. But God's got you, Landon, and His love is true."

Tears slipped sideways from Landon's eyes, dripping down onto her bent arm. "I'm wiped out, but I'm afraid to go to sleep."

## Chapter 25

*Sunday*

Landon didn't even try to get out of bed for church Sunday morning. Every muscle felt like she'd wrestled a bear, and her brain was a thicket of brambles. Even the brilliant sunshine after yesterday's storm couldn't energize her.

In part, it was the emotional toll from being abducted. Threatened. Facing death—again.

But, as she dragged herself into the shower around noon, she knew the root was Zander. How could he do what he'd done and justify it? What would happen to his soul?

Hot water provided no answers and minimal comfort, but it engaged her autopilot to go downstairs to eat.

Meaghan was elbow-deep in sudsy dishwater. She whipped her hands from the sink for a hasty dry on her apron, then crossed the flagstone-patterned vinyl. "What can I get you for brunch? We pamper you today—Anna's orders."

"Where is she?"

"Church. And I think an errand. She'll be back soon." Meaghan took Landon by the arm and steered her to a chair at the table. "This wasn't what anyone wanted to happen. But thank you for finding out who killed Dad."

He'd died because of Landon. Or because Zander wanted revenge for Gord's treatment of Landon. She clenched her teeth. She could not wear this. Like Roy had said to Ciara last night, what Zander did was not her fault.

Meaghan stood looking down at her, compassion in her blue eyes. Wisps of red hair framed her forehead. "I can sleep at night now, knowing there's not someone from his old gang coming for me next. And that it wasn't Hart."

"Did you really think it might be him?"

Meaghan's full lips flattened, and she nodded. "I know you don't like him, but he's better without Dad leaning on him. We're going to be okay."

"I'm glad."

A motor sounded outside, and soon Anna bustled in, hands full of cloth grocery bags. "You're up! I'm not a fan of Sunday shopping, but today, we celebrate."

She unpacked while Meaghan made Landon a simple omelette and toast.

Landon was still finishing her coffee when Anna answered a tap at the back door. She returned to the kitchen with Dylan in tow. "He promises it's a social call."

Dylan's soft brown suede jacket paired with a collared shirt. Jeans and glossy brown cowboy boots made Landon check his hands for a cowboy hat. A grin softened his lean cheeks, and he touched fingertips to temple in a sort of salute. "You doing okay?"

She hiked a shoulder. "Still processing, I guess. But you must have been half the night at Orran's. What are you doing up and out?"

"Heading for the station to finish the paperwork. But until I get there, I'm off duty, and I thought Anna might have better coffee than I'll get at my desk."

He accepted a double-sized porcelain mug from Meaghan. "Thank you. Landon, the sun feels good. Come outside for a bit? I promise, if I say anything work-related, you can have my coffee."

"I'll hold you to that." She topped up her cup and followed him out onto the deck.

Bypassing the patio table, he descended to the grass. "All the times I've come here, those chairs in front have called me. How about we sit out there and watch the water?"

With the sun warming their backs, they trailed along the edge of the driveway and across the still-damp grass to settle in the twin wooden Adirondack chairs on the lawn.

Landon set her mug on one of the broad armrests. The grass sloped toward the inn's signature green fishing dory, its orange marigolds and yellow pansies battered after yesterday's storm but still vibrant. Across the narrow strip of pavement, ocean waves danced far below.

She rested her head against the chair and inhaled the fresh salt air. "Good idea. I tend to leave these for the tourists."

Dylan drank, then held his mug at chin height as if filling up on the aroma. "Much better than I'll get at the station. Especially on the weekend."

"Thank you for yesterday."

"I'm sorry we took so long to process you. But we're not going there today."

"Shaun's leaving in the morning. He'll be in the States by dark. Just so you know."

"If you bring up work, it doesn't count."

That brought a small giggle. "Fair, but he wanted me to tell you. He and Ciara are out on a day trip. He's a self-proclaimed jerk, but he's been good to her. He even kept Moxie last night."

"Well, that qualifies him for sainthood right there."

The rhythmic swell of the waves and the glint of sunlight on each one made Landon's eyelids heavy. When Dylan left, maybe she'd nap right here. She drew in a lungful of sea air and sat straighter in the chair. Swallowed more caffeine. "Can you tell me how Zander's doing today?"

"Hey, you're not getting this coffee. End of story. And no, I haven't heard. I left instructions with the hospital last night that if you called they could update you on his condition. You're sort of family. You're not permitted to visit or communicate with him, though."

His mug clunked on the armrest farther from Landon. He extended both arms overhead, then dropped his palms to his jeans. "Faith isn't my thing. Can you help me understand why a Christian would want to kill people to keep them from God? Isn't that kind of the opposite of what you believe?"

"The why's easy—ultimate revenge. On the victims and maybe on God." She shivered. "This one's on my no-fly list for today, okay? I owe Zander so much, and to find out he's done this—I think my faith's okay, but I'm a mess."

"I hope you can work it through. Anna seems like a good one to field those questions. Maybe I'll come ask her later."

"Or talk to our pastor. Dylan, I know Jesus is real and He makes all the difference in life. You'd love Him. It's just, right now, the people. I don't know."

"People. Maybe this isn't a good time." He braced his forearms on his knees, fingers laced. "I'll say it anyway. Before you find your way into another active investigation."

"Can I not?"

"You tell me." He tapped a pointed toe in the grass. "I'd like to take you out for dinner one night. Not snacks as friends, but an actual date."

Landon's head whipped sideways. Bobby had laughed at her assurance that Dylan's attention was big brotherly. "Dylan... I'm not date material."

"Maybe let the guy asking be the judge of that."

"I like being single. And I don't want to saddle a good man with my baggage."

"So... friends for now. Maybe when you heal more..."

She couldn't help a rueful laugh. "I am healed. And I'm healing. And I will be healed. It's complicated. But it means a lot to know someone like you could be interested. Thank you."

He sat back with a slow smile, brown eyes steady. "Tell me I'm not the first man to make a move on you since you got here. Your getaway driver sure doesn't seem to be pining for his girl in Ontario."

"They broke up, but he knows I'm not open to a relationship. So, yeah."

His nearer shoulder lifted. "I've been trying to test the waters, but you're good at redirecting."

"I thought you were playing the big-brother-slash-cop-protector role."

"I can do that. And if you decide you want more, one date isn't a marriage contract. I know a sweet Italian restaurant in the city." He winked at her, then pushed his palm against the chair arm to stand. "I'd best take my empty mug in and get on to the station."

When she started to rise, he held up a hand. "Stay put and relax. You've earned it."

She was dozing in the chair when Shaun's motorcycle ripped the silence. He stopped in the driveway, and his passenger hopped off the back.

Ciara removed her helmet and shook her short hair free, happiness radiating from every line of her body. She ran to Landon. "I'm going to have a sister—and a brother."

In the background, Shaun sent Landon a gauntleted thumbs-up.

Ciara dropped the helmet and perched in the chair beside Landon's. "That's why they wanted my stuff out of the house. To make a nursery. And Mom's been so hard to reach because she's high-risk. They've poured everything into getting pregnant for years, and I never knew. Now she is, and Phil's gone uber-protective."

She sprang up and twirled in the grass. "Babies I don't have to birth myself!"

"That's great, Ciara. Do you think your folks will want you to stay now that their secret's out?"

"Free babysitting. They need me." Her round cheeks glowed. "Kimi told me I had to go see Mom and not take no for an answer. She and Ken called last night while we were waiting for you. They'd had Mom and Phil in for dinner, and Kimi noticed the baby bump."

The rapid-fire words had Landon's head spinning. "So that's good, then."

"Yes, and I know why Ken and Kimi were hanging around so long too. He's buying a business in Bridgewater. He wanted a few weeks to assess it because they'll be staying in BC where their grandkids are."

"I hope I see them before they go. They're a nice couple."

"They'll be here tonight. Anna invited them."

Landon squinted at Ciara's silhouette against the electric-blue sky. "Tonight?"

"It's a celebration. The cops are invited too. Because even though it's sad about Orran and Tait—and weird about Zander—you and I are safe, and we have our lives back. I'll even get my bangle and the rest of my things once they're processed. Think of how many people will have their lost treasures come home! You might even get a reward."

Astride the motorcycle, Shaun revved the engine. Ciara ducked her head into her helmet. "Gotta go. This bike beats Bobby's Corvette any day. And Shaun's more fun."

Shaun had texted Landon a promise to reveal his identity to Ciara before leaving—but after he gave her a day with the man he might become.

They sped away, Ciara clinging to his waist.

~~~

Anna and Meaghan had barred Landon from the kitchen. Her brain refused to tackle homework or to shut off and let her sleep, so she lugged one of the deck chairs down to the grass to a shady spot near the trees. The orange stray avoided the deck, but sometimes he'd approach if she sat out here.

The wind swished in the treetops, a sound like distant waves or a car passing on the road. The occasional pine needle floated in a languid downward drift. Today was one of those September glory days, warm and balmy, whispering that winter was still a long way off. She'd chosen denim capris and a buttercup-yellow top in agreement with the day's promise.

She queued a few different worship songs on her phone, but nothing seemed to resonate. God hadn't changed. Neither had she, but this... pause... in her spirit chafed like a wrinkled sock in a boot.

Earbuds still in place, she closed the music app and navigated to the library's online borrowing portal. Pecked out *Robert J Hawke*. A string of covers filled her screen, including a match for the paperback upstairs in her bedroom. Audiobook as well as ebook. Sweet.

She tapped to borrow, then started the narration. Reclined in her chair, she watched the movement of the trees. The first bit was familiar since she'd struggled that far in print. The publisher had chosen a good narrator, and his delivery carried her into the story.

A weight landed on her thighs. Landon gasped, her arms and legs flinging wide.

In her lap, tall and bold, sat the marmalade cat. His crooked ear pointed to the side, but his eyes measured her. Daring her to reject him.

She eased the air back into her lungs. "Hey, there, Mister. You could have given me a heart attack."

He stretched his chin high, exposing a creamy white patch at his throat.

"That's not something to be proud of."

The crooked ear flattened. Then he padded in a half circle and lowered himself onto her legs. His tail swept in to tuck under his nose. Dare she stroke him?

Bobby emerged from the path between their homes. "Look at you."

"I didn't see him. Lucky I didn't jump up, or he'd have clawed me."

A lime-green gift bag dangled in Bobby's grasp. "Lost in your music?"

Landon pinched an earbud free and offered it up. He dipped his head to catch the sound, squinting in concentration. Then he straightened with a grin. "Reading the classics, I see."

She closed the book and wrapped the headphone wire around the phone. "I needed to get out of my head. Audio's easier than print."

He stepped back, studying her. "How are you? Really?"

"Mostly okay... Some faith puzzles." Her shoulders crowded her ears. "I'll have to testify against Zander. See him in the courtroom."

"He sure levelled up the forgiveness challenge."

"I'm still processing the extent of what he did. Kind of horror-sad, if that makes sense. It hasn't left space for anger yet."

Bobby's lips thinned. "I've got that end covered for you."

He swung the gift bag from his index finger. "This is for you. But first, I want to talk about the elephant."

Landon's thoughts were too messy today to decipher his meaning. Pointing at his shirt, she went for the joke. "It's a manatee. With a monocle."

Mouth wide in mock horror, he looked down and slapped a palm to his chest. "So it is. Must have missed my own memo."

She offered a faint smile. "An elephant-sized conversation sounds like it needs a chair."

When Bobby set one of the padded deck chairs nearby, wiggling it until he found a flat spot on the lawn, the cat swivelled his head for a quick inspection.

The feline scrutiny turned to Landon. This was her chance. She reached out, hand hovering close, but not touching. His neck extended, nose brushing her fingertips. When he drew back, it wasn't as far.

She risked a gentle touch between his ears. Eyes narrowed, he pressed up into her fingers, elevating his nose as if inviting her to stroke the length of his spine. When she did, he lowered his head to his paws as if nothing unusual had happened. Slowly, carefully, she spread her hand and settled it on the cat's back. He seemed to nestle deeper onto her lap.

Bobby's grin must mirror her own. He gave a gentle nod. "Trust has been given."

Trust had been taken too. By Zander. She wouldn't go there again today. "So... elephants? Is this a Travers thing?"

Bobby's manatee shirt rose and fell in a deep breath. Pink edged into his cheeks. "Totally a me thing. I brought the elephant into the room when Jessie came, so let's deal with it. Yesterday pushed us closer than we should get, and I don't want that to crash the party tonight. Or to trample our friendship going forward."

Fingers splayed white against his jeans, he held her gaze. "You don't love me." One corner of his mouth quirked. "If that should change, do let me know. But you told me your past meant no decent guy would want you. As a card-carrying decent—if non-heroic—guy, I'm living proof that's false. Can you receive the evidence and be free of the lie?"

Dylan had said the same thing earlier, without his heart on the line. Landon's vision misted. "Bobby, you're a hero to me and a fantastic person. It's just—my heart is so scarred, I don't even know if I could fall in love. If God has a romance for me, He's going to have to hit me with it right between the eyes."

"He's not always subtle." A smile ghosted across his lips. "Knowing you don't want a relationship, period, makes it easier. I don't have to worry about how it'd feel to watch you start a life with someone else. Say, a good-looking cop or a rebel biker. I promise I won't push or expect anything more than friendship."

"I don't deserve a friend like you." Landon stuffed that humbling thought into a deep corner of her mind and mimed a handshake. "Friends."

Bobby stood and leaned to grasp it. "Friends." As he sat, he picked up the bright bag from the grass. "This is a gift. Friend to friend. Ordered before the elephant tiptoed into the room."

"Why?" Landon reached beneath the tissue paper.

At the rustle, the cat cracked an eye open at her.

She drew out a bundle of soft grey fabric. A tee shirt. Any shirt connected with Bobby must have some kind of image. Awkwardly unfolding it to see the front without dislodging the cat, she held the shoulders aloft.

Instead of a goofy drawing or slogan, a battle-armoured woman stood tall, blond hair flowing around her shoulders. One hand gripped a ferocious sword, the other a metal shield with a huge silver cross. Behind the warrior loomed an enormous, radiant angel with wings unfurled.

"I know novelty shirts aren't your style. But I saw this the day you lit into Shaun at The Ovens, and I had to get it."

"Shaun called me terrifying." She grinned at Bobby. "I'll wear it tonight."

JANET SKETCHLEY

## Dear Reader: What's Next?

You've finished the story, but you don't have to go yet. The following pages include a note about what you've just read, plus questions for personal reflection or group chat.

## Author's Note

Ruth and Tony Warner "visited" the inn from my Redemption's Edge series. **If you're curious** about their story, you'll find it in *Heaven's Prey*. Ruth appears again in *Without Proof*. If there's another of my characters you'd like to see on the guest list, send me a note at info@janetsketchley.ca. It could happen!

**Human trafficking** is all too real a problem, both for sex and for labour. It's possible for survivors to heal as well as Landon is healing, but I didn't find very many positive reports. The truth is ugly and frightening, and sex trafficking victims can be girls and boys as young as 12. Or younger. One way to fight back is to support your local programs for at-risk youth.

A few sites for background information:

- Canadian Centre to End Human Trafficking canadiancentretoendhumantrafficking.ca
- Public Safety Canada canada.ca/en/public-safety-canada/campaigns/human-trafficking.html
- Canadian author K. L. Ditmars lists more resources on her website: klditmarswriter.com/resources

**If you are or someone you know is a victim** of human trafficking, please reach out for help!

- In Canada: Canadian Human Trafficking Hotline canadianhumantraffickinghotline.ca
- In the US: National Human Trafficking Hotline humantraffickinghotline.org/get-help
- In any country: in your internet browser, type "human trafficking help" and add your country.

To end on **a brighter note**: The as-yet untitled **novel 4** in this series will be a winter story. I hope you'll come back for Christmas at the Green Dory Inn when that book releases. For **advance notice** of future releases, be sure to subscribe to my mailing list at bit.ly/JanetSketchleyNews or follow me on Bookbub at bit.ly/JanetSketchleyBookBub.

Finally, a favour if you're so inclined: Could you drop a **brief review** on Goodreads or your favourite online bookstore? Nothing fancy, just mention what you liked or didn't like, and why. No spoilers, please!

Thanks for reading!

*Janet*

## Acknowledgements

This book has my name on the cover, but it only reached this stage with the help of many:

Huge thanks to Deirdre Lockhart at Brilliant Cut Editing and Emilie Haney at E.A.H. Creative.

I'm indebted (or my characters are!) to Matthew and Russell Sketchley for significant developmental input, and to my sharp-eyed advance readers, Janice L. Dick, Heidi Newell, Ruth Ann Adams, who caught some final details just in time.

A number of fellow members of American Christian Fiction Writers suggested various options for Ciara's injury, and each one was part of discovering what would and wouldn't work. I'm especially grateful to Ronda Wells, MD, and Tracy Crump, former ICU nurse, for their in-depth information. Any medical mistakes in the book are mine! Thank you also to Nova Scotia Health's Brendan Elliott, John Jenkins, MD, and Robert Zwicker, BScN, RN, MHS for answering my questions about the Lunenburg County hospitals.

Thank you to the good folks at The Ovens Park (ovenspark.com) for allowing me to set a few key scenes there. If you visit Nova Scotia, do plan a day trip at the park.

A special shout-out to instructor (and author) Sandra Orchard (sandraorchard.com) and my fellow students at the Write! Canada 2021 online fiction intensive. If I'd kept the original opening, you might not have read the book.

I rely on my friends and fellow writers in the Metro Christian Writers group for insights, encouragement, and prayer.

And family! Russell, Adam, Amanda, Nathan, Andrew, Adrianne, and Matthew, plus our little one who'll be a newborn when this book releases. Mom and Dad W and Mom and Dad S. And the extended branches on both sides of the tree. My family makes life precious.

Lastly but most importantly, I thank our good God for the privilege to create with words. If anything in this book has touched your spirit or encouraged you, that's an answer to prayer. Anything amiss is my shortcoming, and anything excellent has His touch.

## DISCUSSION QUESTIONS

1. After a brief appearance last book, Moxie the Chihuahua returns, along with Mister and Timkin. Are you more of a dog person or a cat person? Do you have a pet of your own? If not, what would the perfect one be?

2. Is there a particular character in this story you feel a connection with? Or one who troubles you? Who and why?

3. As the story opens, Landon has a guilty fear that she ran away from the conflict with her professor in her previous university. Bobby says she chose a fresh start. How do you discern which is which in your own life? How can you encourage a friend who's trying to decide in theirs?

4. Landon initially jumped in to fight for Ciara for the wrong reasons. In what way does our motivation affect what we do and how we do it? Or does it make a difference?

5. Anna, Zander, and Orran each filled a mentoring role in Landon's or Ciara's lives. Mentors, formal or informal, hold a place of trust in the lives they influence. Who have been some of the key influences in your life? Is there someone you're mentoring now?

6. How would you define forgiveness? What are some healthy ways to step into forgiveness while acknowledging the impact of what was done? How can

we rebuild from there—especially if the individual remains a part of our lives?

7. When Landon realizes her anger at the past is back, Anna says, "It's surprising the things that surface after we think we've dealt with them." Have you ever experienced that? What do you think of the idea that some issues present in layers like an onion, with each recurrence being one step nearer to the core?

8. The human desire for justice can include a need for vengeance. How do you feel about the vilest offenders being saved if they repent? About perhaps meeting them in heaven? What does the possibility say about the love and power of God? About His justice? How can a person trust "Him who judges justly" (1 Peter 2:23) and find their way to peace?

9. In encouraging Ciara not to be defined by her past hurt, Landon says, "If you find the life lesson in it, someday you may even be grateful for it." Have there been experiences like this in your life that led to growth or unexpected benefits?

10. Landon discovers that hard-edged Shaun is wrestling with inner uncertainty. As he says, "We all have stories." Most of us have some kind of wound or weakness. How might remembering that affect our interactions with others?

11. What do you think Shaun will do now? Do you think his "reform" will stick? Do you see him and Ciara keeping in touch?

12. In Ciara's ruined apartment, Landon escapes her rising anger by praying for her friend while she works. When

you need to take control of your thoughts, what strategies help most? Activity? Speaking truth aloud? Prayer? Music?

13. Bobby dismisses his value and downplays the things that make him unique. What might you tell him about how to develop a healthy self-image that neither inflates nor diminishes who he is?

14. Dylan and Bobby would each like to date Landon. Do you understand why her past makes her hesitant? Do you think there's romance in her future? With one of these friends or with someone else?

# YOU MIGHT ALSO LIKE JANET SKETCHLEY'S REDEMPTION'S EDGE SERIES:

### *Heaven's Prey (book 1)*

A grieving woman is abducted by a serial killer—and it may be the answer to her prayers.

Despite her husband's objections, 40-something Ruth Warner finds healing through prayer for Harry Silver, the former race car driver who brutally raped and murdered her niece. When a kidnapping-gone-wrong pegs her as his next victim, Harry claims that by destroying the one person who'd pray for him, he proves God can't—or won't—look after His own. Can Ruth's faith sustain her to the end—whatever the cost?

### *Secrets and Lies (book 2)*

A single mother with a teenage son becomes a pawn in a drug lord's vengeance against her convict brother.

Carol Daniels thinks she out-ran her enemies, until a detective arrives at her door with a warning. Minor incidents take on a sinister meaning. An anonymous phone call warns her not to hide again.

Now she must cooperate with a drug lord while the police work to trap him. Carol has always handled crisis alone, but this one might break her. Late-night deejay Joey Hill offers friendship and moral support. Can she trust him? One thing's certain. She can't risk prayer.

### *Without Proof (book 3)*

"Asking questions could cost your life."

Two years after the plane crash that killed her fiancé, Amy Silver has fallen for his best friend, artist Michael Stratton. When a local reporter claims the small aircraft may have been sabotaged, it reopens Amy's grief.

Anonymous warnings and threats are Amy's only proof that the tragedy was deliberate, and she has nowhere to turn. The authorities don't believe her, God is not an option, and Michael's protection is starting to feel like a cage. How will Amy find the truth?

 **Janet Sketchley** is an Atlantic Canadian writer who likes her fiction with a splash of mystery or adventure and a dash of Christianity. Why leave faith out of our stories if it's part of our lives?

Janet's other books include the Redemption's Edge Christian suspense series and the devotional books, *A Year of Tenacity* and *Tenacity at Christmas*. She has also produced a fill-in reader's journal, *Reads to Remember: A book lover's journal to track your next 100 reads* (available in print only, with two different cover design options). You can find her online at janetsketchley.ca.

Subscribe to Janet's newsletter at bit.ly/JanetSketchleyNews, or follow her on BookBub at bit.ly/JanetSketchleyBookBub.

Manufactured by Amazon.ca
Bolton, ON